UNDER HIS TOUCH

JEFFE KENNEDY

Under His Touch was first published by Carina Press in January 2015.

Thank you for reading!

Credits
Cover: Ravven (https://www.ravven.com/)

Amber Dolors has it bad for her boss. Tall, dark, and smexy, the man has a way of giving orders that... Well, she just melts inside. Even though he's older and getting involved at work isn't smart, especially in her very first job, Amber can't help fantasizing about the delicious Alec, with his English accent and commanding ways. What if he's the one she's been looking for, the man who can initiate her into those dreamy, sensual games she's only read about?

Alexander Knight has obviously noticed his hot young assistant. Amber is as adorably nubile as she is whip-smart. But he hasn't risen to the peak of his profession by indulging himself. Integrity and self-discipline are what he lives by—and those don't allow for seducing a sweet, young co-worker who's likely far too innocent for him. Still, he can't help fantasizing about what he'd do to her, especially when she bends over his desk just so...

When the simmering, repressed passion between Amber and Alec breaks free, they're both caught up in the tide of long-ing—and in sating their fierce desires. But they can't forget that they're engaged in a dangerous dance, one that can't be kept secret forever.

DEDICATION

In memory of my stepfather, Leo,
who actually lost a bet about a port in Oklahoma
for oceangoing vessels.

ACKNOWLEDGEMENTS

Many thanks to the Human Resources manager at my day job. Mary Raynard is not only a terrific asset to our company and a lovely human being, but also took the time to listen to my story idea and help me work through the hypotheticals of a workplace romance. Her timely and thoughtful assistance made all the difference at a time I needed it most.

Del Dryden gets a very special thank-you for making a serious exception for me and *talking to me on the phone*. She assisted with this story at a very early stage when I still needed to talk it through with far too many vague details—and managed to give me exactly the insight I needed.

Heartfelt thanks to critique partners Anne Calhoun, Carolyn Crane and Marcella Burnard, who read fast and under fire, as I screeched under the wire for this deadline. Their input, as always, is invaluable. Anne, in particular, bore the brunt of angst for this book, urging me to forge ahead through my angst and trust in the story. She was so totally right.

Additional thanks to Anne for lending me her transjestered story and for NYC authenticity and fact-checking.

Hasna Saadani and Miranda Neville, two of my favorite Brits, read closely and exhaustively to make sure Alec's language met the test of authenticity. Any remaining errors are either a result of my mistake or my obstinacy. Flip a coin on that.

Thanks to Alexander Pierce who answered my Twitter call for help and suggested Rainbow Dash for Amber's overnight bag. Perfect choice.

Thanks also to Tahra Seplowin—@calixofcoffee—for timely and perfect help on NYC details.

Much appreciation, always, to my wonderful editor Deb Nemeth and the team at Carina Press for all they do to make my books shine.

Love to David and my family, who are all so good to me.

UNDER HIS TOUCH

JEFFE KENNEDY

CHAPTER ONE

AMBER SCRATCHED HER temple, but Kiki didn't see the signal. Probably on purpose.

Her roommate and bestie appeared to be wrapped up in her half of the pair of guys currently chatting them up over cocktails in the never-ending quest for sex, romance and happy ever after.

Pretty much in that order—from easy to impossible.

Kiki looked fully into her guy, flirting outrageously, if the vigorous swing of her blunt-cut Bettie Page bob gave any hint. With her black hair and exotically slanted black eyes, Kiki tended to draw attention. Amber often joked that, when she was out with her friend, all the guys made eye contact with her about a foot to the right—or wherever Kiki happened to be standing. Not that Amber couldn't hold her own, but more as girl-next-door than glam.

She tried catching Kiki's eye again as she sipped her second martini, but her friend gave no indication a mutual-bail might be in her future. And their pact prohibited Amber from leaving alone. Too much could happen. She was well and truly stuck.

"So what's it like working on Wall Street?" The guy gave her what he probably thought was a winning smile. What was his name again? Mark. Steve. Dave. Why did they all have to have monosyllabic names?

"Actually, we're in Midtown."

"But is everyone totally ruthless and cutthroat to make money?"

Resigning herself, Amber tried to return the expression and leaned in. "Totally. I carry a shiv to the office."

He didn't quite get the joke and frowned. "Really? I didn't think the neighborhood was that bad."

Kill me now. Bored senseless, she couldn't help toying with him a little. She widened her eyes and twirled a lock of hair around her finger. "Oh, it is! Just last week one of the partners went berserk and attacked her assistant for using the wrong account code. Blood everywhere."

"Wow, really—did you Vine it or anything?" Then he pointed a finger at her, flashing yacht-club white teeth. "A joke, right?"

"Caught me! You're way too clever for me."

He actually puffed up at that and in despair, she elbowed Kiki and scratched her temple pleadingly.

Kiki, with a resigned wrinkle of her nose, made a production of yawning. "I'm beat and I have to be up early. Sorry to break up the fun, but are you ready?"

"Too bad." Amber grabbed her phone case, stuck her sunglasses on her head and shrugged into her coat. "Thanks for the drinks…"

"Greg." Her guy held out his hand and shook hers with a wry smile. "Should I bother asking for your number?"

Ouch. "Well, I—"

Kiki grabbed her arm. "Own it." She lifted a shoulder at

the guys. "Happy hunting, gentlemen."

They made a quick escape, weaving through the busy bar crowded with young execs of all genders, all remarkably the same in their sharp suits and expensive haircuts. Amber sagged dramatically against Kiki. "I so owe you."

"No, you don't. Not this time anyway."

"Color me surprised. I thought you were into yours."

Kiki rolled her eyes. "Works at a bookstore. Makes nothing and wanted to talk about how YA is failing to serve boys. I nearly stabbed him in the eye with my olive pick."

"Did you tell him you're an editorial assistant at the biggest YA publisher in New York?"

She slid a cagey glance at Amber. "No. I went with shampooer at a salon this time. As a test. A regrettable one, as he wasn't worth the lie. At least I discovered I need some realistic details to shore that one up. Do you think most shampooers are working their way up to stylist—or is it a dead-end job?"

"Sounds dead end to me. Why did you stick so long if you weren't into him? I'd been trying to give you the signal for fifteen minutes."

She huffed with impatience. "So you would give yours a chance! He was cute. And into buying and selling, like you are."

"Boring."

"You think they're all boring."

"Because they *are*. White-bread boy with promising career seeking same, but female, for flavorless sex, possible marriage and production of next generation to feed the prep school his entire family graduated from."

"Seeing as how you meet those criteria, I don't think you can cast aspersions."

"But I don't want to. I don't want a Hamptons wedding to a nice guy who comes with a nicely planned life."

"You know, there's nothing wrong with a nice guy."

"Never said there was. I've dated nice guys. It was very nice."

Of course it wasn't tanned Greg's fault that everything he said sounded like blah, blah, blah to her. Not entirely his fault that she wanted something different than what the Gregs of the world offered.

"I want a guy with more…presence." *Mastery.* A man like her boss.

"Does that mean kinkier?"

"Maybe. Probably. I'm young, unattached, living in the city. What if this is my window of opportunity?"

"Then you're doing it wrong because you're not going to find Mr. Kink at the Z Bar happy hour."

"Clearly I'm not going to find him anywhere at all."

"Normal people probably get in a relationship first, then suggest the kinky sex stuff."

"Maybe. So far that hasn't worked for me."

"There, there, darling." Kiki dropped her head on Amber's shoulder. "You'll find Prince Fetish someday. Probably will have a thing for fucking his horse though."

Amber snorted out a giggle and waved down a cab. "At least he sounds interesting."

"Yeah, well, don't be stupid." Kiki held out her crooked pinky and Amber linked hers with it.

"Don't worry."

But she did worry. At least, the problem remained on her mind as she dressed for work, buttoning up her favorite pink blouse and trying to think about the day ahead and not the several disappointments of the night before. First boring Greg and then the erotic book she'd saved as a treat had taken a bad turn. It had been decent until the heroine decided to quit her job, turn over all her money to her dom and become a 24/7 slave.

Why did these fictional doms have to be such assholes? Surely there was a real-world balance out there, a man who could fulfill the sex fantasies and see a woman as an actual person with career ambitions. Because the kitchen-cleaning porn? Not even remotely appealing.

As a palate cleanser, Amber had pulled out her box set of *Sandman,* losing herself in the painful and sometimes horrific journey of dark and brooding Morpheus, the King of Dreams.

Totally different from the world of high finance.

She did love her job. The rush of it, the huge stakes. Even the routine stuff got her revved every morning. Like walking through the steel-and-glass lobby of her office building, the satisfyingly sharp clack of her high heels on the marble floors, even having to show her ID to the security guard. It was all so shiny and exciting.

So was working for Alexander Knight.

She'd landed in clover with this job. Barely above an intern's salary, but with rich potential.

She was working it. Following the business mantra—make your boss look good. A man like Alexander Knight made for excellent inspiration that way, since he already looked pretty damn good. He had a similar vibe as Morpheus, especially at the end of a hectic day, with his dark hair ruffled from scraping his hand through it, snapping out orders to manage his empire.

If being around him gave an extra sparkle to things, well, all the better.

She could—and would—sublimate her sexual energy into the job. Prince Fetish would be nice, but apprenticing to the King of Dreams…priceless.

SHE'D WORN PINK again. That ruffled cotton-candy silk blouse under the severe lapels of her black suit. The one with the tight skirt that showed off her trim young ass. Absolutely appropriate, modest workplace attire. Not that you'd know it from the prurient direction of his thoughts.

If only he could stop thinking about popping her full breasts out of her bra, letting them be squeezed there amidst the pink, framed in black, while he pulled up her skirt and laid her back across his desk.

Bloody hell.

Alec rubbed a hand over his eyes to erase the image and to avoid watching her sashay down the hall, perfect bum twitching, slim calves like cream under her smooth hose, flashing through the demure back slit of the skirt. Though his computer pinged, announcing the arrival of yet another email, he waited a beat to be sure she'd moved out of sight. If he could figure out a way to transfer sweet young Amber Dolors off his team without unfairly impacting her blossoming career, he would in a heartbeat.

Not her fault she tripped his particular trigger, however. As part of senior management, he knew better than to make a pass at her—or do anything to put a smudge on her fresh and shiny reputation. Sending her out in under six months with no reason? It would look bad.

She was too bright and ambitious for some dirty old man to knock down, just because he couldn't control himself.

Because he *could* control himself. Prided himself on it. Iron self-discipline to govern the baser urges that sometimes threatened to overtake him. Stainless integrity. If he'd caught a whiff that anyone in the company—male or female— entertained thoughts about the junior staff of the variety that plagued him with this girl...well, he'd have them called out on the carpet. Had done so in the past.

Rightfully so. He could and would keep himself leashed.

Safe from temptation until the next time she made a trip down the hall, he focused on his overflowing inbox and gulped his tea. Too hot, but the burn helped him to concentrate. Not to think about whether her nipples would be the same color as her blouse or if he spread her slim, creamy thighs—

"No," he said. Inadvertently aloud, and clearly a little too loudly, because the devil herself popped her head round the doorframe. At times such as this he greatly regretted the firm's open-door policy. He needed a closed door. A solid one. And no windows.

Possibly a blindfold. For himself. *Don't think about how her mouth would look under a black silk blindfold.*

"Mr. Knight—did you say something?" Amber had a mild voice, nearly accentless, American Ivy League. It got under his skin. Everything about her did. A sharp, ambitious mind in a simmeringly curved body. From the shining fall of her waist-length honey-brown hair to her Alice-in-Wonderland blue eyes, alert, wide with inquiry. A bit startled, as if he'd caught her off guard. "Can I do something for you?" she asked, a faint line between her brows.

Firmly he pushed away the sudden fantasy of ordering her to kneel and open that blouse. "No, sorry—was talking to my email."

"I don't think it can answer," she replied in a wry tone. "Unless you've got voice-activation that us plebes don't."

"Heh. I apologize for disturbing you—carry on."

"Yes, sir!" She nodded crisply and gave him a cheery smile, completely oblivious to what that phrase did to him. How he'd relish hearing her say it under other circumstances. Yet another completely inappropriate thought. He scowled as three more emails pinged in.

"The bloody things never stop arriving." Ill-timed again, as his muttered comment stopped the lovely Amber from leaving.

She turned back. Tilted her head thoughtfully. "You have it sorting by conversation threads, right? So the stuff for me to deal with goes in a folder you don't have to look at?"

"I know how to use email, Ms. Dolors." He sounded more irritated than he should have. Not that it daunted her at all. In fact, she took several steps into his office.

"It's just that—" She paused, not hesitating, but clearly deciding how to put it to him. "See, as Joe's assistant, with him on vacation this week, I get his inbox along with Jean's email. We all get the same company-wide stuff. But I'm not getting yours. I check your spam folder for anything that shouldn't be there. I should be seeing the unimportant stuff too. Unless Jean is sorting it? As your admin, I'd think she'd be too busy. That's something I could be handling for you, if they aren't. I'd be happy to."

"Is that so?"

She flushed a little, a flustered rose. "I apologize if I'm overstepping. I'd wondered about this before. You have better things to do with your time than delete emails about the company picnic or the vending machine policy. I could be doing that for you." She raised her eyebrows significantly. "I would be doing that, if your inbox was organized by conversation threads."

Despite himself—uncertain whether his frustration was sexual or technological—he huffed out a laugh. "You're waiting for me to tell you I have no idea what you're talking about, right? And then you'll go post on some forum for Millennials about how your stuffy old boss can't handle his own email."

"Never." She gave him a solemn, serious look. "Millennials don't use forums. Too archaic. I'd tweet about it."

He really laughed then and waved a hand at the screen beneath the glass-topped desk. "Show me then."

A bright light flared in her eyes and she set down her water bottle and came round the desk. Tucking a long, shining strand of hair behind her ear, she leaned over, apparently unaware that her hip brushed his arm, nudging his hands away from the keyboard on its recessed tray. Her fingers flew over the keys and she explained as she reordered the lists. "See, the company server sends things by topic. You don't need to look at the standard-topic stuff, the aforementioned vending machine policy and all the griping about it. I can sort through it for you, then bullet-point what you need to know."

Her scent—something essentially fresh, like green leaves—hit him hard. A mistake to let her get so close, bent over his desk as she was. What the hell had he been thinking? So easy to tell her to grasp the far edge of the desk. To stay perfectly still while he worked her black skirt up over her tight little bum. Or to simply brush the back of her knee, where the skirt slit revealed it, the darling tender crease of it. From there, short work to slide his hand up the inner curve of her thigh. She'd be wearing tights, not stockings, but they'd rip easily and—

"Mr. Knight?"

She'd turned her head, looking at him quizzically, as he'd lost track of her explanation, failed to reply to some question. His gaze locked with hers—and her lips parted, the blue of her eyes deepening. The tension sizzled and, had they been anywhere else, anyone else, he'd have taken her up on the implicit invitation. Closed the scant inches between them and taken that mouth, ripped open her pink blouse—

Enough already.

"Looks splendid." He wheeled his chair back a few inches. "Do you need to do more or—?"

"No, it's, um, all set up now." She straightened, smoothed her skirt and picked up the water bottle. "I'll go take a look and flag anything that looks important. Of course, you'll still have total control of it all. You're the final word."

"Thank you." Was the minx baiting him on purpose? Likely had no idea what fire she was playing with. "Now, if you'd leave me be, I'll attempt to get some work done. As should you."

"Of course. Sir." She gave him a little smile and walked back across the office. He stared at the reconfigured email so as not to watch that enticing bottom swinging pertly under her short jacket. "Mr. Knight?"

"What is it?" He snapped it out, wishing she would leave, let him clear his mind.

"I want to do a good job here." She stood in the doorway, hands demurely folded around her water bottle. "If you have any feedback on my performance, or...corrections. I'd be grateful."

Helpless to do otherwise, he watched her until she went out of sight, dark fantasies crowding into his brain.

CHAPTER TWO

H OLY SHIT. ALEXANDER Knight, of the creamy accent and sleek suits, had a thing for her.

She hadn't mistaken the moment. He'd had serious lust in his eyes when she'd bent over his keyboard. In the moment, she'd been focused on making herself useful, seizing the window of opportunity to bring herself to the big boss's notice. With Joe in Europe for the month and his admin, Jean, so busy with whatever it was the woman spent all day on, the time was ripe to show how helpful she could be. Flirtation had been the last thing on her mind, until he'd looked at her.

Wow.

Her heart still fluttered from it. She'd gone wet, just from the look in his eye when she called him "sir." For an endless instant, when they'd locked gazes, she'd imagined he might be about to order her across his desk. To lift her skirt and spread her legs. Never mind that the door stood open, people walking past the row of glass windows, she'd wanted him to.

But he wouldn't. Whether a personality or cultural thing, he pulled out that icy British disdain with devastating effectiveness. He'd cut it off and locked it down, so fast she second-guessed herself. Wouldn't be the first time her perverse mind read in too much. Her particular twist that his clipped instruction to leave him be and get to work sent a rush of heady desire pounding through her.

In her box of a cube, she sorted through his email, finishing the organizing work she'd started. Locking down the steamy fantasies by distracting her head. Not easy, with that look of his burning through her mind. The way his jaw had tightened when she suggested that he would be in control. That she'd appreciate any corrections.

Totally inappropriate, but she hadn't been able to help herself.

She wasn't even entirely sure the hints had taken. Which was always the problem when you hoped the guy would take charge and make you do things. Once she'd made a bet with her boyfriend of the time, knowing she'd very likely lose. They'd been arguing about whether Oklahoma had a port for oceangoing vessels and she'd laughed when he said so, because she knew full well Oklahoma was landlocked. He'd been certain, though, and it was one of those weird facts that would just have to be true.

Figuring she'd lose, she seized the opportunity and set the stakes for the bet—that the loser would have to do whatever the winner told them to, for an entire evening. Thrillingly, she'd lost the bet.

It should have been a sure thing. She'd dressed for it—sexy lingerie, garters with stockings, sky-high heels—and gone to his apartment in such a state of heightened emotion she'd felt unsteady. What would he make her do? They'd been lovers for a couple of weeks, though all very vanilla. All very nice. Even the oral had been civilized. She'd brought up anal once, in a general, roundabout way, testing the waters, and he'd declared it disgusting. Alas.

But surely, any guy with the chance to make his girlfriend do whatever he told her to would come up with something, right?

Not make him dinner and give him a foot rub.

Seriously.

She'd been so pissed, so damnably disappointed, that she'd picked a fight with him a week later over something trivial and blown the relationship. The worst part was, she'd barely missed his company. Something Kiki gave her all kinds of shit about. Yet another three-week relationship. She accepted that and moved on. Still, there had to be a way to find someone who would want to play some sexy games with her. Without her having to provide instructions or trick him into it.

Alexander Knight would know. She had a feeling he'd be damn good at it, with his exacting standards and that sheen of power he wore, the way he gave orders, expecting instant obedience, raising a supercilious eyebrow at any substandard performances.

Thinking about it just made her hotter. Which was bad.

You cannot have an affair with your boss. Snap out of it.

Even if the dashing Mr. Knight had looked at her like he wanted to eat her up in a couple of greedy bites, he hadn't acted on it. Wouldn't, with his perfect manners and adherence to company policy in all ways. Some of the junior staff gossiped about one of the VPs and his tendency to grope. She'd gotten the advice to steer clear of him on the first day. No such warnings about Knight.

Though he was unattached—divorced, was the word, with an ex back in London—he hadn't taken up any of the women in the office on their varied flirtations. More than a few had tried for him, too. Looks, money, power—what's not to go for? Even Kiki had fluttered her lashes at him when she'd visited Amber, which he'd politely ignored. As he did with all the women in the office. A perfect gentleman in every way. Every time.

Except for today, when his mannered reserve had cracked and she'd glimpsed that something beneath, hot, bubbling and so close to the surface she hadn't been able to help trying to tease it out. Because of her. It didn't hurt her ego in the least that he'd looked at her mouth that way. She wouldn't mind playing it up some. A bit of flirtation never hurt anyone.

And wouldn't get her any closer to what she wanted.

In the end, Kiki was probably right that she'd have to go the internet route. She'd looked at the forums—bit of a lie there, making that joke, but then it seemed a lot of the kink stuff on the web was forum-based—and wandered through a few chat rooms. She also wasn't stupid though, and putting herself out there that way felt risky. Nothing like announcing to the greater world of creepazoids that you were a twenty-two-year-old kink virgin looking for a master. They'd sign up, all right—probably not caring how she looked or anything but getting their jollies.

Next thing she'd know she'd be in some Thai brothel and hooked on heroin.

Okay, maybe that would be exaggerating. Still, the prospect of sorting through the guys who would sign up, every overinflated ego who thought that having a love slave would make him more manly, soured her stomach. How did you find out without actually trying them out? And then it would be only about sex and she didn't really want that.

Oh wait—was it just this morning she'd decided to focus on career and forgo this line of thinking for a while?

"Amazing self-control there, Amber. Way to rock those resolutions."

"Are you talking to yourself?"

Her heart jumped and she actually made a stupid squeaking sound as she spun around, nearly falling out of her chair, graceful as a three-legged dachshund. Knight stood in the opening to her cubicle, cool and formal as always. No glimmer of the man she'd shamefully flirted with. "Sorry to startle you. Just wanted to thank you for the ordered emails. Tons better."

"You're welcome. I'm happy to hear it." *Eyes on the prize, Amber. Good job. Make him look good, you'll look good. The rest is chatter.* She gave him what she hoped was a confident, businesslike smile.

"I like initiative." He murmured the words, gaze lingering over her with a glimpse of what she'd seen before burning through, sending a jolt through her. Not so cool and formal after all.

"Alec!" One of Lily's team hailed him. "Got a minute to look at something? I've got some answers for you."

Was that irritation that flashed on his face? He held up a hand. "On my way." Then he fastened his gaze on her. Seemed about to say something and stopped himself with a wry smile. "Good. Very good then."

And strode off.

HE MANAGED TO avoid her the rest of the day. Going to her cubicle had been absolutely the wrong idea. He'd done it once he had himself under control again, convinced his behavior had been a momentary lapse. The product of too much work, too little female companionship, and the unfortunate proximity of a pretty young woman who pushed all his particular buttons.

To prove it to himself, he'd gone to tell her thank you for a job well done. Junior staff should receive positive reinforcement and he knew well he tended to be abrupt. Had been, very likely, unforgivably curt, ordering her out of his office that way. He'd reckoned to give her a pat on the back—figuratively, of course, as it would be a dire mistake to touch her in any fashion—and reassure them both that he was not some sort of office predator.

And then she'd been so startlingly lovely, making that little sound when he surprised her, swiveling in her chair so her skirt rode up over her knees, just askew enough that the upper curve of one full breast showed plainly through the gap of her blouse. In a flash, he'd gone back to full heat, wanting more than anything to pounce on her then and there.

Then saying that to her about initiative, indeed. If they hadn't been interrupted, he'd have been offering to see her after hours with some corrections.

He was clearly losing his mind.

He even had to viciously rein himself in when Bob called him over to look at the quarterly figures. Something he'd brought to Bob's attention the day before from one of his regular reviews. Important answers he was barely able to focus on.

This could not continue. Short of issuing a department memo banning the color pink or putting a smudge on Amber's record by transferring her out, he had no options other than getting himself the hell under control. Something that should be well within his ability to do.

After finishing with Bob and sending a discreet memo to the partners, he left early, taking advantage of a canceled conference call, unwilling to risk being caught late at his desk by the pink-clad Amber without the buffer of the busy office. Making it out of the building unscathed, he congratulated himself on a successful escape—absurd thought, as if Amber were the predator and not the hapless victim.

Potential victim. He'd done nothing more than entertain unsuitable thoughts and some slightly questionable comments. Bad enough.

At the gym, he pounded through his usual routine and more, hoping to sweat it out of his system. Exhausting the body would let his mind clear. When the running and the weights failed to do the job, he secured an empty racquetball court, playing against himself.

A metaphor for his life, that.

Too much alone these days. Perhaps he'd have to give some attention to his sex life, after all. He'd grown tired of the dance of it, the game playing. Dating after divorce felt even more grueling than it had before. Emptier. Far too much work for far too little reward. The sleek women, the clubs, the endless jockeying for position. At some point it had stopped being fun and became an obligation. Much as his marriage had, toward the end. He supposed he'd have to face that the divorce had left him scarred on some fundamental level.

Or exposed his essential flaws.

The rubber ball, slammed too hard, ricocheted past his head and he barely shied in time to avoid being nailed by it. Another excellent metaphor for his life of late.

"Whoa there, Nelly!" Bill Worstler, one of the partners and frequent gym buddy, pretended to cringe behind the door, offering a genial grin. "Teach me to sneak up on you."

Alec shook his head, clearing it, and strode over to grip Bill's hand. "Sorry, mate. Had my mind elsewhere. Didn't hear you knock."

"You were in the zone, all right. Care for an opponent to work some of that aggression out on? Or would you prefer to pound on Curlew directly?"

Ah, yes. Curlew, who'd screwed the quarterly figures. Bob had corroborated it easily enough, once pointed in the right direction. Whether the lapse had occurred out of laziness, incompetence, deliberate obfuscation or sheer error remained to be seen. They'd spent a good part of the day sorting the mess out, so naturally Bill assumed that was the source of his restless frustration.

Instead of a junior assistant young enough to be his daughter.

"Sure." He gave Bill a savage smile. "Let's go a few rounds."

He won four games out of five—losing the one due to a phenomenally lucky shot on Bill's part—and finally said he'd had enough. Satisfyingly drained, drenched with sweat, he took a shower, surprised to see it had gone past nine. He'd been at it hours then, scarcely noticing the passage of time. Too late to think about calling anyone. Not that he could summon a single face or name he'd want to ring up.

Looked like another solo night for his sex life, which was par for the course.

Back at his flat, he warmed the meal his housekeeper had left and scanned the financials for the day. The stock market hadn't closed at much different than it had been when he left the office. Not much there to interest him.

Unwilling to sit, he carried the plate to the wall of glass overlooking the city, eating quickly and feeling the return of that mean edge. He'd thought to leave it behind in gloomy London, blaming his depression and its flip side, sullen anger, on the fog and rain. It had felt that way for a time. But now it roared back in, demanding release.

He'd hardly be good company for a date or even a one-night stand, if he was desperate enough. That wasn't why he'd more or less abstained since coming to the States. Not entirely. He'd been busy, hadn't he? Working his way into the new position, learning the ways of American culture. Relearning to live by himself. The past couple of years had been a good healing period, getting back on his feet.

Or had he been numb? Kidding himself that he'd left the worst of it behind. Instead it seemed it had simply waited him out, looking to sneak back into his psyche through a sweet-faced girl.

The sudden fixation—he wouldn't go so far as to call it an obsession—with his far-too-appealing young assistant likely heralded the end of his self-imposed isolation. A bell signaling that stage in his life should be over. Time to move on. Begin dating again.

Dating. At his age. What a bloody cliché.

No worse than the one he'd been living, with nightly sessions of porn and masturbation. He was a sorry sod and he knew it. And look where it had led, to an unhealthy interest in a young woman with her entire life ahead of her. She was better than that.

Hell, he was better than that.

CHAPTER THREE

*T*ODAY *I* WILL *not flirt with my boss. Be professional, dammit.*

Amber recited her mantra, refusing to let herself go refill her already full water bottle, just to see if Mr. Knight had come in yet. Usually he was at his desk before she got in, but she'd gotten in early. Awakened an hour before her alarm and bouncing with energy. Thinking about him. Replete with extra time, she'd even curled her hair and taken special care with her makeup. Not because of Knight. Okay, not only because of him.

And, because it looked to be a gorgeous spring day and was Casual Friday, she put on a silk dress, teal and sprinkled with rosebuds, instead of one of her suits. The swirling skirt showed off her legs, especially with a pair of strappy sandals. As a nod to the pervasive office air conditioning, though, she added a matching pink cardigan with pearl buttons.

It felt a little prurient, though, sorting his emails and carefully not reading the ones she shouldn't. Like walking through his empty office and rifling through the drawers. The day before he'd been her boss—the big boss—remote, admirable and holding the reins of her future. Now she saw him in a different light.

How wrong would it be to have an affair with her boss?

Wrong. Very wrong.

But holy hell, so very hot.

She heard his voice before she saw him, resisting the urge to pop her head over the cubicle wall—then kicking herself for the blown opportunity when he finished his conversation and moved on without passing her cube. Which, of course, he did. He'd only ever stopped by her cubby once, the day before, and she'd acted like an imbecile, nearly falling out of her chair. And look at her, mooning over him instead of focusing on her work.

This is why it would be wrong.

Resolutely, she typed in a private memo to herself—*Never Shit Where You Eat.*

"Good morning, Amber." Her immediate boss, the one she should really be concerned about, rapped her knuckles on the cubicle divider, a parody of door-knocking. Jean raised her eyebrows. "You look nice today. Hot date after work?"

"I wish. No—just felt springy. And Casual Friday, right?" Abruptly uncertain, especially when Jean seemed to be frowning at her cleavage, she glanced down. The wrap dress covered everything, but maybe it was too clingy.

"Right." Jean gave her a close-lipped smile, indicating her own khaki pants and crew-neck sweater. "Casual. Not garden party."

Another excellent reason to think work, not flirt. Dammit. "I apologize. It won't happen again, Jean."

Her smile thawed a little. "You're young yet. And open-toed shoes aren't exactly against dress code. But, as women, we have to think about the impression we give." Somehow she managed to make "impression" sound like "stripper." "I have to leave early this afternoon and, since Joe's out, you'll have to take notes at the partners' meeting at four. Hopefully that won't interfere with that hot date you claim you don't have."

The better part of discretion there would be not to argue. "Not a problem! I'm happy to do that. Also, let me update you on what I finished yesterday."

At least Jean left satisfied that she hadn't been shirking her work. Fridays were always busy, with all the department heads preparing their reports and week-end summaries for the partners' meeting. The frenetic pace kept her distracted well past Jean's departure at two, right up to the meeting time. Amber took a minute to hit the ladies' before the meeting, in case they went on a couple of hours and didn't take a break.

The dress wasn't that bad. No cleavage showed anyway. To be safe, she buttoned up the cardigan, adding that extra layer. Nothing to be done about the shoes—she could hardly wear her subway sneakers into the partners' meeting. Live and learn.

Undocking her laptop, she carried it into the fishbowl—the exec conference room situated in the middle of their floor, with glass walls on all sides. Though no sound leaked out of the room when the doors were shut, the partners felt the glass added a sense of transparency, part of their official corporate policy. Getting to be actually in on the meeting would be very interesting.

In her eagerness—clearly the code word for the day—she got there early. Being first let her get set up at the corner desk. Lily Straven strolled in not long after. Senior woman in the firm, Lily wore her dark hair up in a severe French twist and, glory be, strappy high-heeled sandals with her red power suit.

Her dark eyes took in Amber over the gold wire frames of her elegant glasses.

"Adorable shoes," Lily commented. "Amber, isn't it?"

Somewhat shocked that the woman knew her name, and uncertain if the shoe comment was sarcastic or not, Amber stood and shook her proffered hand. "Yes, ma'am. I'm Jean's assistant's assistant."

Lily pursed her lips. "Jean left early again, did she? And call me Lily. You make me feel like my Atlanta granny when you say 'ma'am.'"

Apparently not needing an answer on Jean—to Amber's great relief—Lily set down her tablet and turned, leaning against the table and folding her arms. She tilted her head, gold knot earrings winking. "Tell me about yourself, Amber. I know a little from your resume and hiring profile. You went to Yale?"

"Yes, business. Dad's footsteps, all that."

"Not an MBA?"

"Not yet. My dad thought—well, I thought, too—that I should get my feet wet first. See if I like finance. Or if I should do law or…something else."

"Else?"

"Yes. Um. Like maybe something I haven't thought of yet." She'd become a blithering idiot, withering under that sharp-eyed perusal.

Fortunately Lily glanced over her shoulder as two of the other partners arrived, saying hello to them. It didn't help Amber's equilibrium that right behind them walked in Alexander Knight, wearing a silver-gray three-piece suit, who didn't so much as glance at Amber but gave Lily a mock glare.

"Don't grill my assistant, Lily. I don't want her scared off already."

Lily made an unladylike snorting sound and kept her back to him, keeping Amber pinned by raising her perfect black-winged eyebrows. "Nonsense. I'm not scaring you, am I?"

"No, ma—Ms. Straven."

She rolled her eyes dramatically and shook her head. "Gracious. Now I'm my maiden Aunt Rachel." But she smiled more warmly and took her seat. The other female partner, Hai Lin, had already settled herself and taken out an Excel printout. Bill Worstler, senior partner and CEO, gave her a cheerful smile and nod.

The four horsemen, some of the junior staff called them. If so, Alec would be Conquest, with his intense eyes and cutting words.

"Record on?" Bill asked, bringing her back to reality.

"Ready," she replied.

And they got to it.

HE SHOULD HAVE picked a seat where he didn't have to look at Amber. Would have, if there'd been any other chair available on that side of the table. He'd timed it badly, making sure to get there late so as not to be alone with her, and not considering that meant he wouldn't have his pick of chairs.

When Jean sent him the note that Amber would fill in, he'd nearly kicked himself for not predicting the repercussions of that. Between the partners, they rotated whose assistants and admins would take notes for the Friday afternoon meeting. But, given the timing, none of the partners insisted if someone wanted to trade the job away. Jean always managed to offload the task to Joe, who did it efficiently and cheerfully enough that Alec had never given it a second thought.

Of course it had to be Amber, right at the end of his day, sitting behind Lily, looking as fresh and sweet as one of the rosebuds on her dress. He'd avoided seeing her all sodding day and here she sat, long legs crossed, pink toenails matching her high-heeled sandals, delicate fingers flying over her keyboard as Bill reviewed the stats for the week.

She'd curled her hair today, so it lay in glossy ringlets over her shoulders, tucked behind her ears to keep it out of her face as she worked intently. No doubt she thought the little cardigan looked modest, all buttoned up, but the way it hugged her narrow waist and flared over her generous breasts—

"Did Bob confirm the errors you spotted, Alec?" Bill asked. "I suspect your memo was deliberately vague."

With a mental sigh he forced his mind to the figures. At least they let him look somewhere else. "Sadly, he did confirm. I spent most of the day reviewing. It could be a rounding error, but looks to be edging into approximately two million."

"Approximately?"

"Depends on how you slice it. I've not yet determined what happened."

"But it's Curlew's account."

"It is, yes." He raised his brows at Lily, keeping careful focus on her and not the young woman assiduously taking notes behind her. "As he's yours, I thought it worthwhile to wait for this meeting, get your take on how you want to proceed."

"I'd like to proceed by kicking his worthless ass," Lily snapped, swiveling idly in her chair. "Do you think he's skimming?"

Probably. But dicey territory. "We'd want to build the case if so. Could be lousy attention to detail. He hadn't accessed the timesheet edit reports for nigh on four pay periods. Possibly longer."

Lily hissed between her teeth. "So at worst he's embezzling and at best he's lazy. How do we determine?"

Either way, he understood her anger. They'd channel it into a finely honed weapon in this particular battle. Curlew seemed to be an okay bloke, but this would be a substantial hit on the company's integrity. Even if this was all. If it were only the tip of the iceberg, however...

"We need to determine the scope of the problem," Bill decided.

"That's best," Alec agreed. "Audit all of his accounts for the last several years."

"Fine." Lily pulled off her glasses and rubbed the bridge of her nose. "I'll cancel my weekend plans and go—"

"It should not be you," Hai Lin spoke up. "If we determine it's fraud, we'll have to bring in an outside auditor, but it's best if Alexander continues the review, to avoid any appearance of you having covered for Curlew."

"As if I would, that fucker." Lily spun her chair to Amber. "Delete that expletive, please."

Amber glanced up and flashed a sly smile. "I never heard one."

When he'd walked in, the young woman had been practically squirming with discomfort under Lily's notoriously acerbic interrogations. She'd recovered quickly, her sharp intelligence back at the fore with enviable resilience.

"No, that's fine." Lily turned back and folded her hands on the table. "But I think we need to move quickly and I hate to ask you to give up your weekend to this, Alec."

"I had no particular plans." Or plans at all, except the vague thought of attempting to revive his sex life so he could get his head on straight again.

"Still, you'll need help." Bill frowned. "No reason to go it alone and a second set of eyes and hands can make a difference."

"Bob can—"

"No," Hai Lin interrupted. "Already gone to New Hampshire."

"Have Amber help." Lily spun again to look at the young woman. "You've already heard the details, so we don't have to air this further, which is a plus. A good opportunity for you. Unless you have plans you don't want to cancel?"

"Lily—don't put her in that position," Alec protested.

"I'm not putting her in any position. Amber is a big girl and can say no. I'm giving her an opportunity. She knows that."

Over her shoulder, Amber was nodding, bright-eyed and eager. "I'd love to help. I don't really have any plans to cancel. I can work all weekend."

"It's really not necessary," Alec tried again. "I can work fine by myself."

Bill gave him a concerned look. "Do you object to Amber's

assistance for some reason? I know she doesn't have much experience yet, but she's available and I hear she's a hard worker." He smiled over at Amber with a paternal expression Alec quite envied. Clearly it hadn't occurred to his CEO that anything untoward could occur. Which, naturally, it would not. Jesus, he could keep his hands—and thoughts—off the girl and focus on work, couldn't he?

"No, of course not." He tried on the same fatherly expression and felt filthy doing it. "If Amber is willing to give up her weekend, I'm happy to have her help."

"It's settled then," Bill gave Amber a nod of approval. "You get what you can over the weekend. And we'll discuss on Monday. I don't have to tell you two to work discreetly on this, right?"

"No, sir." Amber looked very serious and revved at the same time. Sometimes he thought her enthusiastic ambition turned him on as much as the thought of reddening her creamy white skin. *Stop that.*

The meeting broke up and Amber carried her laptop off to proof the meeting notes, promising to log the draft as confidential. He managed not to watch the seductive brush of her blue silk hem against the backs of her knees by pretending to check his phone for messages. As if he cared about the damn things.

"A word with you, Alec?" Lily leaned her hip against the table and pulled off her glasses to tuck them in her jacket pocket. A smart businesswoman and mother, she rarely minced words.

By the look on her face, he was in for a reprimand and he

had to stop himself from wincing. Had she noticed the drift of his thoughts, the way he couldn't seem to not notice Amber in a sexual way? Bloody hell, he hadn't even touched the chit.

"What's your reservation about using Amber?" she asked.

He had to scramble to untangle his thoughts from the ripe vision that popped into his head at the suggestion of using the girl. "I beg your pardon?"

Lily frowned at him. "She's smart. According to your reports and Jean's, she's careful, diligent, detail-oriented. She has the fire in the belly we like to reward around here. If you have a problem with having her work with you because she's female, I think we should lay it on the table right here. It's not fair for you to discriminate against her—even if it's unconsciously done."

A deeper trap, this. He could hardly admit that he dreaded spending the weekend working with the girl because he didn't trust himself to keep his hands off her. And yet, he almost desperately wanted to seize on sexism as an excuse. *Yes, keep her away from me as I'll only treat her badly.* No, it wasn't fair. Not a bit of it.

"Not at all," he told her, taking refuge in a bit of icy politeness. "I happen to agree with you on all counts. I'm pleased to have her assistance."

"Then what was with the throat-clearing and hemming and hawing?" She narrowed her eyes at him. "I like you, Alec. I think you're a great addition to our firm, but I also feel a responsibility to mentor the young women who work here. If you can't treat Amber fairly, I'll take her onto my team."

Knee-weakening relief warred with bitter denial. Amber

would be on another end of the floor, well out of his sight, if not his fantasies. "I wouldn't want it to seem as if she's being penalized for poor performance," he offered, not sure which way he hoped this would go.

Lily lifted a shoulder. "I can make it seem like a promotion. However." She raised an eyebrow at him. "Work with her this weekend. It's settled anyway. If she's not as good or better than any of the boys, let me know and we'll set it up. But I want you to give her a fair shot. Put her through her paces. Test her if you have to. Don't pull any punches."

He gave her a tight-lipped smile, internally reeling that the woman seemed to have no idea of the way his darker nature spun her suggestions. Of course she wouldn't. This was business and he had no reason to let his mind go down that salacious path. "I'm sure I'll be delighted with her performance."

Lily stood, smiling with more warmth. "Thank you. You're a fair man. I know you'll handle this the right way." As she reached the door, she glanced over her shoulder with a wry expression. "And thank you for wading into this mess with Curlew. Good luck nailing him."

"Cheers."

CHAPTER FOUR

AMBER TEXTED KIKI as she walked back to her cube.

Have to bail on happy hour—working on top secret emergency project. ☺

Her phone chimed immediately in answer.

Shouldn't that be ☹? I'm bummed!

Me too—sorry! But good opp. AND working with AK! >:)

OMG! Bonus. Better than time and a half ;-) massage his timesheet for me! Don't be stupid.

Don't worry!

With a laugh, Amber locked the phone. No taking chances with letting someone see that particular exchange. A weekend of all Alexander Knight plus fab career opportunity. The fates had smiled on her today. Maybe the dress was lucky after all. She finished her QA of the meeting notes and filed them for the partners' eyes only. Immediately after, the company IM popped up. Just seeing the "Alec Knight" and the close-lipped, somewhat arrogant smile in his profile pic gave her a shiver.

I have reserved the executive conference room through Monday morning. You can meet me there when you are ready. Perhaps bring your laptop.

She had to laugh at the formal, complete sentences. He couldn't help himself, even on IM. Why the fishbowl though? Good thing he told her as she'd figured on his office. When she arrived, several stacks of files were laid out on the table, with a cartful nearby. Knight had one open and was making notes. He spoke without looking up at her. "We'll put in a few hours tonight, if you're good with that, order in some dinner, then start again in the morning."

"Sounds good to me." She set her laptop down.

"Not there." He pointed at the other end of the long table. "Set up your workstation at the other end. No sense being crowded together."

Hokay then. Maybe he was pissed about Lily backing him into having her help. He certainly sounded frosted. How perverse was she that the tone aroused her as much as it daunted? Both twisty sensations drove her to bait him with the next question. "Do you have instructions for me?"

He paused, the pen stopping its movement across the yellow pad, and he seemed to take a deep breath. But he didn't glance up at her. Didn't deliver one of those searing looks as she'd more than half hoped for. "Since I presume you're better with databases, you'll review those files—both Curlew's working accounts on the shared drive and his officially filed ones. We'll compare those against the hard copy documents. Look for any discrepancies, however small."

"Do you care if I just pull everything into an Excel file? It might be easier to query the Access data for specifics and then cross-reference on worksheets."

"That would be fine. Carry on."

Since his "carry on" had a way of sounding like "shut up and let me work," she set up in silence. It took time to search all of Curlew's folders for relevant files. She didn't really know the guy—other than that he worked on Lily's team and seemed to be generally regarded as a golden boy. Not clear how he got that rep, judging by the state of his files. If someone asked her right this minute, she'd vote for disorganization and possibly incompetence as the reason for the shortfalls. The file names didn't always specify the correct quarter. And some years seemed to be missing, or misfiled. Which shouldn't be right.

At the other end of the table, Knight seemed to be completely absorbed in his task, reading through a file and taking notes with a silver fountain pen that echoed the shade of his gray suit. The man had beautiful hands. Hopefully he wouldn't be annoyed if she interrupted him, but better that than to chase her tail in the wrong direction.

"Sir? Can I bother you?"

"What is it?" he replied, speaking to the file he read.

So chilly. So unreal the way that clipped tone turned her on. *Mind on the job.* "How far back in time are we going?"

"You were at the meeting—to the beginning. Is something unclear about that?"

"Yes, actually." She must have sounded irritated because he lifted his head and met her gaze. For that bare instant, his eyes clawed over her, full of heat, as if twenty feet of glossy conference table didn't stretch between them. She went hot, a little dizzy from the intensity. With the desire to push him, just a little. "I like to be clear on what you want from me," she explained, mouth dry with her audacity, "so I give you exactly what you need."

Across the rows of cubes outside the glass, the setting sun hit the point where its rays streamed in, making the room bright and stuffy at once. The waiting silence grew thick. Then Knight recovered himself, no longer staring at her mouth in that greedy way, icing it down with chilly formality. "Go back ten years then. Depending on what we discover, we'll make decisions from there."

"Well, that's the thing. I don't see ten years in the system. Looks like '09 and '10 are missing. Along with a few months of '08."

"Are you sure you've looked thoroughly?"

"Yes, I've looked thoroughly." When he glared at her, she realized she'd echoed his accent, the way he said it, the way her Boston horse-mad cousin said "thoroughbred." What in hell had gotten into her, to tease him like that?

"Is my accent amusing to you, Ms. Dolors?"

"I'm sorry, sir." *Shit shit shit.* "I love your accent. I'm just frustrated that these files seem to be missing. I wasn't…"

"Mocking me?" He filled in when she trailed off, managing to sound amused, threatening and sexual all at once.

She licked her lips, wishing her mouth hadn't gone bone dry. His hard gaze followed the movement and she felt suddenly like a foolish rabbit taunting the wolf. But did the rabbit ever feel this desperate unwholesome desire to be gobbled whole? He stood and, eyes still on her, pulled off his suit jacket, then tossed it over a chair. In his vest and white dress shirt, he strode down the table, eyes hard and bright.

Unable to bear it—both the dreadful hope and rush of frantic apprehension—she stared at her screen and the unhelpful files. He set his hand on the table next to her keyboard, silver cufflink catching the light. "Well?" he demanded.

"Um…no. I wasn't mocking you. I—"

"Not that." He cut her off. "Show me what you're seeing."

It wasn't exactly a relief, especially with him looming over her, the scent of his subtle aftershave wrapping around her as his lean fingers restlessly tapped on the glass-topped table. And, she realized after a few minutes, he wasn't angry with her, but rather at the missing files. He asked questions, yes, in that clipped tone, as she walked him through the organization—and lack thereof—and showed him the parallels in the files from another of Lily's team.

"Suspicious holes then," he mused. "This is beginning to shade towards deliberate obfuscation. Well done."

The note of warm approval made her flush and she had to drag her mind away from how it might feel to have those elegant long fingers, so close to hers on the table, stroke her skin. She was sweating under the cardigan and wished she could take it off. "How do you want me to handle the missing files?"

"For the time being create blanks for any missing months—can you do that? I want it to be clear those numbers are absent, not counting as zero balances, you understand me."

"Yes. That makes sense. I'll set it up that way."

"The rub is, it will make the job more difficult." He paused. "How late can you stay tonight? I'll see that you get home safely."

"As late as you need me to." She bit her tongue on saying something like "all night, if you ask me."

"Do you need to call someone?" His voice, while still polite and professional, had a deeper tone to it. "A boyfriend, perhaps."

She risked a glance at him, leaning so close. Smiled. "No boyfriend." Was it her imagination or did he look pleased by that? Was he about to touch her? But his eyes cooled, going flinty.

"Pity that." He stood straight, breaking the spell, and returned to his end of the conference table. Pausing there a moment, he unfastened his cuff links, tossing them with bright clinks onto the glass table surface, and rolled up his cuffs to reveal lean, tanned forearms dusted with dark hair. Irresistible.

"Why is that a pity? Do you have a girlfriend?"

His narrow lips twitched and he slanted her a reproving look. "I suppose I deserve that. Very well—no poking into each other's personal business. It will be a long weekend. We may as well buckle down and focus."

Oh yeah. That was going to happen. But she did her best to put her attention on the rows of dry numbers and not on her enticing boss.

HE WAS IN a hell of his own making. Perhaps a weekend of this torment would go some ways toward expiating his many failures. He'd chosen the executive conference room—far more space than they needed—to remind himself that they were on display in their roles in the company. That he, in particular, had standards to uphold and responsibilities to both his partners and everyone under him to behave correctly.

But even putting her at the other end of the room wasn't far enough.

She shifted, sighing in some exasperation at her computer screen and, without taking her attention off of it, began unbuttoning that ridiculously prim cardigan. She shrugged out of it and wiped her brow, full breasts straining against the rosebud-sprigged silk of her dress.

Amber might look sweet and unspoiled, with her fair skin and girlish curls, but she possessed the sensual impact of a siren. Worse, she must have sniffed out his interest because she was definitely flirting with him. Offering up those wide-eyed blue glances and barbed offers. He wanted nothing more than to turn her over his knee and spank her silly until she apologized, then bury himself between her pretty thighs until she gasped out his name.

Bloody hell. He scrubbed a hand over his scalp and glanced at the wall clock. They'd only been working a few hours. Not possible to endure an entire weekend alone with her. How upset would she be if he simply fired her? Maybe not too badly if he then seduced her, stripping her out of her dress and making her purr. He'd find her some other opportunity, some other company, and perhaps explore with her just how much she'd enjoy being given very precise instructions and corrections.

Her gaze flicked up, catching his, the computer screen light making the deep blue of her eyes glow. "Getting hungry?" she asked.

It took him a damnably long time to come up with the correct reply. *Not for her, you fool.*

"Yes. It's half past eight. Shall we call out for something?"

"I'll grab the menus." She stood and stretched, arching her back, and he forced himself to look away. Not to watch the graceful sway of her hips as she walked out, the long, gleaming curls reaching to her waist. Not to picture how they'd look with her naked, maybe with a black collar and cuffs to set off all that white skin. Not to wonder if she'd be as passionately responsive as he imagined.

And—just fabulous—he'd got a hard-on from that image.

Pushing the file away in an abrupt gesture, he headed to the executive washroom. What in the hell was wrong with him? Of course he wouldn't fire her just to have the opportunity to have an affair. Human Resources would have a field day with that one, even if he sank so low as to do it. Which he wouldn't. Neither would he transfer her to Lily's team. He would suck it up and banish these thoughts of her. Find another woman, or several, to indulge his vices. Wasn't this the conclusion he'd come to only the night before? Denied too long, he'd simply built up a head of steam for his favorite kind of sex.

He'd never much cared for the clubs—making a public display of an intimate exchange—and had only gone because Tessa had wanted to. But this situation sealed it. If he couldn't control his thoughts around a naïve young woman in his employ, then he needed to take steps. Not unlike visiting the dentist once a tooth has grown so painful it can't be ignored.

With grim purpose, he locked himself in the washroom and set about taking care of immediate release.

And, if he let himself picture the lovely Amber as he did so, none would be the wiser.

After—which did not take long—he felt more clear-headed and able to settle. More proof that he'd simply bottled up too much and Amber had been the convenient target. He could handle this.

Then he walked back into the conference room to see her perched on the table, elegant legs crossed and idly kicking the top foot as she perused a menu. She gave him that radiantly fresh smile and cocked her head. For a breathless moment it seemed she might be about to say something about what he'd been up to. *Good orgasm, Alec?*

"Burgers, Italian or Chinese?"

"What's your preference?" For something to do, he picked up a cheaply xeroxed Chinese takeout menu. "Pity we've no one on account that delivers a decent curry."

"What is with you Brits and curry, anyway?"

"You wouldn't ask that if you'd had a good London curry on a foggy, rainy night." He found himself smiling back at her, she looked so rapt.

"Do you miss London?"

"Now and again. Some aspects, yes. Others not so much. I like New York and I'd the opportunity to get some distance I needed."

She shook back her hair, honey curls sliding over silk. "Distance from what?"

Oh no, darling, not going to sucker me into a personal conversation. He tossed down the menu. "Since it's the company dime, I vote Italian. Order me the veal piccata and a Caesar salad. And a large espresso."

She didn't take umbrage at his abruptness, pretty mouth curving in a knowing smile. "And for dessert?"

"Mountains of paperwork." He sat, found his place in the file.

"They have cannoli."

"Fine."

"Yay!" She hopped down from the table in a rustle of silk and went to her phone, laughed softly at some message she saw there, the sound both sweet and arousing. Then she was all friendly efficiency, exchanging pleasantries with whoever took the order, promising to meet in the lobby when they rang up and giving the company account.

"Did you just order the same thing I did because you wanted it or because you're being careful?" He couldn't help asking as he made a note about a client letter from 2004.

"Caught me." She had a smile in her voice. "It seemed impolite to order anything more expensive, but if I ordered something cheaper, then I'd be missing out on the best I could have. Besides, easier on them for me to order two of everything."

"Indeed."

"Is that...okay?" She sounded more tentative. She was a fascinating blend of brash confidence and that delightful earnestness.

He made himself give her a reassuring smile. "Of course. Now tell me what you've found for 2004."

CHAPTER FIVE

T HEY FINALLY STOPPED around eleven, though she could have kept going for hours, as revved as she was on sugar and high-voltage caffeine. Still, Alec called it quits, suggesting a fresh start at seven. She'd have preferred to keep going and start later, but he insisted on seeing her safely home, as he'd be using the car service regardless.

Definitely an improvement over the subway, to have the sleek silver car waiting out the front doors for them, complete with driver who opened the car door for her. She ordered them for him regularly, but rarely enjoyed the benefit. Knight asked for her address and relayed it to the driver through the open window. A shelf attached to the partition held a small television screen and a rack of current business magazines and the morning's *Wall Street Journal.* Also the London *Financial Times,* with its distinctive salmon-colored pages. Picking up the latter and clicking on a reading light, he proceeded to completely ignore her. But then walked her to the front door of her building when they arrived.

"You know," she said, "I come home late by myself all the time."

"Yes, but at the moment you're my responsibility." Though he didn't smile, he had a teasing note in his voice. "Besides which, I thought it best to ensure that you went home and not out dancing, so you'll be in top form in the morning."

"Slave driver."

"You have no idea. But I'll bring breakfast." He nodded to the doorman, swept his jacket back from his narrow hips and tucked hands in pockets. "I'll watch you in."

So old school in some ways. Gentlemanly, but more in a paternal way than a romantic one. Turning in the elevator, she could see him out on the sidewalk still, idly chatting with the doorman, eyes on her. As the doors snapped shut, she caught a glimpse of that wolfish hunger on his face.

He was definitely a hot-and-cold kind of guy. One moment she could swear he was about to go for a kiss—or far more—the next he'd be back to his icy reserve. Maybe the age difference worried him. Or the whole work thing. Which, really, she should be thinking about more than she was. Still, if he translated that tendency to be masterful in the office to the bedroom...the job might be totally worth it. She could have drinks with all the Gregs in Manhattan and never meet a man like this one.

What if Alec had experience that way? The possibility pretty much rocked her world to contemplate. Maybe she wasn't just spinning kinky fantasies about her boss but picking up on a vibe. It certainly got to him when she said suggestive, submissive things to him. What would it take to push him into revealing a bit more?

A restless night of very sexual dreams—and a buzzing brain from the late-night espresso, not her best decision ever—had her resolved to test him, just a little. At least to see if she could entice him into opening up some about his personal life. Despite his cool reserve and overall genial nature, he had a kind of sadness about him. Could be the divorce had wrecked him. That was what Nancy in accounting said, that he'd lateraled over from a sister firm in the UK after his ex cleaned him out.

Though he seemed far from destitute. Maybe Nancy meant cleaned out emotionally or some such. Heavens knew her own folks had divorced over twelve years before and her dad had taken years to recover from it, though he'd finally remarried. Her mom did a lot better, but women did, didn't they? Hung out with their friends and went on girl vacations—or with Amber and her sisters—but her dad had spent a lot of time alone. Or at work. Just like Alexander Knight.

She debated a bit over what to wear. Alec hadn't said. Would he be wearing one of his suits? Did he ever wear anything else? No Casual Friday for him, that was for sure.

In the end, she dithered too long if she was going to catch the train in time to get there by seven. So she went with what she wanted to wear—a white halter-top sundress and flat sandals—pulled her hair up into a ponytail high on the crown of her head, and dashed out the door with only minutes to spare.

Then, of course, being a Saturday, the trains ran differently and the weekend desk guard didn't know her, taking forever to check her ID. She blew in ten minutes late, flustered, and was greeted by the ever-unflappable Alec, who raised an eyebrow at her hasty entrance.

"Sorry I'm late!" To make up for it, she plopped herself into her chair, pulled the laptop out of her carry bag and booted it up, pretending not to see the Starbucks bag and venti cup sitting nearby. Restraining herself from offering a flurry of excuses and further apologies.

"Indeed," he said in that coolly polite tone. "I'm most disappointed in you, Ms. Dolors."

Well shit. Perversely, guilt made her feel defensive. "You know, you can call me Amber."

"I don't think that's a good idea." His pen scratched on the paper in the ensuing silence. Not in a suit, but still far from casually dressed, he wore pressed trousers and a soft violet dress shirt, open at the collar. "Have your breakfast, lest it get cold. I forgot to ask what you wanted, but I think I got your usual correct."

Picking up the cup, she deciphered the barista's shorthand. Nonfat peppermint mocha twist. And an egg white wrap in the bag. Bemused she took it out, casting him a long look. How had it happened that Alexander Knight noticed what she typically grabbed from Starbucks?

"Exactly right," she told him. "Thank you."

When he barely grunted in reply, she had to keep going. "It says Alex on the cup."

"Yes. You Americans think it should be Alex and not Alec, as is proper."

"Alexander is spelled with an *x*, not a *c*," she pointed out.

He raised his head, dark eyes sweeping her from head to foot, simmering with something that wasn't impatience, though he tried to make it look that way. "Do you intend to while away the morning discussing nicknames on both sides of the pond?"

She grinned at him, just to watch his eyes narrow. "No, sir."

"Then get to work, lest I be forced to add laggardly habits to your list of transgressions."

Watching him over the rim of her cup, feeling a bit giddy, both from the sexual tension coming off of him and the sugar and caffeine hitting her bloodstream, she decided not to say anything about the items on this supposed list—and what the punishments might be for them. Instead, she said, "Can I call you Alec?"

"No."

"You let some random Starbucks barista call you Alex but not your faithful assistant who gave up her weekend to be your work slave and who found something really interesting when she worked even later last night?"

"You're not going to bait me. The next words out of your mouth had better be something of interest in Curlew's records."

"How about that I think I found the data from the missing months?"

That got his attention. He focused that sharp dark gaze on her, nostrils flaring as if he caught the scent of something. "Misfiled, were they?"

"Mislabeled for sure. You should see."

He hesitated, infinitesimally, then rose and came down the table, peering at the screen and what she pointed out. Walking him through the way the files appeared to have been deliberately buried, her skin prickled with his proximity. And with the certainty that his gaze had brushed over the rise of her breasts from the neckline of the sundress. The exposed back of her neck warmed. The scent of coffee on his breath and his spicy aftershave combined to give her the sense that they were sharing an intimate morning together, perhaps after a long night of sex.

"Well done," he murmured. And touched her bare shoulder.

Barely a brush of his fingertips, a pat of approval, thoughtlessly done perhaps, but it jolted through her as if she'd put her finger in an electric socket. Her nipples hardened in a flash and she went instantly wet. Impossible that such chaste contact could turn her inside out so fast and yet…she pressed her lips together against a soft moan of longing.

Catching his breath, he stopped, hand motionless on her arm, a long, still moment. Then he dragged his fingers up again, stroking against her skin, an excruciatingly slow caress full of sensuality, rounding the curve of her shoulder.

Pausing at the strap of her halter.

Then moving up to feather over her throat. Down to trace her collarbone.

She stayed perfectly still, as if any movement on her part might scare him off. Send him back into his remote formality. He cleared his throat and she heard him swallow.

"Forgive me," he said, voice rough. But he didn't take his hand away, instead, his fingers flexed, dimpling her flesh.

Letting the quiet moan out, she tipped her head back, meeting his intense gaze. So close. Close enough to kiss her and then finish the caress, to slide those long fingers inside to cup her breast and thumb her nipple. To squeeze harder. Vising on her, like his hand on her shoulder.

The one he snatched away then, as if she'd burned him.

"Forgive me," he repeated and took a firm step back. "I apologize for that transgression. Unforgivable, actually."

She swiveled in the chair to face him, tempted to simply rip open that so-correct shirt and run her hands over him until he stopped talking. Instead she smiled. "I liked it. I like you. Alec."

HIS HAND STILL tingled from the velvet softness of her skin, from the way she'd heated under his touch and the fine tremor that had run through her. Even now her nipples made hard points against the white cotton of her damnably innocent-looking sundress, the creamy curves of her breasts only shades darker rising above the clasp of the fabric. She held his gaze, wide blue eyes full of sensual knowledge. He had no doubt that, if he pushed her full skirts up those long, limber thighs, thrust his hand between them, she'd be hot and wet for him. And she'd drop her head back again as she just had, exposing the swanlike line of her throat and making that throaty moan of approving desire.

"We can't do this," he managed. "I can't do this." He said it to remind himself. Firmly. Then thrust his hands in his trouser pockets, needing desperately to relieve the pressure on his raging hard-on.

Her eyes dropped there, pretty mouth curving before she tilted her head. "Looks like you can." She had a teasing note in her voice, an invitation, but also uncertainty. Not as confident as she'd hope to be then.

"I'm your boss, Amber." He said it gently, so she'd know he wasn't rejecting her. Far from it. He seemed to be totally unable to resist her. To his great shame and detriment.

"I'm an adult. Consenting. We're both unattached. Both interested." She probably hadn't meant that last to be a question, but it came out that way.

With a long breath he sat on one of the chairs ringing the room and scrubbed his hands over his face. He'd barely slept, thinking of her and her graceful gestures, her melodious voice and teasing laugh. She'd cajoled him into eating a cannoli, apparently unaware of how she looked, wrapping her lips around the pastry, then rolling her eyes in ecstatic delight at the flavor, delicately licking crumbs from her fingertips and dabbing at the corners of her mouth. The image had stuck with him all night and, when she'd rushed into the room, cheeks flushed from hurrying and full skirt flying around her dimpled knees, it had taken all his self-control not to pull her into his arms for a long, heated kiss.

Which was why he'd had none left to stop himself from breathing in the sweetness of her skin, from running his hand along the seductive texture of it, to extend that moment of devastating contact.

"It doesn't work that way," he finally told her, when he had a modicum of ability to think again.

She tilted her head, crossing her legs, so her dress revealed a glimpse of the underside of her thigh. "We're not both consenting and interested?"

"No. I mean, yes. That is." He sat straight, instructed himself to handle this better. "Those things don't matter. I hold power over your job, arguably your future career. I can't be interested in you. It would be unfair to you, to my partners, to the company as a whole. Most of all it would be unfair to you." With that he stood, thankfully able to breathe again, and went back to the other end of the table. "We won't speak of this again."

"Not speaking of it won't make it go away," she insisted.

"Yes, it will. Trust me—I know."

"How do you know?"

"Because, if we take our attention off of the idea, we'll stop feeding it. Now that we've discussed the elephant in the room, it can return to a manageable size and be eventually banished."

"I'm not sure I believe that."

"I'm older and more experienced than you are. I know about these things." The temper rose, snapping in the wake of unfulfilled lust.

"You're not that much older than I am."

"Old enough to be your father."

"My father is sixty-three." She smiled sweetly and batted her lashes when he glared at her. "I was a late-in-life baby for him."

"And, let me guess, your mother is quite a bit younger."

"Got it in one." She looked smug, but some uneasiness lurked beneath. Something that alerted him to a weakness there.

"How's the marriage these days?"

She visibly faltered. Transferred her gaze to the computer screen. "They divorced a long time ago."

"Ah."

Her turn to glare at him. "Don't give me that oh-so-British, superior 'ah.' The age difference wasn't the problem. Besides, I wasn't proposing anything more than a hot fuck."

Pissed off now. And, despite his best intentions, hurt. Better for her to be mad at him though. To put an end to this ill-advised attraction.

"Regardless, nothing more than a professional relationship between us will occur. I would not blame you should you decide to file a complaint against me. Or perhaps transfer to another team or division."

He almost hoped she would complain. It would be a mark against him—one he ripely deserved—but nowhere near as severe as it could have been. One inappropriate touch and the consequences would sting enough to get it through his addled brain that he could not, under any circumstances, have her.

"What if I did that?" She pushed the laptop aside and folded her forearms on the table, a position that compressed her lush breasts, the curves tantalizing as any forbidden fruit. "If I'm not your direct report, then we could—"

"Absolutely not."

"Why not?"

Persistent, full of fire and drive to get what she set her sights on, that was his girl. And just young enough not to consider the consequences.

"Let me ask you something—would you call yourself ambitious?"

She frowned slightly, taken off-kilter by the question. "Yes."

"Of course you are. That's why you're here. This job is a

good opportunity for you, isn't it? You'll have figured out your steps, charted the ladder to get where you want to go."

"Well, yes, but—"

"Just listen for a moment. If there are rumors about you, even a whisper or snigger in the copy room that you somehow gained career success by shagging the boss, how will that affect you? Affect what you want?"

"I don't care what people gossip about." But a look of uncertainty crossed her face.

He pointed a finger at her, because she began to understand. "You might not, but it would affect you nevertheless. There's always one or two looking to snipe, to cast aspersions on the bright and successful. You're an intelligent young woman. You work hard and diligently. I can see you doing very well indeed. As well as anyone. CEO of your own company someday, perhaps. Would it be worth it, really, to have a shadow on that because of a passing fancy for a man you once worked with?"

She stared at him, paler than usual. Then firmed her lips. "You're right."

"I know." God, how he hated that he was right. "I'm sorry for it. Sorry for my part in this, but I promise you it won't happen again. *We* will never happen."

She nodded, looking at her screen again, hiding the sheen of tears in her eyes.

"Under the circumstances, I understand if you don't want to carry through on this project this weekend. We can say that you became ill. Food poisoning from Luigi's. No one will think a thing of it."

She brushed the back of her hand under her eye. "We ate the same things," she argued, but her voice trembled and it took every ounce of the tattered will he had left not to go to her and wipe those tears away.

"I'll say you were a pig and ate both cannoli. That alone would make anyone ill."

That made her laugh a little. Watery, but there. "I need to visit the ladies'," she said, standing and shaking out her skirts. "And then I'll get back to work." She met his gaze, defiantly, daring him to comment on her tears.

"Understood." He nodded, then put his focus on the file. Staring at the blur of it until she left the room.

CHAPTER SIX

S HE MANAGED TO get through the rest of the weekend. Barely.

It helped that Alec retreated into a politeness so brittle he sometimes seemed like a robot. They shared no more meals. He sent her to eat with money from petty cash, saying he needed to make some calls from his desk, then went out later to get something on his own. And he told her to go home at four-thirty, commenting only that she'd be safely home earlier than on a normal work day.

By midafternoon Sunday, they'd wrapped up the review of Curlew's accounts. The results looked damning indeed, as Alec put it, with a viciously triumphant smile that he immediately squelched. He offered for her to take the next days off, to make up for her time over the weekend, but it struck her as a salve to make her feel better.

To give her time to feel more herself instead of like a reject-ed, lust-crazed idiot.

She really hated that she'd wept over it all. That she'd lingered in the ladies' room, furiously brushing away the hot spurts of tears that kept coming and then had to fix her makeup. Alec hadn't commented when she returned and the way he studiously ignored her somehow made it that much worse.

She'd practically thrown herself at him and he'd shut her down with logic so infallible it embarrassed her that he'd had to point it out. All his "I'm older and more experienced" crap and then he had to go and prove it.

But she'd learned from the experience and she refused to feel any more humiliated.

So she went to work on Monday—looking sharp as hell if she did say so herself—and, even though Alec asked her to be in on the meeting to report on their findings, managed to hold her head high and treat him as professionally as he treated her. When Lily stopped by her cubicle at the end of the day, her heart tripped a little, thinking that Alec had transferred her over. Or had said something.

Instead, Lily smiled warmly. "You should know you really impressed Alec. That's not easy to do. I imagine he didn't bother to tell you, either."

"No. Well, I mean, kind of. Over the weekend, he said so and, like that." *Shut up already.*

Lily didn't seem to notice her babbling. "Good. I think you'll benefit from working with him, but if you ever want to, I'm happy to have you on my team." She raised her eyebrows with a wry look of annoyance. It wasn't common knowledge yet, but Curlew would be gone as soon as they lined everything up.

The conversation shouldn't have rattled her, but it did. Churning up the memories of the weekend. The heat of his touch. The cold edge of rejection.

"TECHNICALLY, HE DID not reject you," Kiki pointed out ruthlessly, over their second happy hour glass of wine. Her roommate had spent the weekend with a guy she'd met and hadn't come back to their shared apartment until late on Sunday, so she missed being updated until they'd both been rushing out the door that morning. She'd prodded at her to agree to drinks, and Amber had spilled the whole sorry tale before they'd ordered the second round.

"You weren't there. You didn't hear how he spoke to me, like I'm in danger of becoming some office bimbo who sleeps her way to the top."

"Oh, stop that. He did not. He obviously would have loved to jump you—and who could blame him?—but he was looking out for you and your rep."

"'Cause I was too stupid to do it."

"No, a guy like him, he's been around the corporate thing for a while and he's seen how things go down. Also, he's smart enough to know he's got to protect himself. What if he had an affair with you and things went south, you got pissed and decided to file sexual harassment? What if you sued the company? Guys have had careers destroyed over that. Probably women, too, though we don't hear about that as much."

The wine tasted sour in her mouth. "I wouldn't do that."

"Wouldn't you?" Kiki drank her wine thoughtfully. "What if—just hypothetically—what if he had done you? What if you'd fucked like bunnies all weekend long and then Monday morning he'd said, thanks for the good times, see you around."

"He wouldn't do that."

"Because no man has done that ever."

"Fine. I've been there. I didn't go psycho about it."

"And then you get laid off, downsized, or slapped for some mistake. Maybe he weighs in on your performance review and says how you shouldn't use such big words talking to clients because it makes them feel bad."

"Preposterous," she replied, trying to make light of her rising annoyance.

"Tell me that you had zero thoughts just then that you'd want to protest. That you wouldn't wonder if it wasn't because he'd had you and tossed you aside."

"He did toss me aside."

"No. He took the high road and resisted the temptation you offered. Which makes him a damn decent guy, really."

"I know." She pushed her empty glass aside and dropped her head on her forearms. "That's what bites about this. I really like him. I like him so much, Kiki."

Kiki patted her arm. "I know and I'm sorry. Is it too soon for the 'other fish in the sea' conversation?"

"Yes. No. Tell me."

"There are other fish in the sea." Kiki swallowed down her last gulp of wine and signaled the waiter with her empty glass. "You'll meet someone else. Maybe tomorrow, maybe next week. You're young, smart, beautiful. You have gorgeous legs and an amazing rack. Men will be lining up."

She wrinkled her nose. "And here I thought you hadn't noticed."

Kiki tried for an eyebrow waggle, a look that did not work with her precisely arched brows. "You could date a lot more than you do and you know it. You're picky."

"I'm picky," Amber glumly agreed, smiling her thanks at the waiter as he dropped off two more overfull glasses.

"I'm not," he said, "and it still doesn't do me a damn bit of good. The two boys at the bar there—pink tee and pinstriped dress shirt?—offered to buy this round. Sounds like I should tell them to fuck off?"

"Good call." Kiki didn't even look. "Tab is mine tonight. I appreciate you keeping the vultures off my poor dumped friend for the duration."

"Don't worry, honey." The waiter patted her shoulder and strode off, calling over his shoulder, "There are other fish in the sea."

"Great, now our gay waiter feels sorry for me. I'm losing track of the clichés. And I wasn't dumped."

"Isn't that what I've been trying to tell you?" Kiki's eyes sparkled with humor, then sobered. "Okay, seriously. What was it about this guy? It's not like you were in love. I'm not sure you had enough time to call it a crush."

"Isn't the definition of a crush that it happens fast?"

"I think the *crush* part is intensity, not speed. Regardless—why take this so hard?"

She'd been asking herself that very question. Making herself take a long, close look at what she'd hoped for. The sense of tremendous possibility she felt had been within her grasp and yanked away. "You know what we were talking about the other night?"

"No idea. Was I drunk? Refresh me."

"It's weird to talk about, but I got this vibe from him that he'd be into...control, you know? Maybe 'cause he's older or my boss—I thought of that—still, there was this kind of flirtation we did and I thought he'd be really good at that. Like we got each other that way."

"A dom/sub thing, you mean."

"As if you know much about it."

"Hey, I read the same books you do. I must have been drunk because I thought you were joking about Prince Fetish. You're saying that's what tripped your trigger with this guy? That you could get your kink on with him?" She gazed reflectively into space. "I could see it. I mean, I only met him the once, but he does have that you'll-kneel-for-me-and-you'll-like-it thing going."

Even hearing her friend give voice to it gave her a rush. A weird feeling, right there. "I can't believe we're having this conversation."

"Why?" Kiki swirled her wine. "These days it's practically not even kinky. You're dead boring if you haven't been tied up a little bit. There's nothing wrong with you for wanting to explore that."

"I didn't say I thought there was."

"But you're embarrassed."

"I don't know what I am. It's just that, this isn't like telling you I really want a guy who's blond, doesn't work in banking and has a good sense of humor. It's an out there thing to want in real life. In the books you'd turn out to be in a BDSM relationship and you'd hook me up with your dom's freaky billionaire friend who happens to be free."

Kiki sipped her wine, held it behind pursed lips, giving her a long and enigmatic stare. Then burst out laughing, snagging a cocktail napkin to wipe the wine splatter off the table. "Sorry! But the look on your face. Couldn't resist."

"I'm so happy my personal torment provides you with entertainment."

"I know. I'm a cruel and heartless friend." She tapped her French-manicured nails on the table, thinking. "I make that this is a thing with you and you're not going to be satisfied until you find a way to work it out. You fixated on the wrong guy bec—"

"I did not fixate on him."

Kiki returned her gaze evenly. "I figure you've got three choices—you can keep searching semi-randomly, trusting to your subdar or whatever it is, go through a forum slash dating site venue or go to one of these clubs, check it out."

"It sounds so skeezy." She imagined some kind of basement nightclub, with people dressed in black leather and latex. "And kind of scary. Do I look them up on Yelp?"

"We'll do research and I'll go with you." Kiki nodded and pulled out her phone. "I'm making a reminder, because this time I'm definitely drunk and might not remember. That said—want another round?"

"God yes."

GRANTED IT HAD been some time since he'd been part of the scene—and that had been back in London, which was both more discreet and more open about it all—but Alec was amused to find several groups listed online. He'd briefly thought of ringing up Tessa to ask her if she had any contacts, illustrative of his state of mind right there, that he'd considered it. Not that they'd fight. In fact, he'd welcome that instead of the polite distance that seemed to be all they could drum up for one another.

Of course, Tessa felt betrayed that he hadn't understood her needs. Or rather, that he'd understood them all too well and had declined to participate in some. He'd thought it had been the right thing to do, to give her the freedom to explore them with someone else, to set her free of their promises and wish her well. Instead it had dropped the bottom out of their marriage, that he hadn't been jealously possessive.

You're only playacting. If you were really my dom, you'd want to keep me to yourself, under lock and key.

He'd never been able to explain to her how repugnant he found that. He'd never wanted her to be his slave, had never gone along with her fantasy of being locked in the closet the entire weekend while he went on holiday. It had seemed—no, it *was*—crazy unsafe. And hardly fun for him. Sex was about being together, wasn't it? When he'd met Tessa, he'd enjoyed her passion for art, for managing her gallery, as much as their shared interest in exploring kink. They'd been compatible in so many ways that it had been the heart of irony that the sex eventually broke them up.

Ultimately, he hadn't been able to give her what she wanted. What she insisted she needed. And had broken her heart when he offered to open up their marriage.

He'd thought staying together, maintaining their marriage under any conditions was more important than all else. Not so for her. Thus breaking his heart. Though he'd never let her know that. Better for her, to follow her path where it led.

Which, last he heard, was as a pony slave on some compound in Sweden. So very likely he couldn't have called her anyway.

Disheartening to pick a group at random and plan to visit a munch. It felt to be something only a desperate man would do. But then, wasn't he? The Incident—he liked to capitalize it in his head that way—the Incident with Amber had been a wake-up call. She'd handled it like a champ and stuck out the weekend, and the work every day after. He'd hurt her, something he bitterly regretted, that he'd let things go that far, but she'd held up.

At least, she possessed enough poise and composure that no one else should notice her emotional state. He did, as if he'd somehow, just by touching her that one time, by engaging in that truly uncomfortable conversation, plugged into her mind and moods.

There was an artlessness to her. It might be a product of her youth, but it might also be an essential part of her nature. A kind of frank and open honesty that, combined with her eagerness to experience what life had to offer, made her shine with a unique vibrancy. It would be interesting to see how she would be in another ten years or twenty, to witness the ways she became more honed and polished. And how she remained as freshly open to the world.

Participating in how she responded to being sexually dominated, as he felt sure she wanted, would be a magnitude beyond that.

It would be some other man who would know her that way.

And it was better to work off his pent-up frustrations with

women experienced in submissive play. The need lurked in him, obviously, seething and building where he hadn't recognized it, waiting to sabotage him by surfacing at some unexpected moment, as it had with Amber. Touching her had been bad enough, but the way she'd tipped her head back, offering him her throat in such a perfectly yielding gesture, albeit unconsciously done—she had no idea how close he'd been to wrapping his fist in that convenient ponytail and holding her head back while he untied her halter and feasted on her alluring breasts.

Being away from her only created the illusion that he wasn't perched on the precipice of control. She had simply been a convenient target, with her youthful beauty and naïvely teasing ways. It wasn't her, he told himself for the umpteenth time. All his attention had been on work, on the office, and she was part of that. Desire follows attention, thus the solution would be to transfer his attention elsewhere. Somewhere discreetly removed from his business circles.

So, though he found himself curiously dreading the experience—odd, since it should lead to some much-needed sexual release—he made plans to attend a Saturday munch out on Long Island, driving himself there for extra discretion.

Hopefully to shed himself of this gnawing need.

CHAPTER SEVEN

"WHAT THE HELL is a 'munch'?" Amber asked Kiki, torn between laughter and frustration. Why did all of it have to be so weirdly difficult?

"It's sort of a first-timer's orientation session to BDSM," Kiki said.

"Kind of a dumb name."

"I only do the research, but I do it well, so shut up. It's usually lunch and we can go, chat, hang out, and the people in the group or club kind of vet you, to make sure you're not psycho or unstable, that kind of thing."

"What do I wear?"

"This is your first question?"

Amber rubbed her forehead. "You're right. I just can't get these images out of my head of people wearing black leather or rubber. You know."

"I'm pretty sure this is a street clothes kind of thing," Kiki replied in a dry tone.

"Right. I'm not going to pass the not-a-psycho test, am I?"

"You are pretty wound about this." But Kiki sounded understanding, even kind. "You don't have to do this. Wait until you're ready."

"I think I do have to." The fantasies had been eating at her all week. Even the sound of Alec's voice floating down the hall had her flushing. A glimpse of him, jacket swept back and hands tucked in his pockets as he frowned and discussed something with Jean, had sent her turning on her heel and going the other direction. At this rate she might as well look for another job. Even if she could find one as good, she suspected she'd blown it with Alec regardless. He'd feel like he'd driven her out of the company and would refuse an affair.

And then she might not even enjoy the reality of that kind of sex. She had to find out and this was the safest, most direct route that Kiki had found.

"Besides," she said into Kiki's dubious silence, "it's just munch, right?"

"Ha-ha."

THE GROUP MET in an incongruously bland restaurant better known for their all-you-can-eat salad bar than anything else. Kiki confidently made her way to the back room, reserved for private parties, while Amber trailed behind feeling a little ill. Where was the excited thrill she'd expected? This was just uncomfortable and vaguely tawdry, despite the clean, well-lighted restaurant. Nothing compared to the erotic thrill of the executive conference room and Alec Knight's burning caress on her throat.

Which probably showed how twisted up she was.

Heads turned in their direction when Kiki opened the glass-paned doors, a middle-aged woman hastening their way. She wore a sexy dress, but nothing over the top. Fingering a choker of bright silver links, she looked Kiki over. "Do you have an invitation?"

"Kassandra Kurosawa and Amber Dolors. I emailed." Kiki might have been crashing a launch party at a competing publishing house—something she'd dragged Amber to more than once—with the attitude she pulled.

"And your interest?" The woman effectively barred them from entering further.

Kiki gestured languidly at Amber. "My friend is interested in signing up, or however this works."

"Not you?"

"No. I'm her field-trip buddy."

It might have been better had Kiki chosen a less juvenile metaphor, but she was clearly amusing herself with the entire adventure. "You'll have to wait out at the bar then," the woman replied, not unkindly. "Your friend will be safe with us. You can keep an eye on the doors."

Kiki turned her back on the woman. "You know where to find me," she said, scratching her temple with a slight wrinkle to her nose. "Don't be stupid."

"Don't worry."

Tempting to take her up on the signal to bail, especially given the people in the room beyond. They looked more like the sort who'd show up to one of her mother's couples' bunco parties. Disconcertingly bland and quite the opposite of erotic, with their piled-high salad platters and large iced teas. One pretty woman with long blond hair wore a black leather dog collar, but that was as far as it went.

"Do you want to get a plate or talk first?" The woman asked.

"Talk?"

She smiled. "I thought so. I'm Mitzi and this is my Master's group. Let's you and I sit over here." She guided Amber into a chair by the door, well away from the others.

"I meant," Amber explained, "that I didn't know what we'd talk about."

"Do you have any experience with this at all, honey?" Mitzi looked very earnest and more than a little like a preacher's wife, with her powdered bosom overflowing her low-cut dress. "Are you even old enough to drink?"

"I'm twenty-two," Amber said, stung by the implication. "I look younger than I am."

"And are still very young, no matter how you slice it." Mitzi patted her hand. "I'm going to be honest with you. You'd be better off finding a boy your age, have some vanilla sex, then let him tie you up a little, maybe spank you. Work your way up. Don't be in such a hurry."

"That's a lot easier said than done."

"Oh, honey." Mitzi rolled her eyes and tossed her hair. "Believe me—I know. Been there and did not get to do that. It's not at all easy to find a partner, or partners, to play with."

"Well, that's why I'm here, to find—"

Mitzi was already shaking her head. "No. That's what I'm trying to tell you. Nobody here will touch you. You're too young. Too innocent. You don't know what you're doing, and this is an ethical community. No one wants that kind of liability. Even if someone brought you to a party, you'd never get past the lobby. You look like a fifteen-year-old virgin."

The realization that none of the men in the room attracted

her did little to assuage the mixture of angry resentment and dull disappointment. Some foolish part of her had expected to find Alexander Knight's twin brother here and he would have...thrown her over the back of his horse. Still looking for her fetish fairytale.

"What am I supposed to do?" she heard herself asking in a plaintive voice.

Mitzi gave her a pillowed Chanel-scented hug. "What I told you. Your best bet is to date. You're young and lovely. Play the field, play with kink. Don't try for hard core too soon. When you're ready, you'll know. Now I think it's time for you to go."

Kiki, eating a spinach salad and chatting up the bartender, gave Amber a sharp look. "Bust already?"

"You have no idea." Amber slid onto the bar stool, too bummed to think about eating.

"They're all perverts in there anyway," the blond bartender in a blue Ralph Lauren polo shirt offered. "Not a place for a nice girl like you. I get off in an hour and I have a buddy—you girls want to hit a happy hour somewhere?"

Amber pressed her forehead into the palms of her hands to keep from saying something she'd regret.

"Tempting," Kiki chirped, "and yet...we'll have to decline." She paid up and tugged at Amber's arm. "Come on."

"You didn't finish your salad," Amber protested.

"Fuck it. You ever notice that all the vegetables on those things taste exactly the same—what is with that? It's the chicken nuggets of greens, all chopped up, mashed together and pressed into convincing shapes."

Amber laughed. "God, I'm so depressed."

"This is why we're going for pizza. And a lot of wine."

"You can't get me drunk and feed me comfort food every time I have a meltdown."

"Sure I can." Kiki looped her arm through Amber's. "The onus of the BFF. Also? Pizza and wine!"

ON MONDAY, SHE went to work with renewed resolve to focus on her career.

Yet again.

No more mooning over Alec Knight. No more sex fantasies. *You'll meet the right guy when you're supposed to.*

She'd spent Sunday giving herself a series of pep talks—in between nursing a prodigious hangover, napping, eating leftover pizza and bingeing on chick flicks. As a result of falling asleep at the humiliatingly early hour of eight-thirty, she'd popped awake at five. Considering it an omen from the universe, she took the time to eat a healthy breakfast, iron her best suit with the pinstriped pencil skirt, and put her hair up in a hopefully chic and sophisticated French twist.

Settling into her cubby before seven and enjoying the quiet of the empty offices, she began by filtering Alec's emails, so they'd be sorted by the time he arrived. Though Joe had returned, he'd been happy enough to leave the task to Amber. It might be a little creepy, but she liked doing it for Alec. It didn't count as mooning. Never mind that it gave her a sense of closeness to him, to glimpse his daily correspondence, like catching a whiff of his aftershave when he passed her in the hall.

Like window shopping when you were broke. Didn't hurt to browse.

Several documents needing his signature had come through over the weekend so she carried those in to leave on his desk, feeling briskly efficient and making it three steps into the room before she realized he was already sitting at his desk.

Startled by her abrupt entrance, he glanced up without that frosty barricade he'd erected between them, gaze intensifying as it swept over her, before he cooled it, transformed it into a generic smile, only slightly forced. "Good morning, Ms. Dolors. Aren't you the early bird?"

"Delivering the fresh worms just for you, Mr. Knight." She set the documents on his desk. Felt like fleeing immediately, but made herself stay. If he could handle it, so could she. They could talk to each other as normal people did. "Did you have a good weekend?"

"Fine, thank you. And yourself?"

Aren't we so polite? "It pretty much sucked."

A laugh burst out of him, along with a more genuine, sensual smile, as he sat back in his chair. "I admit I wasn't keen on mine either. Thus the pair of us at it early on a Monday morning." His expression dimmed slightly, as if he suddenly realized he shouldn't have referred to them as a pair of anything. Or that he'd admitted to too much. She had no intention of letting him off this particular hook.

"Why wasn't yours good?" She edged a hip on his desk, making it clear she planned to hold him to a civil conversation.

His gaze traveled to her mouth before he yanked it away. "Disappointing. On a number of levels. Such is the off-work fate of the foreign single man in your city."

Disappointing. Amazing how completely that one word summed it up, especially with his particular cadence, that made it sound so spiked. "Well, this single-girl native shares your fate."

He tapped a pen on the desk, glanced out at the empty hall and back to her with a wry smile. "I find that hard to believe. I'd think they'd be lining up to buy you drinks and so forth."

"Back at you. Aren't the women of New York falling over themselves for a shot at you? I could name half a dozen on this floor alone."

"Please don't." He leaned his forearms on the desk, laced his fingers, checked the hall again. Seemed to gather himself and met her gaze. "Surely you know if I wouldn't cross the line for you, I wouldn't for anyone."

Her heart tripped into a faster beat at his quiet confession. One that oddly made her feel better. Funny that they'd been so carefully formal with each other, not referring to that very frank conversation they'd had. Pretending it had never happened. But it had and he'd wanted her, too. He continued to watch her with that somber concern, waiting for her reply.

"I didn't know that. So thank you for telling me." And now she felt that she owed him something in return. "The thing is...see, yes, they want to buy me drinks and take me out and so forth." She said it the way he did, deliberately teasing him with the imitation, enjoying their shared amusement over it. It helped steady her nerves, get her through what she needed to say. "But, I don't want just anyone. I'm looking for something more specific, a particular kind of relationship. Do you know what I'm saying?"

"I do, yes." A shadow crossed his face and he stared down at his laced fingers.

"The worst part of all this is, I think I could have had that with you."

"Possibly." His knuckles tightened and it hit her suddenly that he was concentrating on not touching her. But he hadn't kicked her out of his office, or invoked that icy reserve to shut the conversation down.

"I could look for another job." She threw it out there in a rush. "What if I—"

"No, Amber." He looked up then and his face had filled with bitter regret. "I wouldn't be able to forgive myself. I won't pretend it's not torture to be around you, to see you every day...but I'm getting a handle on that. This is too good an opportunity for you."

"There are other jobs, other good companies."

"As good as this? No," he continued, answering his own question. "We both know it. You'll stay here and we'll be grown-ups about this. Now, if you're uncomfortable around me, I—"

Her turn to interrupt. "I'm not. You seemed like you didn't want to talk to me."

With a sigh, he unlaced his fingers and sat back in the chair. "I was trying to give you some space. So you wouldn't feel pressured. And *so forth*."

She smiled at his emphasis. "It seems to me that part of the point of both of us observing the lines here is so that we can continue to work together. I want to be able to do that.

Without it being weird."

"We won't let it be weird then." He looked both sad and affectionate, gaze wandering over her face more freely, along with the teasing grin as he pronounced *weird* with an exaggerated American accent. "You're absolutely right that the entire point is doing what's proper for your career and for the company. Don't ever be concerned that I'll cross the line with you again. And if I do make you uncomfortable—" he held up a hand to stop her protest, "—if I ever do, by word or deed, say so immediately. Either to me or to Human Resources, or someone you trust here. I insist on it."

"I would say it to you." It seemed painful somehow, the idea that she'd go around him.

"I hope you would. I'd...I'd like to think that we could have enough of a friendship for that. If not friendly, then at least collegial."

"I'd like that. I'm glad we had this conversation. I'm sorry that I got all emotional before. It's not really my style to lose it." *Mostly.*

He picked up the pen again, rolled it between his palms. "Understandable. It wasn't easy for me either. I think you've been handling things with considerable poise. One of the many qualities I find admirable about you. As a colleague," he added, with a meaningful tip of his head. "To reinforce that, and keep things on that level, I think it's time to give you a bit more responsibility. And not only because Lily has been poking at me about it."

"Poking at you?"

He shook his head ruefully. "She's got this idea that I'm

not giving you enough of a chance because you're female, plus she has a hole in her team with Curlew's abrupt departure. If you prefer to work with her, naturally I'll agree. But it feels to me like…"

"A concession?"

"Exactly." He cocked his head. "But one I'm willing to make, as I believe the fault here has been mine. Your decision."

"Is there an early meeting I didn't know about?" Jean stuck her head in the door. "You two are at it early today."

Amber stood. "No, we were discussing our boring weekends. You?"

Jean rolled her eyes. "Lucky you two. I went to twenty-seven soccer games, fifteen dance recitals and listened to the *Frozen* soundtrack nine-hundred-three point five times."

"Point five?" Alec asked, politely raising his brows.

Jean grimaced maniacally. "Halfway through showing nine-hundred and four, I killed my children. So if you need anything from me, ask for it now. The police will surely be here soon."

"I'll keep that in mind."

"Yeah. Laugh." She shook her head and rubbed her temple. "Both of you single, no kids. I'll just bet you had boring weekends, probably partied and got laid. I don't want to hear about it." She picked up the documents Alec had signed and sighed.

Amber dared a glance at Alec, who returned it with amusement. And an underlying burn, again that shared understanding of what they couldn't have. "Guess we all have our problems, huh?"

"Indeed we do, Ms. Dolors. Indeed we do. On that note—" Alec swiveled idly in his chair, "—and by way of lightening your load in case the authorities do catch up with you, I was contemplating giving Amber here the McCloskey account to manage. What are your thoughts?"

Jean looked her over, as if seeing her for the first time, and Amber had to resist the urge to stand straighter. "It would be a help," Jean conceded, but sounded dubious. "Do you think you're ready?"

Alec only returned her inquiring glance blandly, with a hint of challenge. Not going to bail her out. "You'll be around so I can ask questions, right?" she asked Jean.

"Don't quibble," Alec interjected. "Either you think you can or you don't." *Or you can take the out and go to Lily's team.* He didn't need to say it out loud for her to hear the offer.

Fine then. "I'm ready. Sign me up."

Jean reproduced her child-killing grin. "Come with me, my pretty."

CHAPTER EIGHT

AFTER THE LADIES left, Alec sat pretending to read his email, but images of Amber crowded out the orderly columns and viewing panes. She'd been right that he'd been doing more than giving her space. A weakness he could no longer indulge in. He'd begun to think about *Doctor Faustus*, of all things, the classic from his Oxford education coming back with fever-edged intensity. Odd, as he hadn't thought about it in the decades since, with his head in business, not literature.

But the memory of the classroom discussion came back vividly, along with the scents of lemon-oiled wood, thermos-tea and old books. Faustus asking Mephistopheles how he'd escaped from hell and the devil answering, "Why this is hell, nor am I out of it." Ten thousand hells, indeed, to have glimpsed everlasting bliss and deny himself. *Learn thou of manly fortitude and scorn those joys thou never shalt possess.*

He'd taken to repeating it to himself, as a kind of mantra. Not that it had helped yet.

He'd done a lot of thinking over the weekend. Particularly after the disastrous munch on Saturday. Calling it *disappointing* was understated even for a representative of a culture who made an art of understatement. He supposed Amber had the right of it, that he could have found someone there. The women there had been delighted enough to welcome him in—

one inviting him to collar her immediately, to his acute chagrin—and several quite deflated that he declined to join the party that evening.

Perhaps he'd seemed to be a prude, but what on earth had happened to having dinner first?

To be fair, he'd been on their turf and Americans certainly went about things more openly, but he'd felt strangely similar to a trophy. Also somewhat revolted. Not by the potential partners, though none had been particularly appealing, either. Instead he'd begun to feel oddly panicked, as he had in those last weeks and months before he suggested to Tessa they open their marriage, so she could seek what she so craved. What he could not bring himself to give.

He didn't quite understand his reaction, examining it over the long drive back and the lonely hours of the weekend after. Looking back on his life, reviewing his own emotional and sexual history for clues, he could see he'd never been much interested in the public play aspects. That had always been for Tessa. Though he found some of it exciting, largely because she did, he'd always been a quite monogamous soul. Even at university, when his mates had been going on about shagging as many girls as possible, he'd been with only two. *Picky*, they'd called him, and he'd countered with *selective*.

One of those girls, a lovely brunette named Sasha, had liked to be tied up—his first for such games—and he remembered those days with a piercing nostalgia. They'd spend weekends in her flat, experimenting and improvising. He'd discovered how deliciously she responded to being bound and commanded, about the sweet lines between pain and pleasure.

How he, himself, loved the rush of it, the aesthetics and the long, slow build of tension.

They'd had fun with it. Playing, with no awareness of rules or a community that practiced such things as a lifestyle. Both undergraduates, they'd spent time on their studies more than anything, treating sex as a break, a stress-relieving recess from hard work.

They'd loved each other in a similar way, both intensely and exclusively to that place and time, parting ways amicably. It hadn't even been an actual breakup, as they'd wanted different lives after graduation and neither of them cared deeply enough to sacrifice to stay together—or to ask the other to do so. And yet, that affair carried a lovely charge still, of a vital time in his life, shimmering with passion for learning of all kinds—of books and her body. No wonder parsing the puzzle of his sexuality led back to that era and the lines of classical literature, entwined in his psyche with thoughts of firelit rainy afternoons and rope.

It occurred to him that Amber was older now than he and Sasha were then, though it hardly seemed possible. What would he have done, had he not found that girl at that time, to explore his nature, understand his own needs? He wasn't sure.

But he recognized that in Amber and sympathized with her.

I'm looking for something more specific, a particular kind of relationship. The worst part of all this is, I think I could have had that with you.

Her voice repeated those lines in his head, what she very carefully hadn't said, but they'd both understood. It clawed at his heart—and, to be fair, his groin—how much he wanted to give her more than a tepid "possibly" as an answer. But he absolutely could not. Much as it trapped him, too.

The conclusion he'd come to over the endless Sunday was that, for better or worse, his particular bent seemed to trigger mostly off the person and not the kink itself. He didn't crave to master just anyone—just certain someones. And whatever cruel twist of fate had decided to torment him thus, that part of himself had fixed on Amber.

He understood psychology well enough, too, to suspect her very unattainability had more than a little to do with it. Emerging from the dregs of a painful divorce and obsessing on the one woman you can't have? A midlife wish to return to the tastes and textures of youth, of that first vivid love affair? Textbook.

So, it was to be a test, then. Whether by an uncaring universe or his subconscious self, he'd been tasked with overcoming this weakness that made him crave this fresh, unspoiled girl who offered herself to him on a platter.

She would, if he asked her—worse, if he used that channel already formed between them to command her—look for another job. Likely she'd settle for anything, to create the opportunity to salve the craving he could nearly scent on her skin. The skin he'd had to lock his hands together to keep from touching.

And, as anything fresh and perfect, she'd be smudged irretrievably with the touching. All of her bright promise shadowed because he'd failed his personal test of will.

Thus he could not fail. Avoiding her had only added to the

trial, as if he'd gone cold turkey from some instantly addicting drug. So he'd come to work after waking brutally early from sweat-drenched dreams of her, resolved to talk to her, to at least be near enough to wean himself away. He hadn't expected the jolt to his system when she walked into his office, vital, very nearly elegant with her hair pulled up into a sleek coil and her sharp mind already busy with the day—and then the artless pause, the faint flush when she saw him and that flutter that never failed to make him want to order her to her knees, anticipating how she'd smile if he did.

Resolutely, he forced his mind away. The more they inter-acted as colleagues, the more he'd see her as that, and only that, rather than sexually. Having work to discuss and focus on would both occupy their energy and give them topics to discuss that did not lead to boggy territory. She would continue to grow and shine within the firm, rising through her own merit, justifying his mentorship.

After a time, with careful tending, their relationship would be purely professional.

He would pass this test if it killed him. Which it might.

Why this is hell, nor am I out of it.

ULTIMATELY, THE CONVERSATION bolstered her. *Surely you know if I wouldn't cross the line for you, I wouldn't for anyone.* She hugged that admission to herself, even knowing that it shouldn't have mattered as much as it did. Maybe it was a misery-loves-company thing, or a plain ego thing, but she liked knowing that he'd been thinking about her, too. That the zing between them hadn't been her imagination.

Maybe it mainly helped that she didn't feel so young and foolish for wanting him. The oh-so-self-possessed and powerful Alexander Knight had admitted to struggling to get a handle on himself. *I won't pretend it's not torture to be around you, to see you every day.* And that "possibly" of his, the way he'd almost whispered it, so fraught, so full of the longing that plagued her, too.

If not a love of their shared misery, it felt like their joint resolve had united them on some level. Team Heroic Restraint.

She laughed and rolled her eyes at herself.

"You laugh now, but he's not doing you a great favor. McCloskey is a bear of a client." Jean clicked through the files on her computer, sorting out the ones to authorize for Amber's access. "Although you're organized enough to keep them happy. Better you than me, anyway."

"Knight is giving Amber the McCloskey account?" Joe, who'd returned from Europe with a goatee that didn't suit him, came around the partition into Jean's office. "What, did you sleep with him?"

"Inappropriate, Joe. Shut it down." Jean cut him off, before Amber could react, and with the hell-to-pay tone of the mother of four well-behaved children.

"Jeez—a guy can't make a joke around here. Good job, though, Amber."

"I just hope I don't screw it up," she offered. Hopefully he wasn't really annoyed. Illustrative, however, of Alec's point that people's minds went there quickly enough, without having a reason for it. *Actually I'm getting it because I didn't sleep with him—not for lack of trying.* Of course, that wasn't entirely true, either. He was giving her a vote of confidence, showing that she belonged here and that they could work well together.

"If you don't have enough to do, I can arrange to shuffle a few things onto you." Jean gave Joe the hairy eyeball and he pretended to fend her off.

"No, no, I'm good." When Jean turned back to her computer, Joe made an exaggerated gesture of wiping sweat from his forehead. "If you need help, though, ask me. Maybe we could have a drink after work some time."

"Now you're hitting on her?" Jean grumbled. "No interoffice dating allowed."

"What? That's not in the company rules."

"It should be. Go away, Joe."

"Jeez, going!"

FOR THE NEXT week, learning the ins and outs of the McCloskey account, on top of her other work, kept her well occupied. She and Alec had established a tentatively friendly working relationship over the project. *Collegial*, he'd call it, most likely. He kept the tone between them light, without that cold formality. And, for her part, she pretended not to notice when the back of her neck prickled from his proximity, or the way he sometimes coiled his fingers into a fist or shoved his hands in his pockets when she showed him something on the computer screen.

Though tempted, she resisted the urge to tease him, just a little, at these moments. Some devilish part of her very much wanted to. A deeper part, the starving heart, whispered that if she tempted him enough, he might very well give in, that she could drive him over the edge. Most of the time, she satisfied herself by knowing it.

And if he starred in her fantasies at night, no one need know about it.

It all went reasonably well and, during the day at least, she managed not to think about her sex life—or lack thereof—and what her future might hold. And then Lily invited her to join them for drinks after the partners' meeting on Friday. They'd asked her to take notes again and she could hardly bypass that opportunity. Since they finished business in quick order, Bill suggested they hit the happy hour in the penthouse bar, his treat. Amber, spending a few more moments cleaning up the notes, heard the exchange.

"Why don't you come along, Amber," Lily offered. "Don't you think, Bill? A little recompense for all the hard work she's been putting in."

"Of course you should come along." Bill seemed genuine, then wouldn't hear of it when she tried to demur. She felt less conspicuous when they rounded up a few others, a spontaneous reward for those staying late on a Friday night.

She didn't have to sit near Alec in the big booth Lily snagged, fortunately, since the temptation to subtly flirt with him after a cocktail or two might have overwhelmed her. Unfortunately, he sat directly across the table, squarely between her and the dazzling view of the city skyline, unbearably handsome in his navy pinstriped suit. He'd relaxed, a glass of sipping whiskey in one hand, in a conversation with Bill that made them both laugh. Though their words tumbled under the overall din of conversation, enough leaked through to make her think they were debating the finer points of some sporting event. On the pretext of enjoying the view beyond, she indulged in observing him, his easy smile, how he ticked off his points on the long fingers of one hand, silver watch flashing in the lowering sunlight.

So she caught the moment his expression changed. The flicker of irritated tension as a vaguely familiar woman stopped next to him, provocatively tossing long blond hair over her shoulder. With her profile to Amber, the woman pursed her lips in a seductive pout, and said something that made Alec shake his head. An abrupt gesture of his meant to end further discussion. This woman didn't seem to know that, however, and handed him a card, which he tucked in his lapel pocket after dismissing her. He frowned at his drink, lifting it, and his gaze snagged on Amber's. Guilt. Faint embarrassment. It hit her then, where she'd seen the woman.

At the munch. She'd been sitting at the table, wearing the black leather collar. Though she hadn't been wearing it just now, Alec had recognized her and her invitation.

Had taken her card.

None of her business, naturally. But it burned at her. All his protestations of disappointing weekends and the fate of the single man. Total bullshit.

She sucked down the rest of her martini a bit too fast, making her head—already swimming with unreasonable jealous anger and hurt—that much more woozy. Knowing how irrational she was being only made it worse. She made her excuses, saying goodbye to the table at large, never meeting Alec's gaze. If he even tried to catch her eye.

Of course, he didn't come after her.

Which he wouldn't because they had no relationship. He could sleep with, and kink with, every woman in New York City and she had less than nothing to say about it. In fact, she should be congratulating him.

At least one of them was getting laid.

Fuming, she clipped down the stairs to the subway, joining the press of commuters, the push and shove that usually energized her, made her feel a part of the center of things, but instead seemed as overwhelming as all the rest.

She'd known, hadn't she? Of course she'd known that about him, had sensed it or observed it in his small habits. They'd talked around the edges of it. *Possibly.* And what does a foreign single man who's into domination do to get his kink on but visit one of the very communities she and Kiki had looked up? Jealousy, such an ugly emotion, surged in the back of her throat with bitter bile. Yet she tortured herself by imagining him with that woman. Her, naked and kneeling, wearing that stupid, fucking cliché collar, and him standing over her in his crisp pinstriped suit, that coolly amused smile crossing his lips.

He'd probably find her at the bar after the group broke up. They'd flirt and he'd take her home for the weekend and he'd spend it doing to that blonde bimbo all the things he'd done in all of Amber's many and imaginative fantasies. The thought seriously burned her ass.

"Hey, it can't be that bad! A pretty girl like you should smile." A guy whose elbow was casually looped through the upright as he swayed with the train movement gave her what he likely thought was a charming grin.

She didn't bother to reply, only glared at him.

"Bitch," he muttered, turning away.

"Why do they always tell you to smile?" said the woman next to her, readjusting the strap of her laptop bag. "Like they're God's gift or something."

Amber exchanged a rueful look with the woman and, as the train shuddered to a halt, realized she'd missed her stop by two. With a resigned sigh, she got off and made her way to the platform to retrace her steps.

CHAPTER NINE

KIKI WASN'T HOME. She'd texted that she had an after-work thing—a book launch party which looked to go late—and Amber was invited to be her date. At the time, she'd refused, already at drinks with her own work crew. In her turmoil, she'd forgotten about it until she got home and changed into a casual sundress, and then it seemed like far too much effort to go back out again.

Home by seven on a Friday night. Alone. Mooning after a guy she couldn't have. Truly pitiful.

Although, when she considered she could be out with the guy she could have had, who thought she should smile because girls should be perky all the damn time, home alone sounded pretty good in comparison. It still rankled, though, imagining what Alec Knight might be up to. And that woman, having what she couldn't. What—he'd been very clear and honest about—she never would with him. What she greatly feared she would never have.

A vision of the future her parents wanted for her loomed like a Stepford nightmare. They'd have her marry some nice man from an approved family and they'd live in a pretty house in Connecticut, having vanilla sex until she popped out some kids for the trust fund, dutifully using her maternity leave and then returning to climb the corporate ladder. Over time she would come to care more about color-coordinating the couch pillows with the window treatments, attending the dance recitals and soccer games and observing the company dress code than getting laid. Her boring husband—Biff, his buddies would call him—would lose interest in her, find a nubile mistress, and she wouldn't even care.

All too real a possibility, as she'd watched that story play out between her parents.

Okay then.

Amber had never been the type to sit around feeling sorry for herself. Or to let one failure stop her. The munch thing hadn't worked. There were other ways to meet like minds. Time to stop pussyfooting around it. She poured herself a glass of wine and fired up the computer.

With a sense of dipping her toe into water that might be too cold—or, worse, disease-ridden—she went to a BDSM forum and began reading the threads. A lot of subs seeking masters. More masters seeking subs or slaves. Though it made her skin crawl, the language had to be part of it, right? Kind of like branding. People had to give things a label or they couldn't sort out what they were looking for from the mass of garbage.

Still plenty of garbage to wade through, as it was.

She lurked, reading through conversations and hanging in chat rooms here and there. People would sometimes pair off, or form little groups, and go into private rooms to enact scenes. A lot of the submissive types seemed to pick names that advertised them, like slutgirl69 and 4everUrSlave. Amber could just imagine her mother peering over her shoulder. *Do they have to be so tacky?* Tempting to continue to lurk, though that would get her exactly where she'd started—missing her opportunities, backtracking and alone. That dismal future with Biff.

So, when she uncloaked, she simply called herself NYCGirl. A few people waved or said hello. Immediately several sent her private messages.

> *Domme or Sub?*
>
> *Want to be my slave?*
>
> *Take off your panties. Stuff them in your mouth and meet me in this private room immediately or you'll be punished.*

No. No. And no.

Feeling a little ill—and okay, cowardly—she logged out and shut down the laptop entirely. Carried her glass of wine to the window and stared out. She and Kiki didn't have much of a view, but at least the window looked directly across the street and not at a brick wall. She didn't know how to sort it out, how her fantasies of Alec Knight—or even, before him, her favored faceless stranger—could be so compelling, so profoundly exciting while talking to people actually doing the stuff left her feeling soiled. Bereft, even.

Then she spotted him.

Alec Knight.

Looking as if he'd stepped out of a graphic novel. Standing across the street, hands deep in the pockets of his dark topcoat, streetlamp shining on his face as he looked up at her window.

Her heart gave a foolish, even romantic jump and she lifted her hand to wave. He flinched and took a step, as if he thought to flee. She knew him well enough to see him catch himself. He shook his head slightly, then tipped a finger to his temple in a wry salute. She pointed at him to stay there, grabbed her phone wallet and her heels, then dashed out the door.

She ran down the stairs—far faster than the ancient elevator good only for hauling up groceries could go—praying that he'd still be there. Dashing past the doorman, who only gave her an appreciative grin and a wink for her bare feet, she saw him standing there still, leaning against the lamppost. She stopped to pull on her heels, aware that he watched her do it with that bemused expression she caught on his face sometimes, then crossed between cars.

"I waited," he said. "You needn't have run down barefoot. Though I apologize for this. I shouldn't be here."

"Why are you?"

He lifted his shoulders, looking past her at the traffic, the people walking by, anywhere but at her. "Impulse. A terrible one at that. I didn't expect you to come to your window— wasn't even sure which was yours. I'm a bit drunk." His gaze came back to her face, then down to take in her bare toes in the high, strappy sandals. "And now I'm caught in the act. I apologize. I'll go."

"Don't." She'd said it too sharply and his eyes flew to hers. Met and held. Caught. "Maybe we could go get a drink. Talk."

"About the McCloskey account?" He drew out the creamy syllables, full of irony for them both. "We've talked. There's nothing more to say, is there?"

"If there's nothing more, why come looking for me?"

"You left so suddenly. I was worried about you and wanted to make sure you had got home safely." He laughed then, a ragged sound, and ran his fingers through his hair. "And that's a tidy lie. I knew you were upset—about what you saw, though I don't know how you knew—and I couldn't stop thinking about you. I think about you all the time."

"I think about you, too," she whispered, imagining that, but for this wall of rules between them, she could step into the folds of his open topcoat and wrap her arms around his waist.

"*Why this is hell, nor am I out of it.*" He said it softly, gaze drifting to her mouth, almost to himself.

She knew that line, from something. "Dante's *Inferno*?"

"Marlowe's *Faustus*. It's been on my mind lately. Can't imagine why." He shook his head at himself, much as he had when she spotted him out her window. "It's a cool night and you have no jacket. You should go back in. I'll cease to stalk your doorstep."

"There's a bar on the corner. Let's go have a drink."

"We can't go have a drink together, Amber." But he didn't sound firm. Weary, more than anything. An edge of frustrated desperation.

"Why not? We did earlier this evening. Colleagues meet for meals and drinks all the time. If you really want to, we can even discuss the McCloskey account."

His gaze burned into hers. "You know that's not what we'd discuss. Not why we'd go for this very ill-advised drink you're proposing."

"But you want to," she insisted, testing him by edging closer.

"I want a great many things I can't have."

"Tell me about them."

He breathed out a laugh. "Because we're not torturing each other enough as it is?"

Aroused by this conversation as she hadn't been by the much more frank language from the forum, she cocked her head. "You could set the rules. I'll abide by them."

ALEC SUCKED IN a breath, gut punched by her suggestion, by the sheer impact of her proximity. Amber stood far too close, looking much too sweetly seductive from her polished candy-pink toenails to her goose-pimpled hard nipples, clearly visible through her pretty cotton sundress. She should really be wearing a jacket. He should never have given into the impulse to come here.

And yet—to be brutally honest with himself, as he needed to be in this fight against temptation—the illicit nature of this meeting added excitement to it. Just as letting himself stand across the street from her building had, indulging in gazing up at it, wondering which window might be hers, his system zinging with desire he hadn't felt in years.

She felt it, too, soft blue eyes practically glowing in the spring twilight with the challenge. Daring him to set rules for her. So dangerous. So tempting. Maybe knowing how very profoundly he craved exactly that.

"Topping from the bottom, are you, Ms. Dolors?"

"What does that mean?"

Minx. "I think you know. You're manipulating me masterfully enough."

"I didn't make you come here," she pointed out. "Didn't even ask you to."

"For which I've apologized and attempted to rectify. You are definitely the one tempting me to stay, to draw out what we both know can never be consummated."

A hint of stubborn determination to the set of her chin, she pursed her full lips. Considered. "I went to a munch," she said. Then raised her golden brows, daring him to respond.

Which he nearly had no wherewithal to do. "I...I beg your pardon?" Christ, he actually stammered.

"Don't act all politely aghast. Or don't you know what one is?"

He curled his fingers in his pockets, tempted beyond reason to march her back to her apartment and wipe that teasing smirk from her face. How she'd learned to press his buttons, he had no idea. A despairing part of him—Faustus railing against fate—suspected she'd been born knowing how.

"I know what one is." Giving in, he took her by the elbow and escorted her down to the corner pub she'd pointed out. It helped vent a measure of his mounting energy, anyway, despite the pleased smile flirting on her lips that told him he'd played right into her hands. "More to the point—how do you know? And why in bloody hell would you go to one? Two," he snapped at the hostess. "A dark booth, as private as possible."

Amber. Fresh, vibrant and so innocent. Going to a munch where those sodding would-be masters probably drooled all over all the ways to degrade and humiliate her. Did the chit have no concept of what could happen to her at their hands?

She ordered a cosmopolitan, as she had at the bar earlier. And frowned when the waiter carded her, shining a black light on the hologram to be sure it wasn't faked—also exactly as had happened earlier. Then transferred the frown to him. "You don't have to look so amused. I notice he didn't ask for your ID."

"You have a baby face," he said, just to spark her annoyance further. Though it reminded him starkly of their age difference. Humbert Humbert buying his Lolita a fancy pink cocktail. "Now tell me about this munch you went to."

She laced her fingers on the table and gave him a coy look. "Is that an order?"

"Stop it. We're not playing that game."

"What game are we playing?"

"I'm perfectly serious."

"So am I." Gone was the flirty girl. Steel underlaid her tone.

He sat back and considered her as the waiter set his whiskey in front of him. Amber gave the young man a brilliant smile, tucking a glossy curl behind her ear, and he spilled her drink setting it down. The face of a Victorian doll and the hot-blooded heart of a predator. God save him.

His own heart skidded over a couple of beats when she put her lips to the overfull cocktail and sipped at it, watching him through her long lashes. That would be just irony, were he to have a heart attack here, with his much-too-young date. Colleague. Forbidden fruit, either way. "We are here entirely as friends," he told her, making sure to keep his gaze on her eyes and not on the pale curves of her cleavage. "Because I'm concerned you might be engaging in dangerous behavior."

She sat back, slouching a little against the padded bench, and turned the delicate stem of the glass between thumb and forefinger, apparently contemplating the spin of the liquid within. "I wonder what it is," she said, in a musing tone, "about those starchy proclamations of yours that goes straight through me." Glancing up suddenly, she caught his gaze, hers hot. "That makes me want even more."

"You can't have more. Not from me." *Keep reminding yourself of that.*

She lifted one shoulder and let it fall. "So you keep saying. And that, Alec, who wishes to be only and entirely my friend, is why in bloody hell I'd go to a munch." She rolled out the imitation of his accent, making it far plummier than he actually sounded, he felt sure.

Ignoring her bait, he doggedly pursued the important topic at hand. "Do you have any earthly clue what could happen to you if you encountered an unethical person?"

"Isn't that the point of those things? Have a nice meal out in public so everyone can look everyone else over? I went there because I was trying to do the safe and sane thing."

"You have no idea what you'd be getting into."

"I read." She pinkened, whether from anger or embarrassment. Utterly charming. She'd be a naked little lamb to those people.

"Truth is far stranger—and can be far more brutal—than fiction." He attempted to moderate his tone, to make the explanation quietly rational. "Don't go down that road, Amber. Please."

"Oh, stop looking like I've dammed my immortal soul. You would quote Faust." She picked up her glass and took a deeper drink. Steadying herself. "I saw that woman there—the blonde from the bar. That's how I knew who she was. What you'll likely get up to with her."

"Ah, Amber…"

"I know it's none of my business, what you do," she interrupted. "*Who* you do, but that's why I left like that."

He studied her face. Her obvious chagrin and discomfort. "Embarrassed?"

Her lips twisted ruefully and she went back to turning the glass. "Jealous," she admitted. Then looked at him with that artless honesty of hers. "Not my thing usually, but it just about killed me to imagine her with you, having what I can't have. They wouldn't let me in."

"What do you mean?" He understood, though, and the relief relaxed his fears.

"I think you know that, too." She studied him with shrewd intelligence. "I imagine you're well versed in it. They said I'm too young, too inexperienced, and no one with any sense will lay a finger on me. This woman suggested I go find some nice young man to test the waters with instead."

Her frankness both took him aback and settled him. They could discuss this rationally, as friends, indeed. "It's good advice. I heartily concur."

"Oh—is that what you did?"

The whiskey burned in his throat and he nearly coughed. "I'm not discussing my sex life with you."

"We're discussing mine," she pointed out, ruthlessly persistent.

"At your behest."

"As friends we should be able to talk openly about these

things, and right now you're the only person I know who has any real experience."

"You don't know that."

She folded her arms, which unfortunately lifted her breasts enticingly, and glared at him in disappointment. "Really? You're going to take that position? You're concerned about me doing something dangerous but you won't give me any help or advice at all."

Damn it all. Feeling the bite of his collar, he unknotted his tie and coiled it into his pocket, then loosened the top buttons. Leaned his forearms on the table and met that unhappy gaze. "Yes, that's what I did. It wasn't on purpose, but I found the right girl and we…experimented together. That's why I say it's good advice. It's good to start out easy with this sort of thing, dip your toe in, play with it. Don't go hard core straight off the bat."

"When was this—how long ago?"

"College," he admitted, bracing himself for her inevitable response.

"Younger than I am now."

He sighed, scrubbing his hands over his forehead. Coffee would have been better than more whiskey. "I know. But—" he held up a finger to stop her next argument, "—we were both young, the same age, with virtually the same level of experience. It's not the same thing at all."

"Even if you weren't my boss."

"Even so." He sipped at the whiskey to wash down the truth of that.

"So." She signaled the waiter for another drink. "Are you

saying you wouldn't have anything to do with me, even if we didn't have the work thing going?"

"If you have another, you'll be well and truly drunk."

"What does it matter? Friday night. Nothing better to do." She sounded bitter, her soft mouth set. "Which bothers you—the age difference or the workplace thing?"

"Both. And you'll not argue me out of this."

"You want me though."

"Christ." He sipped from his glass, but only a drop remained.

"You said so."

"I most certainly did not."

"Not in so many words, but near enough," she insisted. Sipped from her fresh drink and licked the drops from her full bottom lip, tracking his expression as he helplessly followed the seductive movement. "Besides, I can see it in the way you look at me. I knew it that first time in your office, when I showed you how your email could be sorted. You looked at me like you wanted to throw me over your desk and push up my skirt."

CHAPTER TEN

"**I**S THIS HOW friends talk?" He tried to make it icily reproving, but the heat of her words, the image she evoked, so exactly what he'd been thinking at the time, rattled him. She read him so clearly, trapping him in the web of his own denials. "This has nothing to do with the issue at hand."

She smiled, a slight curve, knowing better than that, too. "I notice you don't say I'm wrong. That's when it started."

"You *are* wrong." He tried to leave it there. Couldn't. "It started for me long before that."

"Really?" She looked delighted, in a flash going from lethal siren to wide-eyed girl on Christmas morning. "When?"

"I am absolutely not putting that weapon in your hands." Giving in yet again, he nodded when the waiter offered him another round, promising himself he'd leave after this one. "Suffice to say, I've had plenty of time to consider my..."

"Desires?" she filled in, eyes sparkling.

"Options," he corrected, with a sternness that did nothing to daunt her teasing smile. "I've made my position on this abundantly clear. What I want has no bearing on the situation. I will not engage in anything more than a friendly and collegial relationship with you. You may put it down to whatever reason you wish. Place all the fault upon me." *After all, I'm damned already.*

"What about what I want?"

"You don't know what you want."

Her expression cooled. "Don't you say that to me. I may be younger than you are, less experienced, your workplace subordinate, but I'm not stupid."

"No." The whiskey had lost its burn. A bad sign, indicating Amber would not be alone in being well and truly drunk. "I apologize for that. But going to that munch was a foolish idea."

She tapped her nails on the slant-slide of the glass. Pink, like her toenails, they shone a shade lighter than the drink. "I don't agree. It was a safe way to explore, and Kiki went with me. My roommate," she explained when he lifted a brow. "You met her once. Anyway, nothing bad happened. According to this plan you all seem to be proposing to me, I should troll the bars instead, trusting to serendipity to hand me the perfect man to explore these needs with."

Safer ground. Or, it should have been. Something warned him to go carefully. "Far better than attempting to access the lifestyle community, yes."

"By sheer chance."

"If it's meant to be, it will happen."

She widened her eyes and lifted her brows into innocently inquiring arches. "How about online forums? Seems like there are lots of willing masters there."

"Good Christ—you aren't seriously considering that!"

She folded her forearms on the table. Leaned in, as if confiding a secret. "As a matter of fact that's what I was doing when I saw you out my window."

He pushed the whiskey glass aside and drank down some

ice water, willing his brain to stop swirling in his skull in that alarming fashion. God only knew what sorts of predators she'd encounter via such a method. Without thinking, he took her hand. "Amber. Please don't do that. Promise me you won't put yourself in that kind of danger. I couldn't bear it."

The blue of her eyes, almost a violet in the dimness, softened, and she turned her hand to squeeze his. "You do care about me."

"This is your conclusion." He had to laugh. He should let go of her hand. Couldn't.

"I won't try the forums again. They were icky."

Icky. She was priceless. "Good. I'll have your promise, however."

"On one condition."

"Blackmail is an ugly thing."

"Not blackmail. You say you're my friend and you care enough about me that you're sitting here when you're certain you shouldn't be. I want to try to explain something." She returned his gaze with all her earnest sincerity, holding his hand so tightly he couldn't have pulled away if he'd been able to muster the will. "There's this thing inside me that's gnawing away. Like a slow burn, feeding on me. Maybe it's always been there, but something about you—when I met you—set a match to it, and it's like I'm on fire now and nothing cools it. I keep thinking it will go out, but it just grows hotter. I'm starting to feel that if I don't give it fuel, something else to burn, it will consume me. I know that sounds melodramatic, but it's the best way I have to describe it. Do you understand at all what I'm telling you?"

He did. All too well. Uncomfortably so. She might have been describing his own sense of damnation. *Why this is hell...* "Perhaps you should talk to someone about this."

"I'm talking to you."

"I mean a professional—a counselor. The company insurance will cover—"

She let go of his hand, finally, and straightened her shoulders, narrowing her eyes. "Are you implying that I'm in some sort of mental or emotional crisis here?"

No, that would be me. "I'm saying I can't help you and am offering an alternative of someone who can."

"I think you can help me." Her gaze burned with the internal fire she'd described. "Be honest with me, as you've promised to be—do you understand what I'm saying, the feeling I'm trying to describe?"

He reached for the whiskey but didn't drink. Stared into it to avoid her avid eyes, that beautiful mouth speaking the words that would drag him deeper into hell. Or into a paradise not meant for him. He was losing track of which it was.

"Do you?" she pressed, voice insistent.

"Yes." He whispered it, hoping she wouldn't hear. Or somehow not take it as encouragement. Forcing himself to meet her eyes, he continued, "That, however, does not mean I—"

She interrupted, winding her fingers together around the stem of her empty glass. "I'll tell you what I think. You say that fate or chance or serendipity or whatever will put the right person in my path. I agree. Further, I think it's already happened. I've met you. You care enough about me to think of my career, my reputation, but you also worry about my safety. Which is more important?"

NOTHING LIKE SEVERAL cosmos over a few hours to light a fire of bravery in a girl. Nevertheless, her heart thudded as she waited for his reply. Watching the play of emotion over his face as he struggled to form the proper response. With his shirt open and his hair disarrayed from running his hand through it, he looked both more fallibly human and, impossibly, sexier than ever. He was truly wrestling with his conscience over this and, while part of her felt the teeniest bit guilty about putting him in this position, a bigger piece of her admired his integrity so much.

The rest of her exulted that his desire for her outstripped even that. A heady feeling and not only from the alcohol.

Finally he drank a long swallow of whiskey and gave her that wry smile. "You may have missed your calling. You should have been a lawyer."

Was he agreeing? Possibly unbending. "I'd be safe with you. You'd never hurt me."

"Well, not in a way you didn't enjoy." His eyes glittered and focused on her mouth, which had gone dry at the flirtation. Definitely unbending.

"I want that, too," she told him, to push a little of that enticement back his direction.

"So you've made clear." He drained his glass and put money on the table to cover the bill and then some.

"I should pay, since it was my idea to—"

He cut her off with a hard glance. "Don't start with me."

Taking his topcoat from the hook on the booth pole, he draped it over her shoulders. "I'm walking you home. Then I'm going to think."

The spring evening hit her with bracing coolness, a sharp breeze cutting through the narrow streets. Him thinking didn't sound like a good plan. He might come up with more reasons to back out. "Do you want to come up?"

His mouth curved in an unamused smile. "That will not happen."

"But—"

"Listen. If we do this—and I've far from decided on it—then there will be rules."

She breathed out a long, hot sigh of longing. "I like the sound of that."

"Immaterial. You'll follow my rules whether you like them or not. We'll do this exactly my way."

"Yes, Sir." A giggle of pure joy welled up in her, but she squelched it as he'd no doubt think she wasn't taking him seriously.

"This isn't a game—don't treat it as one. You've backed me into a corner and we both know it. It was cleverly done, but that's coming to an end, understand?"

"Not really." She shrugged, too juiced to care. "I'm listening."

"I'm going home to think and you'll do the same. I want you to carefully, thoughtfully review all the ways that this could be a complete and utter disaster. I shall do likewise."

"And here I never pegged you for a glass-half-empty kind of guy."

At the corner of her apartment building, he tugged her into the deeper shadows out of the cutting breeze and pushed her up against the wall with a gentle grip on her shoulders. The angled streetlight lit his face from the side, giving it a sharp, almost fearsome slant. Even in her heels, he stood a little taller than she, gazing down with a brooding expression that made her want to kiss him, just to see him relax and smile.

Instead he leaned in and pressed a kiss on her temple, high on the point of her cheekbone, pausing there and inhaling, his hands tightening on her shoulders. "I'm contemplating an action that goes against my better judgment. Enough so that I'm considering whether I may have lost my mind and require professional help. And yet—I can't seem to help myself."

"I don't want you to." She held still, savoring his hot lips barely touching her skin as he spoke, whispering the words, as if moving or speaking too loudly might break the spell.

"I'm going to think," he repeated. "Do you have plans for tomorrow night?"

Holy shit. If she had, she'd cancel them in a flash. Taking a risk, she reached out and laid her palms on his lean chest. He flinched as if she'd burned him, his breath breaking against her temple. But he didn't pull away. "No plans. Shall I come over?"

He laughed, more a gasp for air, and let go of her shoulders, wrapping his hands around her wrists and staring fiercely into her eyes. "I will call you. If I can't talk myself out of this insanity, I'll take you out for a proper dinner and we'll discuss." He set her hands away and let go, stepping well back. "No more touching. I'll watch you to your door."

She shrugged out of his coat and handed it to him, the air

that much colder for its lack, her already aroused nipples tightening painfully. On impulse she rubbed her arms, squeezing her breasts together so he had to look. "Brr."

He dragged his gaze up and gave her a half smile that had a tantalizing hint of cruelty to it. "You know that, if we go ahead with this, I will make you pay for every time you've teased me that way."

She nearly melted. "Oh God—I hope so."

He smiled in truth and shook his head. "Minx. Go."

She took a few steps, then looked over her shoulder to see him standing there, coat draped over his arm, the wind tugging at the dark fabric, a desperate hunger in his eyes. Desire surged through her and something more—anticipation, delight, feelings both hot and sweet. Pressing her fingers to her lips, she blew him a kiss. Then hurried to the front doors, held open by the doorman, who gave her a pleasant nod.

"Good evening, Ms. Dolors?"

"Best ever." She looked back to see Alec still waiting for her to get safely inside. "Looking to get even better."

CHAPTER ELEVEN

ODDLY ENOUGH, HE slept long and deeply. By all rights he should have tossed and turned, plagued by lurid dreams of Amber as he had been for weeks. Indeed, falling asleep with the candy scent of her skin still swirling in his head, he'd expected the fantasies to ride him even harder.

Instead, he awoke refreshed, remembering no dreams and feeling suffused with a vicious optimism. Looking forward to seeing her that night.

I never pegged you for a glass-half-empty kind of guy. No, he wasn't, was he? In fact he must have donned rose-colored glasses somewhere along the way to be contemplating this step, to think it could possibly turn out well. He'd figured on waking early, as usual, which would have given London enough time to advance to a civilized hour for a phone call. Now with it past one there, he hoped he'd be able to catch Luke at all.

"Alec!" Luke picked up on very nearly the first ring. "Have you had enough of the Yanks? I can find a place for you straight away."

Alec stood and looked out at the city, smiling at the sound of his old friend's voice. "Not yet, though I miss London."

"I can't imagine why. Dreariest spring imaginable. You're no doubt better off. Perhaps I'll move there." The sounds of children shrieking filled the background, along with a referee's whistle.

"Wouldn't that be a brilliant idea?" Alec laughed, knowing well that Luke would never leave the company he'd lovingly built through twenty years of solid effort. "How're Suze and the kids?"

"Fine, fine. We're at a football match for Charlie." Luke paused. "You're not one to call me up for chitchat. Since we can't meet at the pub, how about you just come out with it?"

This, then, was why it had occurred to him to call Luke for advice. He wouldn't mince his opinion and Alec needed a strong dose of reality.

"I've a hypothetical for you."

"Is that so?" The background noises dimmed as Luke must have stepped away from the crowd. "Again unlike you, but I'll accept your 'asking for a friend' gambit."

"An older man considers an affair with a much younger woman. Who works in the same company."

"Is she a direct report?"

"Yes, through a few layers, though that could be altered with reasonably little fuss."

"I assume this hypothetical younger woman is on board with both plans?"

An image of Amber under the slanting light in the shadowed alley—eyes shimmering with sexual promise as she gazed up at him, her slender fingers hot through his shirt as she offered to come over—tore through him with swift and agonizing arousal. "Yes," he managed. "We've discussed."

"So much for hypothetical. You don't need me to tell you

this is a bad idea, Alec."

"Perhaps I do, as I've had no success convincing myself."

"Again, unlike you. Is this about Tess?"

"Is there a point at which everything I do is not about my devastating divorce?" Alec replied, with some bitterness. Which Luke didn't deserve.

"Says the man who pulled scorched earth on his entire life as a result of said devastating divorce," Luke pointed out with wry patience.

"It's been two bloody years."

"So, you're saying you're over it? Ready to walk the streets of the homeland again, visit all your old haunts—perhaps look at one bloody photo of her?"

Alec took a deep breath. Luke had sat through many a whiskey-sodden evening at the pub, offering advice and just listening. More than any other, he knew what that divorce had done to Alec, so he couldn't resent that knowledge. Wasn't that why he'd called?

"You're right. I shouldn't do this. Thank you for being the voice of reason."

"I never said that."

"You called it a bad idea."

"It may be that, but it also may be good for you to do something off the straight and narrow. Perhaps this girl is meant to end this self-enforced penance you've toiled under."

That gave him pause. "Is that how you see what I've done?"

Luke sighed. "Hold on." He muffled the phone but his shouted "Well done, Charlie!" echoed through.

"I should let you go—I've interrupted."

"Not at all. Just tossing out the occasional cheer to encourage the boy. Hate to see what a muddle he makes of it all."

"That makes the both of us then." Alec caught his frown in the faint reflection of the glass. He sounded like a sodding loser.

"You, my friend, made a mess of nothing. Tess is entirely to blame for all of it, the treacherous bitch. I've said as much before. One day you'll listen."

"You have to say that, as my friend."

"Doesn't make it untrue," Luke agreed with cheer. "Does this sweet young thing know of your particular predilections?"

"The core of her attraction, in fact. Why else would she be interested in a man old enough to be her father?"

Luke whistled, soft and low. "Tell me she's gorgeous."

"She is. Of the intelligent variety. Looks like a sexy Alice in Wonderland."

"You have to do this, if only so I can live vicariously through you."

Alec laughed—and it felt good, freeing up some of the logjam of feeling as if he might be a Very Bad Person for even considering this course of action. Hell, who was he kidding? He'd never manage to stay away. If the past weeks had demonstrated anything, they'd shown he stood no chance of resisting her another moment. The prospect of being with her that night made him near insane with anticipation.

"And if I destroy my career doing so?"

"Hang on, I'm still mentally undressing my sexy Alice in Wonderland. Ah, yes. If it comes to that, all the better for me—you'll come back to London in disgrace, forced to work for me for slave wages."

"Seriously. What about the workplace landmines—have you *any* useful advice for me?"

"Simple. Get her out from under your supervision."

"Done." Or would be, by Monday.

"Then you have two courses of action. Keep it under wraps or go to your partners and lay it out. I knew a couple did that—in another firm—she with the company and he a client. Asked for and obtained permission to date. I take it you have no company rules forbidding such?"

"None. How did it work out for the couple you knew?"

"Badly. Relationship fizzled, as they do. A reason perhaps to give yours a whirl on the down-low, to see if this is a fling or something more. No sense making a fuss if it's meant to burn out in a few weeks. If you're confident she won't turn on you for harassment. She could, you know."

"I know." Amber, leaning over the table. *I'm on fire now and nothing cools it. I keep thinking it will go out, but it just grows hotter.* "She's not the sort."

"Well, you've always been an excellent judge of character."

"Except for Tessa."

Luke paused long enough for the sound of a goal made in the distance to leak through. "I don't think so. People change, my friend. You had good years with Tessa and you parted ways because you ended up wanting different things. It happens."

Though he knew Luke had the right of it, he couldn't quite bring himself to agree. Somehow his heart couldn't make sense of what his brain understood. And it made him question his own judgment—of character and otherwise. Especially now, with the same unrelenting hunger Amber had described driving him onward.

The hunger he intended to satiate for them both and damn the consequences.

ALEC HADN'T BEEN what you'd call chatty on the phone. Good thing that curt tone seriously did it for her. From him, instructions to be ready at six, that he'd call up for her and to wear a cocktail dress sounded more enticing than all the glad-handing another guy might offer.

Kiki, sprawled on the couch with her reader and an ice pack on her forehead, seemed less impressed. "Short convo."

"It's not like we needed to discuss world politics."

Her friend narrowed her eyes. "You're giddy. I'm going to make you watch *St. Elmo's Fire* again so we can revisit what happened to Demi Moore when she dated her boss. If you sell off all the furniture and I walk in to find you freezing yourself to death, I won't be nice about it."

"Omigod, I can't believe you're using an eighties movie to scare me. We weren't even born then."

"Great cautionary tales never lose their impact. Look at *Les Mis.*"

"Now I'm going to be destitute and cutting off my hair and selling my teeth to support my illegitimate daughter? That reminds me—I'd better buy condoms. Or do you think he'll have them? He'll probably have a favorite kind."

Kiki adjusted the ice pack and groaned. "Do me a favor and don't have sex with him yet. Go out to dinner, okay, try on the dating thing. Hold off on letting him collar you or whatever kink you have planned."

"We have talked. Last night counts as a date. Besides, he's not like that."

Kiki cracked open one dubious eye. "I thought you were hot for him because he is exactly like that."

"Well…" Kiki had a point. But she also didn't know Alec. "It's hard to explain—and I don't have time, anyway. I need to go shopping. Get my nails done. I wonder if I could get in for a body polish at the last minute?"

"Why am I even bothering to attempt to talk sense into you? You're a hormonal whirlwind. Worse than prom night."

"Don't harsh my buzz."

Kiki snorted. "Fine. Whatever. If you can get a body polish for me, too, I'll go. I feel like a turtle, my skin is so scaly."

Amber went with basic black. Nothing wrong with a classic. Or with the dress's full skirt and uneven hem that bared her legs above the knee in front and trailed dramatically to her ankles behind. Though the purchases meant digging into her savings—something that would appall her father if he knew. Of course, everything about this likely would—she also bought new lace lingerie to match. Including an underwire push-up bra that did spectacular things for her breasts in the heart-shaped bodice. On Kiki's advice, she kept her jewelry demure and simple, and left her hair down, though she curled it meticulously.

"Not the red lipstick," Kiki interrupted, handing her a warm-up glass of wine at five forty-five. "The light pink."

"Red looks better with the black. The pink makes me look like a teenybopper."

"And you think he doesn't love that? Trust me."

"Suddenly you're all on board?"

"I'm swept up in the hormonal whirlwind," Kiki replied in a dry tone. "Besides, you look amazing and it's nice to see you so revved. I hope it's what you've been wanting."

"Aww…thank you!" She hugged Kiki's bony shoulders.

"Even if I am a little worried."

"I'll stick to the signal system if I'm not coming home. I'll check in."

"Good. Though at least he's a known quantity, more or less. I'm more concerned about how this could end."

"I can't think about that right now."

"Well, if we did, we'd never color outside the lines. What's youth without at least one disastrous love affair?"

Her cell rang and she pounced as Kiki shook her head at her enthusiastic squeal.

"I've arrived, though I'm early," Alec purred in her ear, sounding considerably less curt this time. "Take your time."

"On my way!"

She grabbed her heels and ran barefoot down the flights of stairs, stopping in the lobby this time to pull them on, then clicking past the grinning doorman to find Alec out front where he'd been watching her through the glass doors, leaning against the car in a dangerously sleek dark suit, holding a bouquet of pink roses. He raised an eyebrow. "Do you never wear your shoes before hitting street-level?"

"The elevator is glacially slow. Stairs and stilettos make for a dangerous combination." She was out of breath from running down so fast. Or from the sight of him and the prospect of the evening to come. Not to mention the swooningly romantic gesture of the roses.

"For you." He handed them to her with a flourish and a self-deprecating smile. "The color made me think of you."

Kiki had called it on the pink. She buried her face in them, breathing in the thick scent, more than a bit flustered.

"You're blushing," Alec observed with a half smile and an intense look in his eye.

"Sorry."

"Not at all. I find it..." He opened the car door and held out a hand to help her. "Most appealing," he finally finished as she stepped in. The hesitation and his altered tone made her wonder what other descriptors he'd considered using.

She arranged herself, making sure her dress wouldn't wrinkle abysmally as he walked around to the traffic side and let himself in. The shaded partition had been raised this time, screening the driver from view. No newspapers in sight— instead the shelf held an ice bucket with a bottle and two crystal flutes.

"Champagne?" Alec asked as the car pulled smoothly away from the curb.

"Yes, please."

He poured for them both and handed her the flute shimmering with golden bubbles, much like the nervous excitement fluttering in her belly. "Cheers," he said, tapping his glass to hers.

She sipped, then grinned in delight at the smooth, perfectly crisp flavor. "Delicious." Remembering, she pulled her phone out of her beaded evening bag and sent Kiki their all-clear signal of two dancing girls.

"What is that?" He narrowed his eyes at her phone screen.

"An emoji. Texting Kiki."

"Say the word again."

"Emoji. It's this emoticon language. Kiki and I have a system worked out for dates with…" She trailed off, realizing how it sounded.

"With strange men?"

"Um. New ones anyway. We set it up when we first moved to the city."

"Probably wise. So what does that one mean?"

"Oh no—I can't reveal the code! What if you took me captive, sold me into a third-world bordello and used the signals to counterfeit that I was safe?" She wrinkled her nose at him.

"I doubt I could find these emojis on your phone in the first place."

"I notice you don't declare that you would never take me captive."

"If I did, I'd never sell you, but keep you for myself." The words and the desire running beneath them set her system humming. A buzz that intensified when he picked up the hand not holding the flute and kissed the back of it, eyes on hers. "You look very beautiful tonight."

"Thank you." From the heat in her cheeks, she knew she must be blushing even harder. "I didn't expect all this."

"All of what?"

She hesitated to use the word *romance*. This might count more as seduction in his book. As if he needed to employ those methods with her. "Flowers, champagne, fancy dress. I don't know." She shrugged when a line formed between his brows. "Don't get me wrong—I love it. I…" *Am screwing this up.*

"Thought this would be about sex?"

Isn't it? "Maybe?"

He nodded, a bare dip of the chin, as if confirming something to himself. "We may have come to this evening via a rather crooked and treacherous path, but I'm not a fellow for casual sex." He shook off some thought and continued. "If we're going to do this—as it seems we are—we shall do it full out. We'll be exclusive for as long as it lasts and, issues of discretion aside, I plan to treat you as my girlfriend in every way. If that's not acceptable to you—why are you smiling that way?"

"I just kind of love it when you tell me how things will be, the way you say it. All formal and didactic."

He squeezed her fingers, then let go to add more champagne to her glass. "Then you shall enjoy the evening ahead."

CHAPTER TWELVE

S HE'D EXPECTED TO have a great time, but not to be entirely swept off her feet. Apparently when Alec made a decision about his personal life—as he did in the workplace—he committed himself to that direction without reservation.

At the restaurant, the maître d' escorted them to a private room via a quiet hallway. With its discreetly curtained doors and soft chamber music, it felt sealed away from the rest of the world. A waiter brought more of the same champagne—after Alec confirmed she wouldn't prefer another—and left them to peruse the menus.

"So," she said, wavering between the prawns *en croute* and the espresso-rubbed lamb, "is this a secret affair?"

"Because of the private room?"

"That and not coming up to my apartment."

Alec set his menu aside and tipped his head in acknowledgment. "The private room, yes. I'll explain how I think we should go about this, subject to your approval, naturally. Your flat—" He looked chagrined. "I didn't mean it as such. It felt…invasive to breach your personal space that way."

She dipped some bread into the herbed olive oil, amused with him and his manners. "If we're going to do this—as it seems we are—you'll be invading a lot more of my personal space than that."

"A point," he agreed, raising his flute to toast her, but with an ironic touch. Then set it down and studied it. "I find myself still experiencing the unsettling notion that I'll be somehow despoiling you."

"I'm hardly a virgin, Alec." The laugh, like the champagne, bubbled giddily through her.

He glanced at her, obliquely. "There are levels of innocence."

"And what you have in mind will divest me of what I have left?"

His lips curved, expression going from chagrined to cruelly sensual. Her belly fluttered and she nearly squirmed in her chair at the sudden certainty that at that moment he imagined her engaged in something deeply debauched.

"Yes."

He rose and went to the doors, pressing a button to lock the door and signal they should not be disturbed, then came to stand behind her. Just as, she realized, he'd stood that day in the conference room. "Eyes forward," he directed. "Hands folded in lap. Don't move."

The flutter in her belly became a hard thumping as she obeyed. All those dark fantasies shimmered in her mind, resolving with bright clarity into this moment, into the thrill of the reality. Of not knowing what he intended and throwing herself into his power with utter abandon.

His fingers brushed her arm and he might as well have touched her between her legs. Shivering, she bit back a moan and held still as he stroked up, repeating that first caress. Over her collarbone, smoothing along her throat. Aware that her breasts rose and fell with her heated breathing, she felt his gaze there as a tangible sensation.

The hand on her other arm startled her into making a small sound. Not distress, exactly, but he hushed her, fingers repeating the same path, until both hands feathered over her throat, tracing the line of her jaw, then down again, brushing the upper curves of her breasts.

Her nipples so hard they ached, she arched a little, willing him to go farther, to dip those elegant hands inside her dress and fondle her there. With a soft whisper of a laugh, he took his touch away altogether and, turning off the privacy light, sat across from her.

"What have you decided to order?"

Gathering her wildly scattered thoughts, she frowned at the menu, almost unable to make sense of it. "I have no idea now."

"Good."

"Why did you stop?"

He made a tsking noise. "Several reasons. First, because we haven't agreed upon the rules yet. Second, because you attempted to direct me, which will be against the rules. And third—"

The waiter entered, interrupting him and tempting her to stomp on his foot with her high heel. She ended up ordering the *en croute*, as it was the only menu item she could retrieve from her churning brain. When the waiter left, having delivered a dish of caviar and poured her more champagne, she prompted Alec, "Third?"

He simply reached for the caviar and handed her a cracker

dressed with crème fraîche and glistening with the black eggs. Then sampled his own.

"Delicious, don't you think?" he inquired, all politeness, but with a hint of a dare beneath. Apparently asking him what he'd been about to say counted as directing him. Fine then.

"Yes." She savored it, then used her ring finger to dab some crème from the corner of her mouth, licking it slowly while holding his gaze, eyes as innocently wide as she could make them. Two could play this game.

He laughed under his breath and shook his head slightly. "Is it any wonder I couldn't stay away? Third, because I enjoy leaving you hanging. Something you should be aware of before we engage more fully."

"Seems to me that's a double-edged sword—doesn't it mean denying yourself, also?"

"Oh yes." He murmured the words, eyes dark on her over the rim of his flute. The King of Dreams, with his shadowed gaze.

"'Why this is hell, nor am I out of it,'" she quoted him.

"More true than you know."

"Then tell me. Why *Faustus*?"

"How about we discuss my proposed rules instead? Then we can proceed with a better shared understanding."

"Do I get veto power?"

"Absolutely. As do I. Until we've sealed negotiations. Then your only veto will be a safeword."

"Lolita," she offered promptly.

He choked on his champagne. "I beg your pardon?"

Got him with that one. "My safeword. I thought it would

have the appropriate chilling effect."

"Already she knows how to devastate me with a single word."

"You're not so difficult to figure out. But it can be something else. I just wanted to tease you a little."

"And so you have. Lolita it is, to my everlasting chagrin. But, be aware, Ms. Dolors, that soon you will hand me the power to tease you within an inch of your life. Something to consider as you bait me, which you seem to so enjoy."

"Duly considered." Perverse of her, too, that the warning enticed her to bait him more. But she restrained herself.

"And your other safeword?"

"I need two?"

"I prefer it. You can have *Lolita* for a full stop, but I'd like you to choose another for slowing down, negotiating and reconfiguring. Something with a less chilling effect, if you please."

She considered as the waiter delivered their meals, bringing a chilled chardonnay to accompany the seafood they'd both chosen. Alec raised an eyebrow at her expectantly.

"Morpheus."

He paused, searching his memory. "The Greek god of dreams?"

"I was thinking more of Neil Gaiman's character in *Sandman*, but yes." When he continued to look puzzled, she rolled her eyes. "Oh come on. Famous Brit writer? Graphic novels. With your penchant for damnation, I'd think you'd be familiar."

"No. But it's a decent enough safeword, as it's unlikely to

be uttered otherwise. All right. Here's what I propose. You inquired about secrecy. On Monday I shall see to it that you're transferred to Lily's team and out of my direct supervision. Nonnegotiable," he said, when she opened her mouth to interrupt. "I shall do it regardless, as I consider myself already compromised."

"And here I thought I was the one to be compromised."

"Funny girl. As Lily has already badgered me to have you on her team, I believe I can navigate that as a favor to her and without besmirching your reputation."

"I like the sound of besmirching."

"Hush. You, however, may decide upon the relative secrecy. I can go to the partners and obtain permission for our affair, which means everyone in the office would be aware of our business."

"Hopefully not the sordid details."

"One would hope."

"I don't really like the idea of everybody knowing." Worse, all the gossip, questions and eyebrow-waggling that would ensue.

"Nor do I. My preference is to keep this discreetly quiet. This makes sense to me as…" He covered not finishing the thought by sipping his wine.

"As?"

He sighed, quirked a brow at her. "Let's be honest. Once your curiosity is satisfied, you'll likely want to have done with me." He held up a hand. "Which I understand and am prepared to face. You have your entire life ahead of you."

"You hardly have one foot in the grave, Alec." All that

lovely arousal and desire fizzled like champagne gone flat. First Kiki, now him. She didn't want to think about how this would end when they were poised on the brink of such an amazing beginning.

"Yes, well, believe me when I say that endings come along whether you plan for them or not. If what is between us burns as hot and fast as it promises, we'll be calling it a lovely fling and go on with our lives. My argument is that it's better in that case that no one have known of it, outside a circle of trusted friends, naturally."

"I can go along with the discretion plan, but I want to log a protest." She waited until he met her eyes, his expression that cool blankness that maybe meant he hid how he felt rather than that he didn't feel at all. "This isn't about curiosity for me. Not entirely," she amended. "It's mainly about you. I have a serious thing for you."

He smiled faintly, even indulgently. And bypassed the declaration entirely. "Discretion it shall be then. We shall neither arrive at nor leave the offices together, unless in the company of others. To keep our focus on the work, we shall see each other only on weekends."

"No sex on school nights?"

He let that one pass. "All interactions between us in the workplace shall be professional and nonsexual."

"Can I still enjoy the subtext?"

"Whatever do you mean?"

She grinned at his pompous tone and finished off the last of the delicious fish. "I kind of get off on it when you boss me around. But then, I think you knew that."

"There shall be plenty of that—outside the workplace."

"Pity. I'd kind of had this fantasy worked up involving your desk."

"I believe I shall sorely make you regret baiting me this way. Will it please you to know I have a home office also? There's a certain scene we could reenact—to both of our satisfaction."

She almost couldn't catch her breath. He watched her, taking in her reaction, eyes glittering with his own spiking desire.

"That would be acceptable," she managed in a reasonably cool tone. And gulped her ice water as he laughed softly.

"I give you permission to enjoy the subtext then, but not to bait me at the office. That will result in punishment."

"What if I bait you outside the office?"

"What do you think?"

"Gotcha."

"Otherwise, the rules are simple. You do exactly what I tell you to. I decide what will occur and what the punishments for infractions shall be. I make all the rules and they can be as arbitrary as I like. If you object to anything at all, you can say 'Lolita' to call a full stop, at which we'll drop all role-playing. Saying 'Morpheus' will allow us to negotiate and modify the scene, while still enjoying the power exchange."

"Sounds good." In point of fact, it sounded amazing. She might be able to orgasm just from him talking about it.

"No questions? You don't need to think about it?"

She met his gaze levelly. "Alec. I've done nothing but think about this since I met you—and quite a bit before that. Sign me up."

"You're sure?"

"It's starting to sound like you aren't. I know I pushed you into this. Do you want to back out?"

He hesitated fractionally and for a panicked moment, she thought he might. Then he blew out a long breath. "I'm here because I can't bear the thought of it."

"I'm really glad. More than I can say."

The waiter came in, cleared their plates and set a silver tray bearing cannoli on the table. He left and she gave the dessert a significant look. "Really?"

"It seemed appropriate, given that I couldn't properly savor what you inspired on the occasion of our other meal. Go set the privacy button and come here."

Arousal zooming, thighs watery with excitement, she walked the short distance to the door and set the privacy lock. Alec had moved his chair back from the table and she went to him, breathless with the anticipation.

"That's a beautiful dress," he told her, "but I aim to see you out of it. Turn around."

She obeyed, heart leaping like a wild animal against her ribs, head swimming as he slowly drew the zipper down. The pads of his fingers brushed up her spine, teasing, electrifying her flesh, and eased the cap sleeves off her shoulders, encouraging the dress to slither to her feet.

"Step out of it and lay the gown on your chair."

Acutely aware of his gaze on her near-naked self—and desperately pleased she'd sprung for the fancy lace underwear— she did as he said.

"Hands under your hair, behind your neck. Lift it and turn for me. Let me see you."

Slowly pivoting, she reveled in the charged eroticism of it. His casual command. Exposing herself to his avid gaze as unknowing restaurant staff and diners went about their business outside. Even more mind-blowing than she'd fantasized.

"So very lovely. Come to me. Wrists crossed at the small of your back."

A whisper of silk as he drew off his tie and wound it around her hands, binding them tightly there. An unnamable emotion rose in her chest, something like a sob of grief but pounding with sexual desire so intense she thought she might shatter with it.

"Sit on my lap." His voice had gone dark and gravelly. He eased her onto his thigh, hand hot on her waist, and lifted her chin. His dark eyes, always intense, looked nearly black in the candlelight, his face showing new lines of stern arousal that would have undone her even without the rest. "A kiss," he whispered, "to seal our agreement."

Saturating herself in the experience, she relished Alec's obvious desire as much as her own. It felt so perfect, to yield this way, to be half-naked on his lap, held in his grip as his mouth lowered to hers. To know he'd control the kiss and at the same time craved the taste of her. Trying to be gentle, he brushed her lips with his, but his hand tightened on her hip, fingers digging in, and he made a sound she would have called despair in another circumstance, from another person.

Heady with the moment, with him and the way his mouth

sank into hers, she returned the kiss, leaning into him with a sense that she might die if he stopped. His hand on her chin shook and he transferred it to the back of her neck, winding it into the fall of her hair and twisting, pulling her head back so he kissed her more deeply. He tasted of wine and desire, kissing her so hard, the attraction they'd both banked until now meeting and opening like their mouths, feeding on each other and fusing in a nuclear reaction, slamming them into each other and into a blaze of need.

Finally he wrenched his mouth from hers, mainly by the hand fisted in her hair, holding her still as he pulled back a few inches and, breathing hard, stared into her eyes. Without speaking, he reached for the cannoli and held it to her mouth, the command implicit. Feeling deliciously sensual and naughty, she parted her lips and wrapped them around it, well aware of the sexual imagery and the way his eyes fired as he watched her mouth. She soaked in the way he experienced her, as she sank her teeth into the crisp, flaking pastry, then into the sweet cream.

Unable to use her hands, she couldn't prevent the shower of golden crumbs onto her bosom, the smear of cream around her lips. Seeming mesmerized, he set the cannoli aside and, tugging her hair so she arched her back, lifted her lace-encased breasts to his avid mouth as he slowly licked the crumbs from her skin.

CHAPTER THIRTEEN

H E LET THE moment wash his brain clear of everything except her. The white curves of her high breasts rising and falling with her charged breathing. Her delicately pink mouth open, the lipstick delightfully smudged, dabbed with smeared cream. How she arched her swanlike throat to the pull of his hand in her spun-silk hair. Her hot little cunt grinding against his thigh.

A few shimmering flakes still gleamed in the cleft between her breasts and he touched his tongue to them, imagining that her skin tasted sweeter beneath. Seduced by her texture, by the plunging of her heart beneath his lips, he kissed his way up, dragging his tongue along her center line, up to the hollow at the base of her throat. She breathed hoarsely, blue eyes staring blindly at the ceiling, totally pliant but also fighting to stay still. If he slid a finger between her legs right then, she'd probably come immediately.

Not yet. He wanted this as mind-blowing for her as for himself.

Hell, it turned out, had a great deal in common with heaven.

Or perhaps he'd lost track of his moral code entirely, spinning away in the delirium of holding the luscious Amber in his arms, hands bound and deliciously yielding. Watching her move—so graceful and lovely, with those golden curls tumbling down her back to brush the tops of the scandalously sexy black lace knickers—had pushed him nearly to the edge. Touching her skin, so creamy white, nearly steaming with the heat she radiated, had sent him past it, into some realm where he no longer recognized that right or wrong even existed. Those considerations shattered in the sheer erotic gestalt of not just finally having her, but of having her willingly give herself in to his power.

She'd lost that Alice-in-Wonderland mien early on—though when he'd fetched her, she'd looked disconcertingly like a teenager dressed for prom—and now she simmered under his touch. All sensual woman.

Demanding even as she obeyed him.

Moaning in encouragement as he ran his tongue over her satin flesh.

The taste of her both fueled his rapacious hunger and filled him with a pervasive dread that he might never get enough of her, that no matter how much he indulged in her, satiated every sense with her company, he would be forever starved for more. That, when she inevitably moved on, she'd leave him even more empty than he'd been these last couple of years.

Due penance for succumbing to his craving for her.

All the more reason to take whatever she offered, to glut himself on her and shunt aside the prospect of that dismal future.

He nibbled his way up her throat, a fleeting thought crossing his mind that he should pay attention to her sensitive spots, which undid her the most. He lost it again in the pounding haze, as if he'd become some sort of sexual berserker and had lost the ability to do anything but feast on her. Taking her sweet mouth again, he devoured her flavor—cream, roses, lipstick and something essentially her that reminded him of new leaves in spring or the fresh bite of a slightly green banana.

Bite. Inhale. Consume.

She moaned, an agonized sound, and he recovered himself enough to relax his hold, thinking her neck might be getting sore, but she fastened her blurred gaze on his and parted her smudged lips. "More," she demanded.

Never mind that, under the rules, she should not be directing him. This might not last beyond the one night. If it did, he'd torment her with the games of will and discipline. In the blaze of this moment, he had little ability to deny her much at all—or himself. Picking up the cannoli, he held it to her soft lips. Holding his eyes, she opened suggestively wide and gently licked at the end, then sucked the pastry deeply into her mouth, keeping it there so he could see, before closing down on the too-large bite.

The brittle crust shattered, pieces going everywhere. Overcome, he fastened his mouth over hers, taking some of it, the sugar explosion somehow electrifying through the sensual miasma, making his already throbbing cock painfully hard.

He could have her here. Bend her over the remains of their dessert, pull down the tease of her lingerie and plunge into her. She would let him. More, she encouraged it, moving her body in supplication, making those pleading sounds deep in her throat, her mouth feeding on his, tongue stroking him, urging him deeper, wordlessly begging him to take more.

God knew he wanted to.

But not here.

Not for their first time together. Maybe later—if this lasted any time at all—he'd bring her back here and have her in all sorts of deviant ways while people politely dined outside. He might make her believe he'd left the privacy off and titillate her with the thrilling fear of being discovered helplessly bound and exposed to his desires.

Sentimentality aside, that sort of suspense wouldn't work on her tonight—she was too far gone to know it, and that sort of premise relied heavily on her awareness of the world around her. He could likely march her naked through the restaurant and she wouldn't notice. In fact it took her a long moment to realize he'd stopped kissing her and stood them up, steadying her as she swayed, waiting for her to come back from that dark, dreamy pool and focus on his face.

"What—"

"Turn around." He undid the tie around her wrists and put it back on, knotting it simply. "We'll continue this at my place. Do you need to check in—send one of your emojis to tell Kiki that you're okay?"

"Yes." She looked around for her bag, as if she'd forgot its existence entirely, delightfully unaware of how gorgeous she looked in her black lingerie and high heels. Finding her phone—girlishly bedecked with a pink rhinestone case—she swiped the screen, then gave him a hesitant look. "Am I...staying the night?"

"As far as I'm concerned."

She smiled, dazzling, and selected a symbol, sending it with a whooshing sound effect. Then put the phone back in her beaded clutch and reached for her dress.

"Did I tell you to put your dress back on?" He deliberately made the question softly menacing. She stiffened, roses blooming on her cheeks, returning arousal deepening her gaze as her eyes widened, staring back at him without answering. "I asked you a question."

"I'm sorry."

"The correct response should be 'no, Sir.'"

"No, Sir." She breathed the words, her nipples hard through the black lace of her bra. They'd be pink, like her mouth.

"I want to see your breasts."

She reached behind her for the hook.

"No," he snapped, making her flinch. "Pay attention to what I tell you to do, understand?"

She narrowed her eyes at him, not at all the picture of obedience. Torn between laughing and tossing her over his knee for a brisk spanking, he kept his expression stern and raised a cool eyebrow at her.

"Yes, Sir," she replied and waited. Better, though she looked impatient. Hell, so was he.

"Kneel down."

A tremor ran over her, excitement on her face, and she knelt. So fluid and supple.

"Without taking off your bra, pull down the lace and tuck it under each breast, one at a time. Then put your hands behind your neck, under your hair, back arched."

She obeyed, fingers shaking. Penetrating her mind now, how she would look. That she'd be displaying herself because he commanded it. More of an edge to it, with the dose of reality and distance. She'd have to be wondering just how far he'd ask her to go.

But she hadn't pulled out either safeword, so full steam ahead.

Good thing he'd sat again as so much blood fled to his groin at the sight of first one perfect breast and then both that he went a bit dizzy. When she submissively put her hands behind her neck and arched as he'd instructed, his vision sparked at the perimeter. Impossibly perfect globes, with flawless pale skin drawn tight by her crinkled nipples. Anything but meek in her demeanor, however, she stared at him in proud challenge, blue eyes hot and bold.

"Very nice," he told her. "Leave your bra as it is, but put the dress back on and summon the waiter. Then sit in your chair, fold your hands in your lap and sit up straight. When the waiter comes in, I want you to look him in the eye and think about how it would have gone if I asked him to come in right now. Imagine telling him about what I made you do and how much you liked it. Don't say anything. When he asks you how you enjoyed your meal, I want you to look at me and tell me how much you liked this exact moment. Go ahead."

A little unsteady, she climbed to her feet, naked breasts bobbing, and pulled the dress over her head. She struggled with the zipper and he let her, enjoying the way she shimmied and imagining how the stiff silk bodice might be stimulating her nipples. With the dress finally in place, she crossed to the door, sliding him an unreadable glance as she did, turned off the privacy again, hit the call button and sat, following instructions perfectly. Though the impish gleam in her eye belied the ladylike impression.

The waiter entered and she blushed, exactly as he'd hoped, then wriggled in her chair, so overcome he thought she might not be able to pull it off. But she managed to look the man in the eye and smile.

"How was everything, miss?"

Amber transferred her gaze to his, with such searing sensuality that he nearly fumbled his wallet. "So amazing it left me starving for more."

Alec managed to pay, signal the driver and offer her a hand out of her chair, then draped his topcoat over her shoulders. Pleasing himself with arranging her hair over it, honey gold against the black, he bent and kissed the side of her neck, thrilled at her shiver of response.

"Please tell me you're going to fuck me tonight," she whispered, as if speaking softly kept her from breaking the rules.

"Just for that, I shouldn't. Perhaps I'll string you up naked where I can look at you and watch you suffer as I satisfy myself."

She looked up at him over her shoulder, leaning back against him. "But you won't. Not tonight."

"Why do you think so?"

She licked her bottom lip, eyes intent on his. "Because if you are even a tenth as turned on as I am, you won't be able to help yourself."

"Hush." He took her hand, but instead of lacing his fingers

with hers, he wrapped his around her slender wrist, easily encircling it. "When I do this, it means that I expect you to be silent unless specifically asked a question—or to use your safewords, of course—and to obey as if we are in a scene, though we're in public. When I let go, you'll behave normally."

She bit her lip and nodded, blowing out a sigh between her pursed lips, as if mastering some response. Perhaps her long anticipation added to the charge for her, but he couldn't recall another woman so devastated by the smallest gestures such as this. Glancing up at him, she smiled, seeming to follow the train of his thoughts with wry acknowledgement.

Tightening his grip slightly, just to feel her shiver of reaction, he led her out of the restaurant, took his topcoat off her shoulders and handed her into the backseat of the car. The privacy partition remained up and Amber sat demurely, hands folded in her lap, clearly vibrating with anticipation. He flicked on the little cabin light.

"You can take your dress off again," he told her, amused to see her start of surprise. She hadn't expected that and hesitated, eyes flicking to the partition, then the window. "No one but me can see—unless you hesitate again and I'm forced to put down the window to teach you a lesson. Kneel up on the seat facing me and do it. I'll keep your purse."

She looked a bit mulish but gave him her little beaded bag and reached for her zipper again, glaring at him when he refused to help, folding his hands on his knee and smiling pleasantly at her. As the bodice loosened, her bare breasts came into view, bouncing enticingly as she struggled out of the dress, rewarding his gambit and then some. When she had it off, her face and breasts flushed and hair in disarray, he held out a hand for the gown and she gave it to him, looking off balance. Something about this made her nervous more than being in the same state of undress in the restaurant. Interesting.

"Cross your wrists, in front of you."

She started to glance at the partition but stopped herself and obeyed, though her outstretched hands trembled. He took his time folding her dress so it wouldn't wrinkle, setting it down on his other side, where she'd have difficulty reaching it, should she be so disobedient as to try. Fixed on his movements, she watched him unknot his tie and slide it off, chewing on her lip a little in dismay. He bound her wrists tightly, more so than before to communicate the escalation, and paused when she opened her mouth, expecting at least the slowdown safeword.

But she searched his face and said nothing, clearly uncertain, but with that open trust she'd offered him so freely from the beginning. Slowly so she'd wonder what he might be doing, he reached into his pocket and drew out a gold hook, cool against his hand, and looped it through the black silk binding her wrists. She frowned a little, curious, then her eyes widened when he lifted her wrists over her head and hooked them to the garment hold.

She struggled against it, reflexively more than anything. Whatever it was about being in the car that made her feel less in control seemed to be amplified with the vulnerable position. With her arms strained above and behind her, her pretty breasts were even more on display, something she seemed to be aware of, looking down at them and up at him, emotion in her eyes. If he'd allowed her to speak, she'd be pleading with him.

It might be nice to know exactly what she'd ask for—or rather, how she'd phrase it—but he suspected being forbidden to use her smart mouth and wit to duel with him contributed to her current predicament, so he'd continue it a bit longer.

Having her wrists attached that way put her back against the door, so she sat askew on the seat. She nearly flinched when he leaned forward, so he slowed, wondering what she'd been anticipating. Not his hand wrapping around her ankle. She resisted as he lifted it and he raised an eyebrow at her, the expectation implicit. Either yield or safeword. Visibly relaxing herself, she blew out a breath and let him raise her leg so her severely bent knee rested against the seat back, the sharp heel digging into the leather. He picked up the other foot and she whimpered a little when he hooked the heel into the bracket meant to hold a newspaper.

Splayed for him now, the narrow scrap of black lace riding deeply into the folds of her cunt, she looked charmingly helpless. She wanted to struggle, to close her legs—that much was clear from the way she panted, the flush over her breasts, the half-wild glazed look in her eyes. For a moment, he thought she wouldn't be able to stand it, would have to do something to adjust the way he'd arranged her.

But she stuck it through. If she hadn't pulled it together, he'd have called a halt himself, to make sure she wasn't simply being stubborn about her safewords. He wouldn't—not only because she'd passed some threshold, but because stopping without her say-so at this point might trip up the trajectory of whatever internal voyage she'd embarked on. She wouldn't thank him for interrupting the spell, having reconciled herself to it.

Her self-discipline somehow soothed him. Or perhaps he felt calmer, more in control now that he knew she wouldn't back out. At least for tonight, she belonged utterly to him. He could simply ride around all night and have her this way, pliant to his will. Craving another sampling of her skin, he touched her where he hadn't yet—setting a finger on the inner curve of her thigh by her knee and sliding down the impossibly soft glide of it. Stopping close enough to her open sex to feel the heat, but not enough to touch her.

She moaned and moved her hips, trying to push herself into his hand, so he pulled it away. Shook his finger at her, in the style of an annoyed professor.

"Tsk-tsk, Ms. Dolors. One would think you've paid no attention to the rules at all, have you?"

Something like a sob escaped her and she closed her eyes. "No, Sir," she got out, sounding miserable.

"Open your eyes and watch," he ordered, fascinated by how affected she was.

He set the same finger on her other knee and, with a moan of despair, she fastened her gaze on it, eyes full of desire and a kind of dread. The play of emotions had him so rapt that he watched her face instead of her gorgeously displayed body. The seductive satin of her thigh drew his hand down and she shuddered under his hand. Nearer her crotch, her skin grew sticky with moisture and he stopped when he reached it. Unable to resist teasing more, he paused there.

"You're very wet, aren't you? Have been for some time now."

She met his gaze, still blushing fiercely, but her tone had some defiance. "Yes, Sir."

"Hmm. A pity to ruin such pretty knickers, but I need to see for myself and you look so lovely I don't want to move you. Hold still."

He reached for the shears he'd stowed in the newspaper rack, hoping for an opportunity such as this—big, showy brass ones. Riveted, she stared as he slid the cool metal just over the top of her mound, letting her feel it.

And snipped the gusset free.

CHAPTER FOURTEEN

WITH A SNAP, the panties gave way. They'd been cutting with sadistic pressure into her aroused tissues ever since Alec spread her legs like that, fixing them in place with her own stilettos so her feet felt as bound as her hands. Much as the underwire and displaced cups of her bra constrained her breasts, so they ached with the combination of constriction and arousal. The abrupt loosening—along with the cool air on her splayed pussy and Alec's gaze on her as palpable as a touch— nearly sent her into orgasm right then.

In truth, she'd felt on the verge of orgasm since he'd first undressed her, with his deep kisses and infuriatingly light touches everywhere but where she craved them most. The antithesis of every lover she'd had, who'd all predictably homed in on the hot spots, ignoring the rest of her, Alec seemed frustratingly oblivious to them. Instead he touched her waist, her arm, her throat and now—damn him to whatever hell he'd sprung from—with her pussy naked and desperate to be stroked, she had to suffer without. Worse, he wore that intently interested, slightly supercilious look on his face, as if he enjoyed watching her face as much as anything else.

And seriously got off on tormenting her.

He left the scrap of her panties hanging ignominiously

around her hips and set the wicked shears aside. Then set that same finger on the inside of the knee wedged against the car seat. With excruciating lightness, he slowly ran the pad down her inner thigh, barely making progress. Seeming to relish the way she couldn't catch her breath. A high keening noise filled her head and she wasn't sure if she was making it out loud, but she suddenly lost it, finding herself thrashing against the silk of his tie and sobbing. "Pleaseohpleaseohplease."

It had the effect of making him pause, giving her a mock-astonished scowl as he took his hand away. "Oh, Ms. Dolors. That was badly done indeed. Such a simple rule, too."

Shaking his head as if disappointed, he sat back and poured himself some champagne, smiling in cool condescension. "We'll give you a moment to calm down and think about what you've done."

So cruel, as she'd obviously never be able to calm herself in her current state, especially not bound and displayed this way, with the city going past out the windows and the driver only feet away. She'd expected a great deal—but not such an obliterating mind-fuck. On one level, a (very) small objective part of her brain could appreciate his technique. Her instincts that he'd be both talented and experienced at this had proven right on target. With his devastating combination of romance, understanding, domineering cruelty, voracious hunger and playful teasing, he'd systematically taken her from her usual composed self to...someone else. Some animal state where she had no inhibition but simply responded to his least caress, shattered by the most casual reprimand.

And more desperately aroused than she'd ever been in her

life.

"Would you like some?"

She stared at him, the words making no sense, and he smiled indulgently and stroked her cheek. Shuddering, she pressed into his palm, needing the contact.

"My poor little girl," he crooned. "You're quite desperate to come, aren't you?"

"Yes, Sir." She infused the two inadequate words with as much feeling as she could manage, knowing full well she only handed him more power over her, if that were possible.

"Knowing, however, that I shall not let you, would you like a sip of champagne?"

Miserable, she nodded and he held the delicate flute to her bottom lip, the icy bubbles bright in her mouth. Following the cool glass, his mouth followed, kissing her gently, with loving care, all the while careful not to touch any other part of her. "We're nearly there," he murmured. "Shall I make you walk naked into the building? Perhaps offer you to the night doorman, as a tip?"

She had to close her eyes against the image, knowing in the rational part of her mind that he wouldn't do that and he planted the suggestion only to further the mind-fuck, and yet that open, receptive part of her answered, "Yes, Sir."

He laughed, dark and warm. "I should, if only because you think I wouldn't."

A tug on her wrists and he unhooked her from the grab handle—something she'd never look at the same way again—and, slipping the hook out of the repeated layers of his tie binding her tight, he tucked it into his pocket, as another man might stow a pen for later use. "You may sit up and close your legs. Might as well slip the shreds of your knickers off, lest you drop them on the pavement and shock some decent citizen."

Knowing the polite suggestion to be an order—another insidious part of his game, tricking her into unknowing disobedience—she used her bound hands to wriggle the destroyed lace over her hips and down, snagging the soaked fabric on her heels. It wasn't easy to do, but then he clearly liked that, watching her struggle. Pity about them indeed, but she supposed her investment had been worth it. She wadded them up in her hands.

"I'll take those." He held out an imperious hand, raising that eyebrow in his annoying way when she hesitated. Hell, she had no reason to be embarrassed. They both knew how aroused she was, how wet. As much as he was, if the insistent bulge of his cock against the perfectly tailored trousers gave any indication. That and the nearly feral glint in his eyes despite his coolly composed expression. A couple of times she'd thought he'd been about to leap on her and fuck her right there in the restaurant.

And she would have let him, too.

No, just another dare, a way to open her up and leave her with no secrets from him. Already it seemed as if he possessed an uncanny knowledge about what she was thinking. Relentlessly, he pushed for more. Holding her head high, pretending he couldn't see right through her, she deposited the ball of shredded lace in his hands. With a quirk of a smile, he made a show of unfolding and fingering them, suggestively stroking the soaked gusset as he hadn't touched her, watching her press her naked thighs together.

The car came to a halt and her heart thudded into panic. Here she sat, wearing only fuck-me heels and an underwire bra that covered nothing and instead lifted her naked breasts almost obscenely, her hands bound with a man's silk tie. He wouldn't really order her to get out naked, would he? She'd use the safeword. Probably.

Yes, definitely.

He watched her closely, folding the ruined panties and tucking them in the kerchief pocket of his jacket, waiting to see what she'd do. What if the driver opened the door? But he wouldn't—hadn't all evening. Alec smiled, just a little, and picked up his topcoat, wrapping it around her shoulders and buttoning it up. If anything, wrapped naked and still bound under the smooth silk rocked her that much more. "Can't have you getting a chill," he murmured.

Then he picked up her dress, smoothed it over his arm so it draped like a discarded jacket, and opened the car door. Standing outside he curled a finger at her to beckon her out and she scooted over the seat carefully, making sure not to dislodge the too-big coat. He took her arm through the fabric to help her, then put an arm casually around her to hold it all in place and keep the empty arms from flapping.

"Good evening, Jorges," he greeted the doorman, who smiled genially and seemed to have no idea of the game Alec was playing. They entered the elevator and, as soon as the doors closed, he turned and pulled her into his arms for a long, dreamy kiss, his hand sliding inside the coat and stroking over the outside line of her thigh, over her hip, to settle in the small of her back and press her hard against him. Her nipples chafed even against the smooth silk of the lining, no doubt because they'd been unrelentingly hard for hours, and the pressure against her swollen breasts made her nearly frantic. With her hands trapped between them, she struggled to urge him on for more, but he ignored her squirming, his hand winding in her hair to hold her still while he kept the kiss tortuously languid.

The elevator dinged and the doors opened onto a hall with a door at either end. "My neighbor is in town, or I would have stripped you in the elevator and made you crawl to my door, so I could watch. Perhaps some other night."

He loved to do that, speak casually of what he might put her through, in the same tone as mentioning that, on another evening, they might stop for gelato. As it was, he kept his arm inside the coat, around her naked waist as he guided her down the hallway. Someone approaching them might glimpse her nakedness beneath, but from behind she might appear to be wearing some short dress. His hand on her belied the casual teasing note in his voice, fingers stroking her skin with hungry repetition.

Once inside, he bolted the doors and hung up her dress in the hall closet. "You won't be needing this for some time," he said, his voice rough, strained somehow. "Or this, if you're sufficiently checked in." He held up the little evening clutch and set it on the shelf. Not out of her reach, but symbolically so. He unbuttoned his coat, took it from her and stowed it, too.

Then he took a deep breath, the line of his shoulders tight, and turned to look at her, almost reluctant—except that his gaze raked her with such ferocity she took a step back. Moving slowly, he pursued, cornering her against the wall, then shoving her bound hands over her head in an abrupt movement, hard enough to make her gasp, his grip fierce and on the verge of painful. He pressed hard against her, his suit rubbing against her skin making her very aware that he remained clothed while she was naked, totally in his power. A surge of hot moisture pulsed between her legs. If she hadn't been aroused already, she would have been instantly, just from this.

He was breathing hard, lips pressed to her temple, not moving further, and it seemed he was wrestling for some sort of control.

"Last chance to back out." The hoarseness of his whisper gave the warning a lethal sound. What was he telling her? And why did she have the odd urge to reassure him? She paused, uncertain if she should answer within the rules or not.

"Tell me what you're thinking, sod it." He gritted out the demand.

"Are you saying you won't respect my safewords?"

His grip loosened, ever so slightly, not enough that she could break free, but relaxing that feral edge. "No," he breathed the word, lips hot on her temple. "I'd never ignore your safewords. No matter how...extreme I seem. Do you want to use one now?"

"I'm fine. You're fine. Keep going."

"This is a lot for your first time. I don't want to push you too hard."

"I'm not an innocent and I'm hardly a doormat. If you do something I don't like, I'll say so."

"Promise?"

"I promise."

He pulled back far enough to be able to see her face, searching her eyes for the truth. "Maybe we should call it for the night. I could take you home."

She might die if he did that, but she didn't say so. "Is something wrong?"

"Just—" He leaned his forehead against hers, closing his eyes. "Seeing you naked here, locked in my flat, it's...I want to ravage you."

She shivered, knees weak enough that she sagged in his relentless grip. "Oh God, Alec, don't send me home. I want that, too. I'm yours to ravage. I trust you."

He sighed, ragged. "I hope I'm worthy of it."

Backing off, he lowered her hands and, face intent, he plucked the knot free. "I need a moment. I'll get us a nightcap. If you need to use the facilities, they're just down the hall. Then go into the living room and sit on the couch to wait for me."

Grateful for the opportunity, she headed for the powder room, aware he watched her naked bottom as she went.

"Amber," he called out as she reached the door, sounding more in control again. "I don't have to tell you no surreptitious frigging in private, do I?"

Her face went hot as she'd been considering that very thing, to take the edge off. "No."

"No, what?" His voice had gone icy, making her perverse body leap with desire.

"No, Sir."

He nodded and walked off. Finding the switch, she shut herself in, dashing for the toilet to pee. Cleaning herself after was a torture. Had she ever been so slick and swollen? It would not have taken much to make herself come, but she'd keep to the rules, at least for now. Her reflection in the big mirror over the marble vanity left her a little shocked. She looked like she'd crawled out of bed from a night of wild sex. Her lipstick smudged and mascara smeared, hair a tangled mess. And her breasts, bright pink and thrust up by the bra. She hadn't felt self-conscious before, but she couldn't go back out there like this.

She knew better than to take off the bra, but she finger-combed her hair. The curls had largely fallen out, so it cascaded in a sleek mass down her back. With a tissue folded into thirds, she used the corner to clean up her eye makeup and lipstick. She couldn't do more without her purse, but at least she looked less disheveled.

When she adjusted the bra a little, her hand brushed the sensitized skin and the sensation made her knees buckle. If Alec touched her breasts, she'd come apart. Not that he seemed inclined to yet, unless he lost the control he clung to. Not done tormenting her, drawing things out. Working her over even as he indulged himself, kept himself leashed that way, perhaps. At some point she'd be reduced to begging him—pretty much had already—and she'd probably offer him anything. Anything at all.

And mean it.

Strangely hesitant to face the next phase, uncertain why, she made herself leave her sanctuary and go to the large formal living room. Glass windows filled one wall and she hesitated. He liked threatening her with exposure, probably recognizing the way the prospect both thrilled and terrified her. Moving quickly, she picked a seat on the couch with her back to the view. Just in case.

When Alec finally entered, he carried two snifters of brandy and had doffed his suit jacket, but still wore the black vest. He'd opened the dress shirt by a few buttons and rolled up the cuffs to reveal leanly muscled forearms. His eyes remained dark with that dangerous glint and they ate her in greedy sweeps. Setting the snifters down, he sat and picked up her hands, examining the red marks where the silk had cut in when she pulled against it, stroking them with light fingers. "Does this hurt?" he asked softly.

"No." Though she might feel it more tomorrow. At that moment her aching breasts and vulva disturbed her more. The insistent craving to be sated.

"Liar." The accusation snapped out, a reprimand, and she reflexively tugged at her hands, but he held them tight. "I expect honest—and complete—answers from you."

"They really don't hurt. Other things bother me more. Not in a bad way. More distracting."

"Is that so? Such as?" His expression sharpened, that fascinated look he got when observing her, looking into her responses.

"My, ah, breasts. With the bra this way, they..."

"What?"

Another kind of exposure, this, sitting on the leather couch, telling him how his little torments made her feel. "They ache.

They feel hot and tight. Almost unbearable."

He smiled, not a pleasant one at all, and surveyed the objects of discussion. "They are quite red. I have some ideas there. I wonder if you've truly come close to 'unbearable' yet. In the meanwhile, open that box." He let go of her hands and nodded at the wooden box on the table.

Maybe she should have asked for a slowdown. Still could, she reminded herself. He'd regained his composure but the raging desire beneath ran wild and bubbling, palpably intense. He'd never hurt her, but he very well might shatter her composure. Not might—would. It felt odd to be on the verge of falling apart, much as she'd wanted it.

The sight of the black leather cuffs in the box gave her pause, made her heart run faster. Fear or desire, she didn't know. Some amalgam of the two. She lifted one and Alec plucked it from her hand, wrapping it around her wrist and buckling it. Lined with soft velvet, it didn't cut into her skin like the tie had, but it looked…startling. The black made a severe contrast to her skin, and loops embedded in the leather seemed so very sexual that she nearly moaned as first one, then the other tightened.

"Ankles," Alec ordered and she set her feet on his lap. He slid off her shoes and cuffed her ankles, then fondled them. "I've imagined how you'd look in something such as this since the first day I laid eyes on you."

Shaken, she couldn't answer. Didn't need to because he picked up a dish of gold trinkets. Looking at its contents more closely, she saw it held a rather dizzying collection of hooks, chains and clamps. He selected a short chain and used it to attach the ankle cuffs to each other, where it gleamed prettily against the black. Then he told her to sit on the edge of the couch and to put her hands behind her back. A clinking sound and he set the dish down beside her. He must have chosen another hook, because he quickly connected her wrists, then had her turn around and straddle him.

Not easy, with her ankles so close together. She ended up more pitched forward on her knees with her thighs parted widely by his. He took his time adjusting her to his liking, sitting back against the couch, her bottom suspended in the air, her breasts at the level of his face. Picking up a longer chain, he felt behind her and hooked it between her wrists, then, making her arch her back, attached it to the one between her ankles. Pushing most of her hair behind her shoulders, he kept out a long strand and, with a wicked glint in his eyes, brushed it over one taut nipple.

It might as well have been an electric shock, the way she jerked. But she couldn't go far. Could barely move. Face intent, he did the same to her other breast, avoiding the nipple this time and dragging the ticklish hair over the surface of her skin, over the top curve and to the underside. She squirmed and he held her in place with a hand on the tight chain behind her.

"So very sensitive," he commented. "I can see what you mean. But unbearable? Hmm."

"Oh, please," she whimpered, but he kept to his game, using the long silky edge to slide here, the more prickly ends to poke her there. All while her pussy ached, empty and ignored.

At last he let go of the lock of hair and left it to hang between her breasts.

She was out of breath, sweating. He was all cool control again and showing no sign of relenting, despite the pause. Instead he set a finger in the hollow of her throat, much the same as he'd touched her in the car, bringing it slowly down between her breasts.

Far from done with this.

"Oh God. Alec. Enough already."

"I don't think so." With devastating lightness, he touched the underside of her breast, circling inward, spiraling toward her nipple, without ever quite touching it. Holding her fixed as he did it. Ignoring her pleas, which grew increasingly frantic and incoherent. Trading hands, he held the chain with one and used the other to mirror the torture on her other breast.

The pressure built inside her, but she'd never be able to come this way. Just hover on the brink of it.

Then he replaced his finger with his tongue and she lost her mind entirely.

Oblivious to anything but the slow stimulation of his tongue on her tender breasts, feeling that at any moment she might begin bleeding through her pores, she dropped her head back, trying to absorb it. Sounds came out of her. Delirious moans and whimpers, but she gave up wondering when he'd stop this. Gave up thinking about needing an orgasm like water in the desert. She only rocketed with each tortuous lick, unable to resist in any way.

When his mouth closed on her nipple and bit, she came.

The orgasm took her like a lightning bolt. Unheralded except for the static cloud that had built so slowly and imperceptibly that she hadn't been able to prepare. Instead it caught her in its convulsing current and she screamed, thrashing in Alec's hands, wild and mindless. He switched to her other nipple, sucking and biting it as she bucked on his lap.

CHAPTER FIFTEEN

THE ORGASM TOOK her so hard he was pressed to keep her from pitching off his lap. Not many women could come from only nipple stimulation, but Amber was extraordinary in so many ways. Her unconditional trust had steadied him, made him feel he might be able to maintain.

That and the quick trip to relieve his raging hard-on. Only a few strokes of his hand and he'd spilled like an adolescent. He hadn't planned on it, but it helped him level, cooled him enough to keep his head and make this good for her.

A measure of reserve he lost by degrees as she came apart, sweet flesh in his mouth, tasting fragrantly of woman and mindless passion. Letting her ride it out, he moved from one breast to the other, salving and stimulating, bracing her as she shuddered and coaxing her back to arousal. When she whimpered, moving her hips pleadingly, he knew she was ready for the next phase. With the knife he kept in his pocket during scenes, just in case quick release became necessary, he sliced through the bra straps and the band in front, giving her trapped breasts some freedom.

She sobbed a little, mostly relief, looking down at them. "That was really expensive lingerie," she said, voice full of sensual rockiness from her screaming.

He laughed, cupping her breast and rubbing her velvety nipple with his thumb. She filled his hand perfectly, full and taut. It hadn't been easy to wait to touch them, but he'd made it. Conquering her body by degrees.

"I'll buy you more, if you like." If there were more after tonight. "We'll make a game of it. You can go shopping, take pictures of yourself in the mirror and show me later. Then I'll go buy my favorite while you wait in the car, and I'll make you change into it."

"At which point that lingerie won't last any longer than this set did."

Sliding a hand behind her neck, he pulled her down to kiss him. Off balance, she fell against him and he followed her. "Then I shall have to buy three sets of each," he murmured, feeling he could kiss her hot, avid mouth forever.

"Why three?"

"One to rip off of you as soon as possible. One to make you wear around the flat for decoration. One for you to wear to the office, so you can think of how I cut something exactly the same off of you."

He couldn't seem to take his hands off of her, but he made himself. She lay on her side, her ankles pulled fetchingly up behind her, watching him with those wide, sex-drenched eyes. Putting his hand on her bum, he stroked it, enjoying the perfectly round curve and how she squirmed with pleasure, fighting the bonds. "Can you get free?"

"You know I can't."

"Show me."

Halfheartedly, she struggled. To encourage her, he put his

hand on her mound, the light dusting of silky hairs there drenched with her arousal. "Show me," he told her, in a harder tone.

She fought in earnest now, more to get his fingers where she wanted them than anything. A glorious sight.

"Good girl." He patted her bottom, tempted to redden that, too. But, despite the way she'd thrown herself into the experience, regardless that he might not get more of her than this night, he thought better of it. Not everyone responded to that kind of punishment the same way. Unhooking the chain that hogtied her, he released her ankles and wrists, too, helping her to sit up.

He made a tsking sound, which always seemed to get her dander up. "You're too woozy to walk. Best crawl to the bedroom, don't you think? That way."

He'd shocked her a little with that, just as he had when he suggested he'd make her walk naked into the building, or from the elevator to the door. It rocked her foundations in the most delightful way and he relished how she obeyed, desire suffusing her face as she slid off the couch and crawled on all fours in the direction he'd indicated.

Picking up the brandy snifters, he followed, wishing he could record her on more than the screen of his mind. Unbelievably beautiful naked, with the black cuffs as obscenely harsh against her translucent skin as he'd imagined. Her pert bottom high in the air, she crawled quickly, but not so fast that he didn't have an excellent view of her slick and swollen cunt, flushed between her creamy thighs, begging to be repeatedly plundered.

Desire for her roared up through his head, making him as dizzy as she'd acted. Taking a long sip of the brandy to distract himself, he wondered how he'd manage to satisfy her without spending too humiliatingly soon. Not something a man with a much younger mistress cared to contemplate.

Coming again would be his best play. At this rate he should have no trouble getting it up a third time. Would she be into being forced to suck him off? Dicey sometimes. But he'd know it if she didn't really like it. He hoped.

God knew, his cock strained against his shorts at the image.

"Kneel there, palms flat on your thighs," he told her softly when she reached the bed. She looked up at him as he set his snifter down and cupped her chin, holding the brandy to her full bottom lip. "Yes?"

"Yes, please." She sipped, eyes of drowning blue on his, her pretty pink-tipped breasts rising below. Rubbing his thumb over her lower lip, he set that snifter down, too. Then smoothed her hair back from her face, studying it. So perfectly yielding, as if she'd been doing this for years. Perhaps she had the right of it, that it came naturally to her.

"Undo my trousers."

Her eyes darkened and her sweet tongue passed over her bottom lip as she reached to obey with all the eagerness he could wish for. A quick learner, she stopped after lowering the zipper and waited, though her gaze was focused on his groin. Feeling a bit desperate, he grabbed the brandy and took another drink of it. Christ, he'd lose it the moment she put her hands on him, much less her mouth.

At his hesitation, she glanced up, amused. Clearly reading

him as well as—or better than—he read her. Sod it all.

"Suck me off then," he ordered, setting the brandy aside and making himself think about the damn McCloskey account. Which helped not at all because it reminded him immediately of how she'd smiled when she suggested they could discuss that over drinks, sly and full of that—

"Holy Christ," he gasped as she freed his cock and closed her hot mouth over it.

She worked the shaft with her delicate fingers, taking him deep into the depths of her clever mouth. His balls clenched as she sucked the climax out of him almost instantly. Unthinking, he buried his hands in her hair, held her head and thrust himself into her mouth. Mindlessly emptying himself.

As the miasma of it cleared, he looked down her, pink lips rounded around his cock as she'd done with the cannoli, eyes enormous in her pale face. Appalled at himself, he let go of her, pulling out of her mouth, though she kept the suction tight, sending a last orgasmic shudder through him as he popped free.

"I beg your pardon," he managed and she laughed.

"Honestly, Alec, you are a piece of work." She gave him a cherubic smile and flicked a finger at the corner of her mouth, just as she'd licked away the cannoli cream, then sucked on it suggestively. "And you have a beautiful cock. How do you plan to use it on me next?"

Staggered, he lowered himself to the edge of the bed. "Does nothing shake you?"

"Plenty." Seeming to feel released from discipline for the moment—as he supposed she was—she followed him, kneeling up and running slender hands over his thighs, then unbuttoning his shirt. Opening it, she licked at his belly with a hum of pleasure, then glanced up at him, assessing, sensual as a cat. "I've discovered I like being shaken off balance as much as I hoped. You haven't done anything to me I haven't been starved for, my gorgeous man." She climbed up him, pushing the shirt over his shoulders and running her hands over his naked chest, then bit his shoulder, the sharp pain clearing his head. "But Alec? If you don't fuck me sometime in the next century I'm going to lose my mind. I won't be responsible for my actions."

Delighted with her, he cupped her face and held her still for a long, deep kiss. "Then you'd best remove the comforter and pillows and spread-eagle yourself on this bed immediately. Or I shall punish you by making you wait hours more."

She sucked in a tight breath and jumped off his lap, tugging the pillows—an arrangement meticulously created by his designer and repeated faithfully each day by his housekeeper—and tossed them willy-nilly. Watching her sleek, nubile body as she crawled over the bed, he pulled his shirt the rest of the way off and peeled off his shoes and socks. She pulled the comforter down and scooted into the middle of the black sheets. He'd chosen the color to set off her skin, as the cuffs did, but now he leaned toward gold for her in the future, to complement instead of contrast. Shimmering like her hair and the subtle scattering of fawn freckles he'd found, a treasure on the pale skin of her cleavage.

Disobediently kneeling in the center of the bed, curls tumbling around her so she looked like a painting of Thumbelina, she looked him over and raised her brows when he refastened his trousers. "Isn't that the wrong direction? You should be taking them off, too."

"Trying to take control, Ms. Dolors?" He made his voice icy. It worked, too, because she shivered, her nipples hardening. "I'm rather distressed by your disobedience and poor attitude."

"Sorry, Sir." She scrambled to obey, spread-eagling herself on the sheets, looking a bit shocked to see herself reflected in the mirror over the bed.

"Too late for that." He made a show of looking disappointed, opened a drawer and took out a strap. Carrying it to the bed, he slapped it lightly against his palm and watched her face closely for her reaction. She blanched slightly, showing some trepidation. Also glittering interest. Her eyes flicked from it to his face, searching with earnest innocence, and back to the strap. "Anything to say to me?" He kept it in character of the scene but made the offer sincere.

She swallowed. Licked her lips. "No, Sir."

A surge of something hot and dark filled him. She'd let him strap her adorable bottom. He couldn't believe his great good luck and welcomed whatever damnation might follow. "Turn over," he told her softly, loving the way her face showed her nerves, her full and swollen mouth trembling and her eyes dark with sensual anticipation. She spread herself into an X again, without being told. Setting the strap to drape over her bottom so she could think about it, he attached her cuffs with chains to the four posts of the bed.

Taking his time adjusting them so she'd be evenly displayed, letting the anticipation spin out, he moved around the corners, tightening the chains by increments, so that she was stretched to the utmost and still perfectly centered. She made little moaning sounds as he worked, her body undulating as she accustomed herself to it, setting fire to his blood. When he selected one of the designer pillows and wedged it under her hips, positioning it to lift her delicious bum in the air, she segued into those panting moans she made in the extremity of arousal.

"Turn your face to the side," he instructed, then smoothed her hair back from her face when she did, studying her expression. Totally transported. He brought over a standing mirror, angling it so she could see her reflection in the overhead mirror, then picked up the strap and stood next to it. "Can you see both me and yourself, from above?"

She nodded, pressing her lips together against her frantic breathing.

"I need you to answer me out loud, Amber. So I know you're in there and okay."

"I'm okay," she whispered. "I can see."

"Have you ever been spanked before?"

"When I was little. And bad." She laughed, a breathy sound, then trembled. "I remember it hurt."

"It's supposed to. But you can stop this anytime. Tell me your safewords."

"I don't want to stop it." She sounded almost petulant, and oh so very young. God help him, it flooded him with crazed fervor for more.

"You might find yourself wanting to beg me to stop, which is fine, but I won't unless you use the safewords."

"I know."

"Say them anyway, so I know you remember."

"Morpheus and Lolita. I'll say them if I need to. Please, Alec."

"All right then. Time to punish my naughty girl." Far from having a chilling effect under these circumstances, hearing the name *Lolita* roll off her tongue, with all its sordid implications, made him feel that much more wicked. Her adorable, pristine ass, utterly vulnerable and perfectly white, begged to be defiled.

With a sense of power, he cracked the strap in the air, loving when she flinched, then smacked it down over her bottom.

Her mouth made a perfect O and her eyes, riveted not on him but on her reflection, looked astonished, then filled with tears. Her gasp of shock followed long after, the delayed sound of thunder after the lash of lightning. A stripe of pink appeared on her skin, gratifyingly marring her unblemished whiteness. He strapped her again and she cried out faster, a sound of high pain with an undercoat of a woman's arousal.

Born for this, indeed.

Keeping himself on a tight leash, though he quickly became as fiercely aroused as ever, he worked her slowly, varying the speed and strength of the strap. Making an art of reddening her snowy flesh, watching her eyes go blind with the sensory overload, her body squirming in a frenzy of need. She wept, seeming not to notice and cried out for him, little pleas to stop and for more tangling together. When he did stop, and set the strap aside, she kept moving the same way, her body entreating him to end the torment and send her to the full catharsis she craved.

Shucking his trousers, he pulled a condom from the dresser and put it on, then knelt between her spread thighs. Running his hands over her steaming skin, he relished the way she moaned at the touch, pushing herself against him, her delicate cunt unfurled like a rose, glistening and gorgeous. Knowing how close to climax she'd be, he positioned his cock at her entrance, slid one hand beneath her to cup the outside of her mound, and braced himself with the other.

She stilled, cognizant enough now to anticipate, her breath hitching with tears and moans of encouragement. In one swift movement, he buried himself in her and slipped his fingers into her slick tissues, to press hard on her clit.

As he'd anticipated, she convulsed, wrenching as the orgasm took her. To his surprise, he nearly came, too, barely hanging on, digging his fingers into the sheets as her body milked him. He managed to make it until she crested, enough to ease himself into stroking in and out of her, finding her rhythm, bracketing her clit to ease her through the crash and prolong her arousal. She responded as a thoroughbred racehorse, ramping into another rise and climax, her body shuddering and her cries going from despair to delight.

He had it now, so that she'd remember the drenching pleasure that followed the pain. The orgasmic catharsis completing the gutting one of being restrained and tormented. He held out until her third climax hit, this one so strong that her internal muscles vised on him, spinning him into his own orgasm much as her talented mouth had done, pulling it from him with an edge so jagged it wrenched a cry from him as heartfelt as any of hers. Stars pinpricked the blackened edges of his vision.

Utterly spent, he collapsed over her, face buried in the honey silk of her hair.

CHAPTER SIXTEEN

H E LAY THERE in a delirium. Aware on some level of her sweet, slim body crushed beneath him, her bottom hot against his groin, her muscles still clenching on his softening cock. Hazily he knew he should move, get the condom off before it leaked, release her from the bonds so she wouldn't cramp or stiffen. But his body seemed fundamentally disconnected from his brain and he couldn't seem to make it do anything.

"Oh. My. Fucking. God." Amber drawled out the words, punctuating them with her uneven breaths.

That galvanized him. With an apology, he managed to wrench his hand from the soft trap of her folds and get it to the condom, keeping it in place as he withdrew from the delicious hold of her body. Quickly he dispensed with it and returned to release her from the chains, holding out a warm, wet cloth as she rolled over onto her back, limbs flopping in disarray.

Scowling at the hair draped over her face, she blew at it and he chuckled, brushing it aside for her as she seemed disinclined to move. Awareness returning to her eyes, she took him in, sitting naked beside her on the bed. "I wonder…" she said.

He raised an eyebrow and, since she hadn't taken it, set the cloth within her reach and used another to clean himself.

"I wonder how it can be," she tried again in a musing tone, "that you can drive me out of my fucking mind like that, with everything you did to me tonight, ending up with chaining me to your bed, strapping me silly and fucking me within an inch of my life—but when you say 'beg your pardon' in that starchy tone, I get hot all over again."

Arrested, he stared at her, unable to think of a response. She giggled and sat up with surprising alacrity, tossing her hair over her shoulder and snatching up the cloth. "The look on your face."

She bent her knees, letting them flop bonelessly apart and set to cleaning herself, hissing as she shifted her bottom. "Wow—that stings, now that I'm coming down."

"Let me see." Had he gone at her too hard? He'd been careful, but it had been some time and he had a tendency to lose control around her. "Turn over."

"I'm fine. Don't worry so much." She looked fine. Indeed she looked saucily pleased with herself, full of enviable vigor.

"I believe I gave you an order, darling."

Her eyes flickered and she quivered a little. "God. I don't know how you do that to me." With the appearance of obedience, she slithered over his lap, positioning herself with her bottom over his thigh, bracing on her elbows so her back arched gracefully, then glanced coyly over her shoulder, blue eyes bright. "How does it look?"

He ran his hands over her reddened skin—fading to a hot pink, as it should—and checked for bruising or anywhere he might have broken the skin. She sighed with her whole body relaxing and eyes going dreamy. "I love the way you do that.

Like I'm precious. Like you enjoy just touching me."

"I do enjoy it," he murmured, indulging himself in the curves of her delicious bum, since she seemed to be all right with it, trailing his fingers into her cleft, so seductive and steamy. "You're a beautiful woman, Amber. I don't know that I could ever get enough of touching you."

She moaned a little and wiggled her bum, encouraging him and nudging her thighs apart when he dipped his fingers into her, dropping her forehead to the sheets. "Call me selfish, but I hope you never do. Oh God—just like that."

He had a thumb inside her tight channel, pressing barely enough to arouse gently, stroking the outside of her clit with bracketed fingers. Less intense this way, a lovely rise and gentle fall to help her settle out the last of the high-voltage arousal. She came with a long, grateful moan, rocking her hips and humming deep in her throat.

"Magic hands," she murmured.

"Fancy a hot bath?"

She rolled onto her side and eyed his partial erection, wrapping her slender fingers around it. "What about this?"

"This," he said, firmly taking her hand away, "should be let alone for a bit. Thrice in a few hours is plenty." Realizing his error, he scrambled for a way out of it, but she was far too perceptive, crawling up to straddle him and push him onto his back.

"Thrice?" she echoed him, with uncanny mimicry. "I only counted twice for you. You jerked off in private. When?"

She narrowed her eyes and set her nails threateningly into his chest. She looked glorious, bare breasts swaying, all that honey hair tumbling around her and her lambent blue eyes full of mock anger. "After we got here, I'm betting. When you nearly lost it in the hallway."

"I did not 'nearly lose it.'"

"You get more pompous and British when you're uncomfortable, did you know that? Tell me when you did it."

"I do not and I shall do no such thing." He grabbed her wrists when she sank in her nails. "Ow."

"Don't be a baby. You tortured me far more."

"Yes, but I don't enjoy it as you do."

"Then I shall have to punish you another way," she said, sliding down his body with a maliciously seductive smile, dragging her nails and nipping him along the way.

He put his hands in her hair, keeping her from reaching her obvious goal. "Don't do it," he warned.

"Hush, or I'll tie you up. Be a good boy and take your punishment. You stole an orgasm from me and I want it back."

He groaned when she took him in her mouth and cupped his balls, chagrined to find himself hardening and rising eagerly—if somewhat painfully—to her ministrations. "I shan't be able to come again. Not this soon."

She lifted her head and tucked her hair behind her ears, lips shining wet. "Whatever. I'll just play with you awhile then. My reward for good behavior."

If he'd harbored any continued illusions of her as an innocent young thing, she shattered them with her exquisite technique. With the leisure to apply herself properly this time, she worked him with tongue, mouth and hands, driving him up and backing off again. Taking him to the brink of the climax he hadn't believed possible, sucking hard and fast on the sensitive head of his cock, then pretending to lose interest and be fascinated with licking the underside of his shaft.

When she swirled her tongue around the tip as if eating an ice cream cone, watching him through her lashes, the telltale clench of momentum warned him. He wrapped his hands in her hair. "Amber, I'm begging you."

"For what?" She gave him that angelic smile and delicately licked the tip, ignoring his attempts to drag her head down.

"Bloody hell, finish me, you brat."

Holding his cock by the root, she held a finger a breath away from the weeping head of his cock. "Is that any way to talk to the girl holding your life in her hands? Tell me I'm pretty."

Unable to watch a moment longer, he dropped his head back. "You are gorgeous. The most beautiful woman I've been privileged to lay hands on."

"And pretty," she insisted.

"And pretty," he agreed. "Please, darling."

"You're sorry you jerked off—especially after forbidding me to do the same."

"I am now."

She laughed. "At least you're honest. All right then, Mr. Knight. Relax and let me take care of this little problem for you."

Her mouth swallowed him, taking his cock all the way down her throat, hot, wet, impossibly tight. With a hoarse shout, he released. She still held him by the root, controlling him so he couldn't pump into her, making the climax that much more intense. Again she swallowed his seed, throat working him, milking the orgasm that was both ecstasy and agony.

HE COLLAPSED UNDER her hands, going limp in every way. Such a gorgeous man. She'd thought it was the suits, but seeing Alec naked was even better. He had that lean, longly muscled build she loved. Pale skin contrasted with a smattering of sable-colored hair, though it shaded even darker at his groin, neatly trimmed to frame his truly beautiful cock.

Normally she didn't think about men's cocks as aesthetic or not, but his was amazing. Long as the rest of him, thick, smooth and perfectly shaped. She played with it while he recovered, licking the velvety texture and admiring its clean lines, even in repose.

His hands tightened in her hair. "No more. I mean it."

"The creature lives."

Transferring his grip to her arms, he pulled her up and rolled, trapping her under him, holding her wrists beside her head. "Yes. And if you persist I shall paddle you until you can't sit."

"Promises, promises," she taunted, making him smile.

Lowering his head, he kissed her—something else he'd turned out to be very good at—smoky, dreamy and full of sated sexuality. She sighed in the sheer shimmering delight of it all.

"You're tremendously talented at giving head," he said, nuzzling her cheek.

"Skilled, thank you. One thing the guys I went to bed with

would let me do. I got lots of practice. I can even deep throat."

"Believe me," he said, sounding amused, "I noticed."

"I couldn't the first time with you, because I have to be able to control the movement, to relax the gag reflex."

"Perfectly understandable."

"Are you laughing at me?"

He lifted his head, gazing at her with those brown eyes that looked nearly black when he was near—or over—the edge. "Not even remotely, darling. I find you delightful in every way. You've entirely shattered me."

"If there's a next time..." she tried, mouth going dry at the possibility that this might be all he'd agree to. She'd used his lust for her rather ruthlessly to corner him into this much. At some point, with the edge of his desire blunted, his better judgment might kick in again. "Next time, we could try it with me kneeling, now that I know your shape better."

He let go of her wrist and stroked her cheek. "Would you want there to be a next time?"

"Very much so," she breathed, deeply moved by the look on his face, the tenderness of the gesture. By the hope that maybe his interest would outlast more than an encounter or two.

"Who am I to deny you?"

She found herself smiling. No, grinning like an idiot. "Now I fancy a bath."

"I shall inform the staff."

"You have staff? Where?" Hopefully not anywhere close enough to witness. The condo was huge by city standards and she certainly hadn't seen all of it, but...realizing, she smacked his arm and his straight face dissolved into a teasing smile.

"Of course I don't have staff."

"You have a driver," she pointed out.

"That's only practical." He levered himself up and began unbuckling the cuffs she'd forgotten she wore.

She watched the process with fascination, remembering how it had blown her mind when he put them on. The fastening was complex enough that she would have a hell of a time taking them off her wrists with one hand. The ankles she could at least get to, but they'd take a while. Engineered to be applied and removed by someone else—a deliciously simple method for taking away control. Because thinking about it made her go wet again and she didn't want him to think she was some kind of nympho, she went for lighthearted.

"Uh-huh. It's a wonder we have public transpo. Everyone should have a driver instead. Fifty bucks says you have a housekeeper, too."

He inclined his head at her score and turned her wrists over, probably checking for any remaining marks from the tie.

"Alec." She sorted through what she wanted to say, feeling full of some precious emotion that pushed to be expressed but might be bruised if she tried to fit it to the wrong words. He met her gaze seriously, searching her face with concern. Not what she had meant to do. She laid her hand on his cheek and leaned in to kiss him, showing him how she felt, what she couldn't—or shouldn't—articulate. "I really liked tonight. Everything. It was…more than I imagined."

"Good," he answered softly.

"And I imagined a hell of a lot," she added and he laughed,

as she'd hoped.

"You'll have to tell me some of them."

Abruptly, she felt shy about that. Some of her fantasies went pretty dark. It was one thing to have him come up with the ideas. Quite another to describe hers and introduce the possibility—no, the probability—that he'd take her seriously and act on them. Or, worse, think less of her. She stretched. "Wow. I'm sore in places I didn't know I had."

"Then let's get you in the tub and let you soak."

"Will you join me?"

"Wouldn't miss it for the world."

She used the facilities, surveying her pink bottom with satisfaction. She suspected he'd gone quite easy on her, as these things went, and still it had hurt insanely. The pain had affected her in this crazy-making way that sent her right over the edge into a kind of shadow world where she deserved to have this powerful man punishing her. Where she lived forever chained to his bed, the sight of her naked body stark in the mirrors, her own struggles as arousing as the sensation of leather on her flesh.

They weren't thoughts that bore close examination. Certainly not now, with her body sore from his ravages in the most transporting way. Enough time to ponder later. And to decide which of her darker desires she could confess to him. Difficult to decide how to balance it all—to take most advantage of however long she held his interest, to fully exploit that he enjoyed the same things she did. That he not only didn't judge her, but wanted that from her. She also didn't want to rush things, to go into the deep end faster than she was ready. And, who was she kidding? They'd gone deep and fast already.

Finally—who knew what the boundary of judgment might be? He liked that she was new to this, fresh, innocent. That much was obvious. A virgin, he'd called her. If she ruined that image of herself, would he lose interest faster?

Too much to consider. *Live in the moment, chickie,* Kiki would advise. Because it was smart advice. Taking it to heart, she went to find Alec.

And savor what he offered.

CHAPTER SEVENTEEN

S HE FOUND HIM in a rather spectacularly large bathroom off the hall, separate from the master bath, that mainly held an enormous free-standing tub shaped like half an egg, which she'd seen in design magazines. The tiled floor alternated black and white squares in a chessboard, and mirrors in gothically scrolled frames studded the walls. Bloodred towels gave splashes of color to the otherwise monochromatic scheme.

Already in the tub, Alec watched her walk naked across the room with the lazy attention a sated lion might give a deer. He looked at her in a different way than the younger guys had, with full attention and almost as if he appreciated her form in an artistic way. Not that he hadn't demonstrated his carnal interest as well. And not that it didn't turn her on profoundly.

She stopped and twisted her hair into a rope and tied it into a topknot so it wouldn't get wet—and to let him look his fill. It wouldn't hold forever and, in fact, immediately sagged under its own weight, but it was the best she could do.

He held a hand up and she took it, stepping gingerly into the hot water. Very hot water. She hissed breath through her teeth and nearly stood again when her bottom stung as if she had sunburn, but he snagged her against his side and kept her there with an arm around her shoulders. "It's good for you."

He pressed a kiss to her temple. "Consider it part of the program."

"Easy for you to say—your part of the 'program' doesn't involve doing everything the other person says," she grumbled.

He brushed a lock of hair off her already steaming forehead, taking her seriously. As he always did. Something to remember. She wasn't in the habit of being taken at her word. Certainly not by guys. But Alec wasn't a *guy*, was he? He was more a man. All along he'd treated her like a woman, even called her that when she mentally thought of herself as a girl still.

"Not true at all," he said. For a moment she thought he'd responded to what she'd been thinking, then had to backtrack. "Never think you have to do everything I say," he clarified. "In sex, yes. But only if we're playing that way. You should always feel free to disagree—or alter terms. In fact, I insist on it."

She smiled at that and he realized what he'd said. "Did you just order me to not always follow your orders?"

He shook his head and wiped a wet hand over his face. "I'm hopeless. But I do mean it."

"I know you do." Her body relaxing in the heat, she agreed it felt good. "There's a line from a song that goes something like 'if you told me to jump off a cliff I totally would because it would be a good idea.' Do you have that in Britain? The thing where mothers say that you'd jump off a cliff if all your friends did?"

His fingers idly stroked her shoulder and he had his head tipped back, eyes closed. "I believe they usually say jump in the river as that song—by an Irishwoman, as I recall—actually says."

"Whatever." She couldn't help teasing him. "It's an old song. I don't know it that well."

He sighed. "It's from the mid-eighties."

"Before I was born," she pointed out in a breezy tone.

"Good God. Don't say things like that." He paused and she waited, knowing he wouldn't be able to stop there. "When were you born, anyway?"

"July 29."

"The year, darling." He flexed his fingers into her skin in warning, giving her a shiver.

"Ninety-two. A very good year, I'm told. I'll be twenty-three in a few months."

"Somehow that doesn't help."

"Where were you when I was born?"

"London. My first job after graduating from university. Much as you are."

"Did you get to fuck your boss, too?" She squealed when he squeezed her breast under the water, pinching her nipple.

"I might be past fucking you at the moment, but I'm plenty capable of doling out more punishment. Or using something else on you."

"Such as?"

"Are you daring me?" He still had his eyes closed, but that seemingly languid tone promised a great deal if she kept pushing him. Tempting, but she was pretty sore...

"No, Sir." She tried to make it sound meek.

He cracked a golden-brown eye open. "You are far too cheeky. Clearly I didn't strap you nearly enough. Please note I can do a great deal more in this room than simply bathe."

Curious, she sat up and surveyed the room again. She'd been all eyes for him when she walked in because, now that she looked, it became clear that the walls had all sorts of rings embedded. Chrome structures she'd taken for extra towel racks—and who had extra towel racks?—upon review seemed suspiciously intended for other purposes. Both arousing and daunting.

Alec watched her keenly, eyes on her face as she took it in. She sank back. "Duly noted."

He chuckled, caressing her shoulder. "Only ever what you want, darling. I didn't intend to alarm you."

She wondered if he had any clue that, rather than being alarmed, her brain had filled with pretty good ideas of how all those might be used. Also, though it made her uncomfortable, she forced herself to face that a man with this kind of equipment—and experience and obvious sexual bent—did not spend his weekends alone. She might be the sweetmeat du jour, but this was hardly the spectacular adventure for him that it was for her.

Which she'd known walking into this, and that was okay. He'd promised, and requested, exclusivity for the duration of the affair. That was more than some guys offered. So she would banish the shades of other women.

"What did you mean," he asked, relaxed again, "when you said fellatio was one of the few things your lovers would allow?" The way he pronounced the word gave her even more of a kick than that he'd asked the question.

"Well, pretty much no guy turns down a BJ."

"I imagine that's true." His tone was measured, but she knew he was amused by her. Something else she had to offer. She made him laugh and that was something.

"I don't know—it's what I was trying to explain to you before. A lot of guys act kind of horrified if you suggest something non-vanilla. I mean, I don't get it, it wasn't their asses I was—anyway. Even the ones who wouldn't go down on me would let me do that. So...I used them for practice."

"Practice?"

She felt kind of silly. Did other girls—women—do this? "Okay, see, I figured that if I ever found a guy, a man who had real experience, like you, then he'd be a certain kind of man. One who would expect his lover to be able to deep throat and all. So I wanted to be good at it. If and when."

"If and when."

"Stop echoing me. I feel stupid enough as it is."

"And how else is this 'certain kind of man'? What else does he expect?"

"You tell me," she retorted, feeling sulky.

"Darling." Alec sighed and turned over, water sloshing in the tub, and pinned her against the sloping side. "I don't expect a bloody thing. Understood? Deep throat if you enjoy it—or if you enjoy having me make you do it—but not because you feel the need to keep some kind of accounting between us." He slid a hand under the water up between her thighs, stroking the inner curves so she parted them invitingly. But he didn't go for the gold, just smoothed his fingers over her skin. "You'll likely tease me about giving you more orders, but I have to know that you'll tell me if you don't enjoy something. If you don't really want to do it."

She tried wriggling closer to those tantalizing caresses, but he wouldn't let her. "Some things I might not know if I like them if I don't try."

"Fair enough. But that's why I employ the slowdown word, so we can discuss how something is working for you. Something you didn't use once tonight."

"It all worked for me."

"Is that the only reason?" He scooted her a little higher in the water so her breasts emerged, and he placed a gentle kiss on the upper curve of one, inching his hand higher.

"Yes," she sighed. Then protested when he moved his hand back down again.

He gave her a mocking smile. "Tell me the truth if you want your reward."

"That's unfair."

"Is it?" He bent his head and took her nipple into his mouth, with unbearable softness, circled it with his tongue, and let go again and met her gaze with a stern look. "I use the methods at hand. Tell me what else."

"I didn't want to break the mood."

He rewarded her by moving his hand higher, still not quite brushing her labia, but tantalizingly close, and gave her other nipple the same treatment. "We can always get the mood back. Having you be honest with me is more important. What else?"

"There is nothing else." And, dammit, he took his hand away, moving to stroke the back of her knee—and nipped her nipple sharply, making her jump. "There isn't," she insisted.

"You're not telling me something." He lifted her higher.

"Reach your arms over the side of the tub—there's rings on the underside. Grab hold of them."

She had to adjust, but she found them. "Handy."

"I've thought so. If you don't keep your grip on them, I'll tie you and I'll punish you a way you won't enjoy so much."

"Aye, aye, Captain."

"Cheeky." He moved between her spread thighs and pushed back her knees, opening her to the hot water, but not touching her pussy. Instead he began licking and nibbling on her over-sensitive nipples, making her eyes roll back in her head. Then he stopped.

"You've got to be kidding."

"Rewards and punishments, my sweet. You withhold, I withhold." He brushed his thumbs along the crease of her groin, the hollows formed by having her thighs spread so wide, and the sensation was unbelievably erotic—and not nearly enough. His gaze remained intent on her face as he did it again, and she couldn't help moaning a little. "What are you worrying about?"

"I'm not worrying! Ouch!"

He'd nipped the underside of her breast and it smarted.

He raised an eyebrow. "I'm not hearing a safeword."

She braced when he bent over her breasts again, but this time he licked the spot he'd bitten, then drew her nipple into his mouth, sucking until she groaned and couldn't hold still. Then stopped and gave her a pointed look.

"You're the devil."

"Thank you, darling. Something else to tell me?" He inched his thumbs closer to her aching vulva. She felt as desperate as she had before the first orgasm—and quite certain he'd keep this up until she caved.

"I just—" No, she couldn't say that. "It sounds stupid."

"Tell me anyway."

She took a deep breath. So much for sophistication. "I didn't—don't—want you to be disappointed in me is all."

"Ah." He slid a long finger inside her, stroking in and out. Better. Not enough, but getting there. She let out a long breath of relief. "I couldn't be disappointed in you. Unless." He stilled the movement, frowning at her when she made a sound of protest. "Unless you aren't perfectly honest about what you want, what you feel."

"I feel very turned on and I really want you to touch me."

"Now there's a start." He resumed the movement, adding a brush of his thumb over the hood of her clit. Electrifying. "Tell me something else."

"That's really all—"

"Shh. Not that. Tell me one of the things you've imagined."

"There's lots of things." Dark fantasies. Not for the light of day. Or the bright light of his bathing chamber.

"Pick one."

She tried to squirm away and he pushed a second finger inside her, sapping her will. "Oh please," she panted, holding onto the tub grips so hard her fingers were going numb.

"Just a little one. Tell me a story."

"I used to fantasize about giving you a BJ at work."

"How would it happen?" He coaxed her with his voice as much as his hands, making her tremble.

"I'd bring something into your office and you'd give me that frown and say I needed correction. You'd tell me to kneel and open my blouse. I wouldn't be wearing a bra and you'd say I was naughty."

"Very naughty."

Oh yes. Hearing him say it made the vision that much more real. "And you'd examine my breasts, pinch my nipples."

"Like this?" He rolled one hard nipple between his thumb and forefinger, maintaining that provocative glide and tantalizing strokes of his other hand.

"Sometimes harder."

He obliged and she moaned.

"Like that. And I'd beg you to stop, that someone might see."

"Because there are windows to the hallway."

"Yes. You tell me you'll only stop if I suck you off and I'd better be quick about it, or—"

"Or what?"

"Or you'd tie me to your desk with my skirt pushed up. You'd spank me and leave me there for everyone to see. And oh God!" The orgasm roared through her, making her arch her back and press into his hand. He responded in kind, working his hand in and out of her, squeezing one nipple and sucking hard on the other.

The climax wrung her dry, leaving as fast as it blew through. Alec told her to let go of the rings and eased her down into the water, running the tap to add more hot, rubbing her shoulders.

"A lovely fantasy," he finally said, kissing her softly.

"Thank you."

"For what?"

"For sharing."

"I thought you might mind, because of the work stuff."

"Far from it. I had one or two of my own. Inappropriate, but there it is. Part of the charge for us, no doubt. The taboo."

"Do you think that's all this is?"

"Wanting what we can't or shouldn't have? That's part of it. Not all, I think. Isn't that what we're finding out? Besides, if we find out that is all this is, what's wrong with that?"

"I seem to recall you making references to some sort of Faustian hell."

"Ah yes. That's another thing entirely and mine to deal with. But the fantasies, the darker desires, no. I truly believe there's nothing wrong with exploring them with someone else who also enjoys them."

"Are you saying nothing would shock you?"

"I don't think it's possible, no. Not that there aren't things I'm not into." He fell silent and some broody thought seemed to take him. He shook it off, cupping her breast and pressing a kiss to her cheek. "You can tell me anything. If I'm not into it, I'll be honest and if it's something you very much want to try, we'll either work it out or find another way to get you there. Fair enough?"

"Fair enough." Though she wondered what he meant by finding another way. "Tell me one of your fantasies then."

"Mine?" He sounded taken aback. Oddly so, considering the conversation. As if it had never occurred to him that she'd ask.

"I showed you mine. Show me yours."

"I'll do one better. Friday next, if you wish, wear that little suit and jacket. You know the one? Black—and the pink blouse with it."

"Yes. The one I was wearing the day I first noticed you had a thing for me."

"Yes. Regrettable." He sighed, then kissed her. "I'm a weak man."

"Oh brother. What else? Wear that to work and what? You said no hanky-panky at the office."

"And I plan to stick to it. The day you wear that, I'll expect you here that evening. And I'll show you one of mine, in spades."

CHAPTER EIGHTEEN

FORTUNATELY THE HOT bath and that last, very hot orgasm ran Amber down enough that she snuggled into bed with him without testing him further. She'd hate the analogy, but she reminded him of having a new puppy—full of energy and revved to try any- and everything, all at once. He wouldn't have thought he had four orgasms in him. It still rattled him that Amber had managed to extract that last one. And that he hadn't dredged up the strength to stop her. Another, however, might have given him a permanent disability.

He didn't know how all those men twice his age dealt with their beautiful young mistresses. Certainly not a venture for the faint of heart. Perhaps they counted on their trophy companions to be satisfied with the money and lifestyle. And pool boys and tennis coaches, if the jokes were to be believed. Sod him if he'd become that kind of fool.

Besides, all of that was thinking much too far down the road. This first encounter for them had been a tremendous release of pent-up energy. Preceding even the catalyst of meeting each other. Amber with her stockpile of fantasies, practicing deep throating on those bone-headed boys who had apparently no clue what a sexual siren they'd been too afraid of to properly savor. And him, with his lonely penance, depriving himself of all but the most basic and boring of sexual interludes.

It had been an extraordinary evening. In the glimmer of lights from the city around them, he could just make out their reflection in the mirror above. Amber's white skin nearly glowing as she lay sleeping on his bare chest, dark in contrast, and her tumble of hair spread in a banner over the pillow she wasn't using. The sheet draped over her sweetly flared hips, her back long and narrow. Sensual and comfortable in her skin, exuberantly sexual, she made him feel at once paradoxically younger and old by comparison.

Even in this moment, when she'd fallen asleep with childlike speed and he lay awake, despite his body's depletion and the late hour, mind buzzing. Brooding again, Tessa would have said, with that impatience of long association. Her remanent in his head had a point. Here he had what many men would envy—a beautiful young woman, eager to let him have her any way he wished. And he couldn't quite let himself enjoy it. The inevitable end of the affair worried at him. Knowing he'd suffer for it. Knowing he deserved to.

Why this is hell, nor am I out of it.

He woke when she stirred, slipping out from under the sheets, morning light pouring in the windows and heating the room. With a stab of pain, his first waking thought was that she was leaving him already. "Where are you going?"

She squeaked—very close to one of the sounds she made during sex—and spun around, her hair a tangled cloud around her naked body, eyes blurry and face still flushed from sleep. He wanted to drag her into bed and ravish her.

She bounced a little on her toes, pressing her thighs together. "I seriously have to pee."

"Carry on then." He flopped back, his reflection staring at him accusingly. What a bloody mess he was. Should he wait to see if she came back to bed or get up and start the tea? Coffee for her, no doubt. Though he wouldn't be able to make the mochas she favored. Unable to decide and impatient with himself for dithering about it, he was still lying there when she—thank all the gods—danced back into the room with a happy smile and dove under the covers to sleek up against him.

"So much better." She leaned up on her elbow to scrutinize his face. "Sorry I woke you."

"You didn't," he lied, faintly embarrassed that she had.

She scraped one of her candy-pink nails over his chin stubble. "You're all scruffy this morning."

"Comes with the territory. I'll go shave."

"Don't. I like it." An impish glow in her much more alert eyes, she kissed him, soft and delectable, tasting of mint.

"You brushed your teeth."

"I found a toothbrush still in the wrapper. I didn't want to be all morning-breathy."

"It's unfair to leave me alone in my morning breath."

She kissed him again and made a sound as if she'd tasted something delicious. "Men don't get morning breath. Just like you wake up with perfect hair and never have pillow creases on your faces. I think it goes back to Adam and Eve."

"If you truly believe that, I have some hedge funds to tell you about."

"Mmm. If you're selling, I'm buying." She walked her

fingers down his chest and slipped them under the sheet, grasping his morning erection. "Is this for me?"

Charmed by her, he tugged at one of her tangled curls and brought her down for another kiss, cranking up the heat of it as she stroked him smoothly. "Apparently so."

"Goody." She started to slide down, but he stopped her and flipped her onto her back.

"Not so fast." He yanked the sheet down to reveal her lovely body. "My turn for that."

"I thought we weren't keeping score." She gasped when he pulled her thighs apart, revealing her shining pink sex, already slick and eager for him.

"We're not. I intend to demonstrate that I'm not one of those boys who wouldn't go down on you."

She tasted as sweet as the rest of her, with the tang of salt and heat. Her breath sighed out as he licked her, shivering under the caress of his mouth.

"Believe me, Alec. You have nothing to prove..." She trailed off into a moan and ran her fingers through his hair, breath hitching when he sucked her clit into his mouth and flicked it with his tongue. She came right then, a long slow wave. So very responsive. She plucked at his shoulders, urging him up, but he wasn't done.

Holding her firmly in place, he drove her up again, a steeper slope of arousal this time, as her body awakened and geared up for more extreme heights. She climaxed with a startled cry and segued into another peak, body trembling as he stoked the fires hotter. This time when she pulled at him, he obliged, pausing only to put on a condom, and slid into her startlingly hot sheath.

She undulated under him, rolling her hips to welcome him in and accommodate his girth. Her face blurred with pleasure, eyes smoky blue with it, she wrapped long, pale arms around him and pulled him in for a kiss. She'd taste herself on his mouth but didn't hesitate, opening there for him as sweetly as she opened her thighs.

He rocked with her, their movements dreamier in the morning light, the shimmering need building more slowly, more of a ripening than the explosions of the night before. When her hips moved more urgently, he levered himself up, breaking her grip to penetrate deeper into her. She dug her nails into his chest, head thrown back and eyes closed as her mind fogged, soft mouth moving with her moans, hair a spill of gold and honey. And cried out as she came.

Capturing the moment with his mind, he tucked the image away, to take out and cherish later. Then let her body drag him over the edge into his own orgasm, into his own version of oblivion.

"YOU KNOW," SHE said some time later, after they'd disentangled themselves from each other, "I would not have pegged you for a mirror-over-the-bed kind of guy."

"It is rather tacky."

She frowned up at her reflection and ran a hand through her hair, hitting a snarl immediately. "It's great for sex, don't get me wrong. Totally hot watching you give me head. But now I can't stop seeing that I have bed head bad enough to make me want to go all Miley Cyrus."

"Your hair is lovely."

"Thank you." She wrinkled her nose at him and sat up, bare breasts pale and perfect. "But you have to say that, especially as you don't seem to have a hairbrush. I didn't think you'd want me using yours anyway."

He ran a hand over the curve of her hip, unable to stop touching her. "We've commingled in plenty of ways. I wouldn't mind, had I one. I've a comb you could borrow."

"God no. Unless you figure out a way to make that sexy, it's pain I'm not willing to endure. I can tie it up and deal when I get home."

Ah. There it was. Time for that, of course. Inevitable. "Need you go immediately, or would you want some breakfast?" He glanced at the sun. "Brunch?"

She broke into a radiant smile. "I would love that. But..." She hesitated, studying his face. She had a bit of whisker burn and she looked delightfully well used.

"But?"

"I don't want to be that girl you can't get rid of. You're a busy man, I get that. You probably have things to do. Feel free to kick me out."

"In point of fact, I was contemplating tying you to the bed so you couldn't leave. I hoped to lull you with food and then go for a surprise attack when you were full of jam."

"You have jam?"

"I can have, yes. We'll order up brunch from the restaurant below and sit on the terrace."

"Um, I have nothing to wear unless you give me back my cocktail dress. Your neighbors might not appreciate that."

"They'd probably thank their lucky stars to have the opportunity to lay eyes on you, but I think I shall reserve that privilege. You can borrow a shirt." He swung out of bed and headed to the closet.

"Alec?" She sounded tentative and he glanced back at her, waifish in the big bed and tangle of black sheets.

"What, darling?"

"Can I get my phone out of purgatory? I should send Kiki a note."

"Of course." Funny how he'd quite forgot that bit of the game in their recent interlude. Vanilla sex, pillow talk and…not romance. But something very near it that had his heart feeling rather raw. "Can't have her thinking I've sold you to a third-world bordello."

She hopped out of bed and down the hall, calling back, "They wouldn't have me—I'm too old."

"You don't look it," he muttered.

"I heard that."

Ears like a cat. He chose one of his white dress shirts and held it out to her as she walked back in, beaded purse in one hand, already scrolling through her messages. Tossing them both on the bedside table—on the side she'd slept on, he noted—she took the shirt and gave him a dubious look. "This is all I get?"

"It's plenty big enough, and the terrace should be warm."

She tilted her head thoughtfully and shrugged into it, buttoning it up and looking at herself in the full-length mirror. The forked tails of the shirt parted over her slim thighs, the final button just above her crotch. She rolled up the cuffs and fixed the collar, then met his eyes in the mirror. "Is this a sex thing?"

Moving closer behind her, he ran his hands over her bare bum, then over the silky hair of her mound and into her wet folds, her clit swelling at the brush of his fingers. "You look charming."

Dropping her head back on his shoulder, she parted her thighs invitingly. "Definitely a sex thing."

He pressed a kiss to the side of her throat, stroked her a bit more, delighted by the way she practically purred in response, and let her go. "I'm definitely about the brunch thing. Let me get the menu."

She mock-scowled at him. "You're a tease, Alec Knight."

"Darling, you have no idea."

CHAPTER NINETEEN

ALEC WENT TO get their food, saying the delivery took too long, which gave her time to be nosy. Within reason. No opening of drawers or cabinets unless legitimately looking for something—like, hello toothbrush in the wrapper, one of five he apparently kept on hand for impromptu sleepovers like this—but anything in the open or not behind a closed door was fair game.

She wandered around, wearing only his shirt, which, though freshly starched and laundered, managed to smell like him anyway. The place had to be professionally decorated, not surprising for a man of his status—more money than time. It gave the condo a slightly formal air, however, more like a hotel room than something really his. The art was interesting. Not the stolid landscapes she'd expected of a stereotypical Brit, either, but eclectic paintings and sinuous sculptures.

Though the colors and subjects varied, they had a consistent enough aesthetic that she'd bet he'd selected every one. They were…tactile. Somehow profoundly reflective of the Alec she'd gotten to know over the past, what, seventeen hours. So interesting to meet the passionately sensual man underneath the cool reserve, as starched as his shirts and as easily removed.

She found a few framed photographs—arms around some

men in a pub, him grinning broadly on a rafting trip of some sort, a pair of kids dressed in far-too-big grown-up outfits mugging for the camera, three women in fancy dress, raising glasses with the ocean behind them—but none she thought were the ex-wife. Not that she'd really expected him to have one, but probably a good sign that he didn't. Not pining for the ex, then, but something got between him and Amber sometimes. Something that both saddened and angered him.

He possessed a broodier nature than she'd suspected, than he ever showed at work. She studied an oil of a demon that flickered in and out of black flames, the pale form of a woman barely visible through the veil of her hair, clinging to him or struggling to escape. He sometimes sank into dark thoughts, him and his obsession with Faust.

Alec found her there, handing her a shopping bag and looking at the painting, too. "I've always liked that one. Interesting. I see different things in it over the years."

"You have another in your office, by the same artist, I think."

He gave her a considering look. "Interesting that you recognize the style, as the subject matter is quite different."

"The eyes are the same." The one at the office was a woman, depicted as a saint in the old style, with a snake skeleton under her feet. But she and the demon shared the same haunted gaze, rimmed in smoke, staring straight out at the viewer. Heaven and hell, flipped sides of the coin, much like Alec's public and private faces. "Is she trying to get closer to him or get away?"

"I never can decide. It seems to depend on my mood." He

smiled and shrugged, tucking that dark thing away, covering it with the sunny. "I brought you some things. You can avail yourself while I plate up the food. Mimosa?"

"Yum. Yes, please."

In the bag she found—God bless him—a boar's bristle hairbrush and a high-end skin-care kit, complete with cleanser and oil-free cream. She took them back to the master and happily desnarled her hair, then tied it back and washed off last night's makeup. Waking up in the previous night's smoky eyes might feel deliciously soiled for a while, but the shine dimmed at the prospect of sunny brunch on the terrace.

"You look fresh-faced." Alec rose when she walked out. With a brush of a kiss, he led her to the table and held her chair.

"Thank you. I feel like a human being again. But that's probably the most expensive hairbrush you could have bought."

"Is it?" He smiled easily, thoroughly composed now, no glimmer of a darker mood as he clinked his mimosa to hers. "I've some idea of how women are about their hair. I imagine it takes some work to take care of yours."

"An odd thing for you to think of."

"Why's that?"

"I dunno. Most guys don't?"

"Well, yours is very long, but also quite silky—very fine and tangles easily. Between the two, I imagine you have to be careful."

"Were you a hairdresser in another life, Alec?"

"No, but I do have three sisters."

"Aha. And where are you in the lineup?"

"I am the older brother—fortunate as my parents could escape the invidious accusation that they must have been trying for a boy. The family, especially my baby sister, jokes that they were trying for a better girl."

"They sound like a fun group."

"They are." He ate his French toast methodically, spearing berries on his fork first, adding a neat wedge of toast, dipped just slightly in syrup.

"Do you miss them?

"I do, yes."

"But you left London anyway."

"They don't live in London. I grew up on the coast, near Brighton. They all still live in that area."

"Why not go back there instead of all the way to New York?"

"It's not exactly the financial center of the universe."

"And you didn't want to stay in London."

He gave her a long look. "Too many memories. How are your eggs Benedict?"

"Amazing." With crab and avocado, a bit of bite to the hollandaise and a puff pastry instead of an English muffin, it might have been the best she'd ever tasted. "Should I not be asking you questions?"

"Sorry." He winced, chagrined, and covered her hand on the table with his. "I haven't been in the habit of talking about my personal life much. Ask. If I don't care to answer, I'll say so."

"All right then." Might as well go for the gold. "I won't

phrase this as a question, but I'm thinking your ex-wife had long hair and that's the real reason you know what to buy."

"Maybe I'm partial to long hair on a woman and so have had a number of lovers as such."

"Vast numbers, no doubt," she said, pointing her fork at him.

"Hardly. I believe you overestimate my stamina. And free time."

"How many?"

His mouth quirked. "A gentleman doesn't keep count."

"I think not knowing the exact number falls into the 'vast' category."

"Are you seriously wanting to have this conversation?" He seemed less offended than intrigued.

"Yes. I think it's very interesting to learn people's histories. I'm fascinated by you. That's no secret." She sipped her mimosa and fluttered her lashes ostentatiously. "I'll tell you mine if you tell me yours."

He folded his napkin and tossed it on the table. "Counting you makes an even dozen."

Mimosas burned like hell going back up your nose. Taking a minute to recover, while Alec watched, highly amused, she waved her own napkin at him, until she could speak. "I cry bullshit!"

He shook his head, slow and even, eyes steady. "For full-on sex, twelve."

"How is that possible?"

Golden brown glittered as he narrowed his eyes at her. "I'm selective."

"Even if you didn't start until, like, eighteen—that's only one every two-plus years."

"I had my first lover at twenty, thank you. Then I was married for nearly nine of those, and dated my wife exclusively for three before that."

"How many since you divorced?"

Raising an eyebrow, he leaned elbows on the table and assumed the patient expression of the interrogated. "Three, counting you."

"You know, you don't need to keep specifying that I count."

"Just making sure you know, darling."

"Are you annoyed with me?"

"Not a bit of it. I find I'm…rather helplessly fascinated."

"Okay, so you have this place with all the gear for bondage, the mirror over the bed, the bathroom set up for water games of all kinds, probably lots more. Subs are hitting on you in the bar, and yet I'm only the third woman you've banged in New York."

"Second, in point of fact. The other was in London. Both were vanilla encounters. All of the gear was here when I bought the place from a friend. He'd equipped it and suggested I'd enjoy…exploiting the facilities."

"But you haven't."

"I've not, no. And no, I don't care to discuss why not. Particularly as I believe you're trying to distract me. I'm anticipating the revelation of your own score. Counting me, naturally."

Well, shit. "I really hesitate to say now."

"I wondered if you wouldn't be digging yourself into a hole. Of course, you're committed. And I shall know if you're prevaricating."

At least he'd set the standard for counting full intercourse only. "Would your number go up if you counted sexual interludes that weren't full-on sex?"

"You're stalling. Fidgeting, too."

She made herself fold her napkin and set it aside. Then met his oh-so-amused gaze. "You make twenty-three." She clapped her hands over her cheeks, to cover the embarrassed flush. "Oh God, I'm such a ho."

To her surprise, he threw back his head and laughed. The totally sunny Alec, eyes sparkling, the sun catching red-gold glints in his brown hair. "Why don't you come sit on my lap?" he invited, patting his knee.

More than happy to, she brought her mimosa and sat, immeasurably pleased when he kissed her, hand settling familiarly on her bare thigh, petting her with affection. "You started earlier, I imagine."

"Sixteen," she admitted. "And, jeez, I felt like I held out! I didn't want to screw up my first time."

"So, you've been methodical—a new lover each quarter, more or less."

"The long-term relationship thing has not really panned out for me, it's true. But, I should qualify that just over half of those were in college."

"Perfectly understandable."

"Not for Saint Alexander, who did, what, two years of university before busting his cherry?"

He tugged her hair, then draped it over her shoulder, smoothing it. "Three—I went to university early. My advantage in academics seemed to be inversely proportional to my success with women. I promise I slept with the first who would have me."

"I find that so hard to believe."

"Yes, well, you're biased." On pretext of stroking her hair, his hand moved over her breast, cupping it through the shirt before dropping down to her thigh again, stroking seductively. "I may have learned one or two things since, as well."

"I'll say."

He moved her hair over her shoulder, exposing her neck, and nuzzled under her ear, hand caressing up her hip under the shirt. Flush now with rising arousal, she angled her head back.

"Now the answer to your other question—how many if I don't count full sex?" Following the curve of her hip bone from her waist, fingers brushing down her belly, he took her earlobe in his teeth. Nipped a little. "Part your thighs for me."

"The neighbors…"

"Can't see past the tablecloth. Do as I say."

The sun hot on her skin, knowing he'd find her as wet as after hours of teasing, she obeyed, shuddering when his fingers slipped into her folds. Methodically, very lightly, he stroked her. "It depends on how you parse 'sexual interlude,'" he said in a reflective tone, as if his hand wasn't working between her thighs, making her squirm. "Not to be Clintonesque about it. Many situations for me are sexually fraught while appearing to be nothing to anyone else. Watching you walk down the hall, for example. Or when you run barefoot onto the sidewalk and stop to pull on your heels, your hair falling over your face and your skirt riding up your lovely thighs. Very sexual."

"Alec," she moaned. She couldn't stay still and dug her fingers into his shoulder.

"Or this moment, with you all hot and slippery under my hand, would hardly rate your parental guidance from the film censors, seen from afar. Really, it's only a bit of petting. Particularly if I stop before you come." He took his hand away and traced down the open vee of the shirt instead, popping open a button. "Keep your thighs open. I never said you could close them."

A tremor went through her, brain getting more rattled. Would he undress her out here, after all? He opened the shirt just enough for her bare breast to show, though her position would block the sight from any onlookers, and returned to stroking the outside of her thigh.

"I'd call this equally as sexual. What say you?"

"Yes. Yes, I would."

"It excites you when I give you orders such as that. Even benign ones." His eyes gleamed, both with that teasing glint and the sensual challenge.

Not something she minded admitting. "It does."

"So then, yes, if you parse it thus, the numbers may be vast indeed. I've been in many, many sexual interludes, from mild to wildly debauched." He lifted his hand under the shirt, to thumb her nipple, watching intently. "Many women enjoy being prepared for submissive sex by another man. Or simply dominated by one. It's not necessary to have full-on sex to have a scene with someone. In this way, darling, if either of us is the 'ho,' it would be me. You would likely be shocked—possibly horrified—by some of what I've seen and done."

"You said there's nothing wrong with exploring those things, with someone else who also enjoys them." She gasped when he pinched her nipple between thumb and forefinger, rolling her hips.

"Be still. I do believe that. But there are degrees."

"Of what?" She tried to keep her thoughts on track, but they arrowed back to what he was doing to her.

"I considered that, with you." He still focused on her breast. "Considered offering to give you a taste in a non-physical style. Act out some scenes and let you feel what you liked of being under someone else's control. It would have been a degree lighter. Less deeply involved."

"Why didn't you?"

His gaze rose to meet hers, and that intensity had returned. The hand supporting her back wound her hair into a rope, tugging so she tipped her chin up, unable to watch as he trailed his fingers back down her center, dipping into her folds again. Excruciatingly arousing. The conversation alone would have done it. With his relentless teasing...

"Because I knew it wouldn't be enough. I'd already discovered that I couldn't resist you. One taste wouldn't be enough. I wanted all of you. To possess and ravish you in every way possible. No, don't come, yet."

Taking a deep breath, she blew it out slowly, mastering the burn. Staving it off. She'd tried practicing this on her own, but it had been a hell of a lot easier that way. "I'm glad," she said, managing to sound somewhat human. "I want you to have me every way."

"A good thing, as I intend to. How many for you, if you don't count full sex?" He sounded politely interested, but the way his clever fingers worked her belied that. "Pay attention and answer my question."

"Not that many," she gasped. "Like five. Once I made the move to have it all, that's what I like."

"Being penetrated." He slid a finger inside her, curling it, driving her to the brink.

"Oh yes." She clutched at him. "Alec!"

"Don't you dare come."

"Then stop touching me like that!" Even as the desperate words came out, she tried to grab them back, but he hushed her.

"Did you just tell me what to do?" His tone had gone icy. "Oh dear. This shan't do at all."

"I'm sorry, Sir."

"Ah, she mouths the words, but she's not truly obedient. How best to teach you a lesson?" His hand continued to stroke her, remorselessly, and the incipient orgasm bore down on her. "Shall I make you come anyway, right here on the terrace, so the neighbors will hear your cries of helpless pleasure?"

She pressed her lips together, as if to stifle those theoretical screams. Focused on not climaxing with every fiber of her being.

"I think we'll make this private," he said, as if deciding on the spot. "Go in the flat, take off the shirt and kneel on the floor, eyes closed, thighs spread nice and wide, and wait for me."

In a haze of relief that the immediate trial had ended, a mix of anticipation and trepidation over what he'd do next and trembling with arousal, she fled into the condo. Whipping off the shirt, she scanned the large formal living area and realized he hadn't said where in the flat. Dammit.

Knowing it didn't really matter, as he'd decide whether to punish her for that or something else, she picked a spot and knelt. He hadn't said what to do with her hands, so she clasped them behind her back. Waited.

And waited.

Funny how the mind-fuck worked. The semi-arbitrary rules, created more to increase her tension and anticipation than to satisfy him. He made her wait because he knew it would work on her as surely as his hands and words had. The threat of punishment kept her on edge, uncertain. Denial of orgasm and prolonging her arousal. She understood how it all operated and yet…

It still drove her out of her mind with need.

Crazy exciting.

CHAPTER TWENTY

MAKING HER WAIT a bit was calculated, of course, but it also let him settle himself. Leash the raging desire to simply plunge himself into her, to have the sweet clasp of her body over and over. She wanted a very specific ride from him. He had a responsibility to deliver that. Hopefully they'd manage it so it didn't affect her career or reputation, but if it did, at least she'd have gotten exactly what she signed up for.

Not him mooning after her like a schoolboy with his first crush.

She got under his skin, with her probing questions and artless honesty. Where other women hid their secrets or gauged how best to play the relationship, she spoke her mind. Asking him if she'd annoyed him, brows raised in earnest concern, skin and hair glowing in the sun as if Venus had stepped off her seashell and into his life.

It had hit him hard, the stark knowledge that she was the first for these games since Tessa. Oh, he'd glossed it, made it sound as if he'd hit the scene recently, the kink, in a non-physical way. But he hadn't. Hadn't wanted to until he laid eyes on Amber. He'd known all along his attraction to her bordered on obsession, went over the top, even discounting the forbidden aspects. At least he'd said "selective" instead of the word that had sprung to mind—"monogamous." Tessa had teased him relentlessly about his monogamous nature. *You're the straightest kinkster on the face of the earth.*

But he'd surprised her, hadn't he? Opening the marriage hadn't only been the last thing she'd expected him to suggest—it had been in the realm of impossibility. Maybe Tessa had been right in her accusations. He'd told himself that he'd been trying to do the right thing by her, but she'd known what it meant.

He hadn't offered to open the marriage so much as acknowledged that it no longer existed for him.

Not something he could think about right now. Particularly not with Amber being so bloody observant and insightful. Detail-oriented, Lily had called her. Understatement of the century. No, he'd keep his mind off his personal issues and his curious lover too occupied to pry further.

Fortunately, he had the perfect tools for that. Moving silently, he rose and halted in the open sliding-glass doors, soaking in the glory of her. She had her back to him, head bowed, and her pert bum showed just under the fall of her tumbling locks. So lovely and self-assured. Twenty-three lovers, indeed. No, he didn't mind a bit—envied her that she embraced life so fully, in fact—but he'd had to choke back the demand that he be the last. All the possessiveness Tessa could have wished for and Amber, she for whom "the long-term relationship thing" hadn't panned out. Ah, the irony.

Just another circle of hell.

She'd sensed his presence, lifting her head slightly, listening. So he walked around her, letting her hear the soft footsteps on the plush rug, anticipating his censure or pleasure. She trembled and he knew he had her, either way.

In every way. At least for a few more hours.

"Ms. Dolors," he said very softly, voice as full of disapproval as he could make it, "when I tell you to kneel, I expect you to put your hands behind your neck, under your hair, tits out."

She complied immediately, nipples taut as she thrust out her pretty breasts, a smile dancing on her full lips.

"Does something amuse you?"

He picked up a switch—a fairly light one in respect for her tender skin—and drew it along the underside of her arm, so she'd wonder what it was.

"No, Sir." Her voice trembled. Repressed laughter? Arousal? Not fear, he thought.

"Don't lie to me." He flicked the switch against the outside of her thigh, a bit of sting that made her gasp in shock, eyes flying open. "Eyes closed!" He'd raised his voice, made it a little angry, and she whimpered, squinching them tight again.

He let her stew, then teased one hard nipple with the switch and she made a little sound of distress. "What were you thinking that made you smile?"

She licked her lips, moistening them in her nerves. "Only that, I figured since you didn't tell me what to do with my hands, that whatever I picked would turn out to be wrong, so you could punish me for it."

He drew the switch along the underside of her breast, a bare tickle, and she responded by arching her back more, raising her breasts higher. "Why would I set you up to fail?"

She hesitated and he flicked the switch against her vulnerable belly. She had to fight not to curl up defensively, but managed to resist the impulse.

"Hold your hair higher and answer the question."

When she'd lifted the glorious waves out of the way, he traced her spine with the switch, drawing it from nape to tailbone as she spoke.

"Because you enjoy punishing me."

"Do I?"

"I think so." She rocked on her heels a little when he teased the cleft of her bum with the tip of the switch, then stilled herself, breathing harder.

"Is that the only reason?" He flicked the switch against one buttock, then the other in quick succession, before she could answer.

"No!" She sobbed a little, caught her breath. "I mean— because I enjoy it, too."

"I wonder which of us enjoys it more." He made his tone musing, moving around her and giving her little stinging flicks, watching her come apart a little at not knowing where they'd land, at not having them connected to a task. They wouldn't hurt so much individually as the stimulation would accumulate, each building on the last. He let a pause draw out, while she caught her breath again, then brushed her nipple with it.

She nearly jumped out of her skin.

Then moaned as he trailed it down over her uplifted rib cage, her soft belly, and tickled her nether mouth. He tapped her there lightly, not enough to sting, but to plant the seed in her mind of what that would feel like. She strained not to close her thighs.

"There is also the disturbing nature of your impertinence to me. I'd feel constrained to address such a problem, whether I enjoyed it or not." He tapped her again and she nearly convulsed. "Don't you agree?"

"Yes, Sir." She was close to begging. Would, if he allowed it, but he wouldn't give her that outlet. She'd gone deep into the head trip. He wouldn't get in the way of that.

"Let's take care of that little chore then. Hands and knees. Crawl forward. I'll direct you. You may open your eyes, but keep them focused between your hands."

She obeyed as soon as he tapped her hip with the switch. Moving ahead of him, she responded instantly to his guiding flicks of the switch, skin and supple muscle shivering at each touch. Her hair fell in a curtain around her head to the floor, so he needn't have told her not to look up. Dependent on him to direct her, she moved with a gratifying lack of hesitation. Astounding how much trust she placed in him.

In the little den, he made her wait as she was while he re-trieved the cuffs and her heels. When he returned and told her to stand, he very nearly pulled her luscious, lithe body into his arms, so he could kiss her sweet mouth and drown in her heat, her sensual hunger. But that would change the mood and he'd promised her punishment.

She bent over to put on the heels as he bade her, something he hadn't exaggerated as being sexually fraught for him. Something in her grace, the fall of her hair, the way she pointed her toes to slide her foot into the stiletto. Going from barefoot girl to elegant woman in the space of a four-inch heel. Straightening, she tossed her hair back over her shoulders and—emerging from the zone a bit—gave him a sly smile. Oh, yes, she remembered what he'd said, and reveled in it.

"See that wall?" He pointed. "That's where you'll be in a moment."

She studied it, bemused and intrigued. Couldn't quite piece together how it would work, the series of hooks, recessed openings and threaded bolt holes set deep into the red velvet wallpaper. Some of the sexual gymnasium of the place was over the top. When he'd bought it, he'd succumbed to George's exhortations that it would be the perfect place for a man on divorce-rebound with his preferred kink.

Neither of them had expected him to become a hermit. Or for his first partner here in these games to be so untouched.

Nevertheless, when he backed her against the wall, the lurid contrast it made to Amber's wide-eyed innocence and lissome nakedness set the blood beating with hard urgency in his brain. As with the demon in the painting, he wanted to devour her. The cuffs he'd buckled onto her wrists might represent a symbolic captivity, but his darkest nature craved more than that.

Pulling her legs apart, he hooked the cuffs to the lower rings, then raised her wrists over her head, choosing the ideal height and spread for each. Her breathing accelerating and deepening, her full breasts rose and fell, hard nipples brushing his shirt, wondering gaze glued to his face.

"Afraid?" He brushed her cheek, unable to quite discern the emotion behind her turbulent blue.

"Of you? Never."

"Then what?"

"I'm not sure. But don't stop."

"I wouldn't." He dropped his hand to her breast and pinched her taut nipple hard enough to make her wince. "I won't stop until I'm satisfied, no matter how you cry or beg me. Understand?"

That did it. She spiraled up into that dazed, heightened state at his words. "Yes, Sir."

Of course, it wasn't true, but it made for a lovely conceit between them.

George had loved his mirrors, so when Alec moved away she saw herself reflected in the full-length one directly opposite. A device that worked nicely on her, kept her riveted and in the moment.

"Up on tiptoes," he told her, holding up the crimson phallus. She transferred her fixed gaze to it and, with what little space she had to work with, raised more onto her toes. He'd figured it correctly and found the threaded hole perfectly aligned below her slick little cunt. She groaned, understanding now, as he screwed the phallus into the wall, carelessly brushing her sensitized and swollen tissues with his knuckles, pretending to ignore how the casual touches rocketed through her bound form.

When he stepped back, to let her see, the thing protruded obscenely between her pale thighs, sticking out horizontally and sitting just below her nether lips after she set her heels down. Close enough for her to feel. Not nearly enough to satisfy her.

She looked her fill and turned her gaze on him, wry intelligence back in a flash, acknowledging as clearly as if she'd said so that the punishment would be diabolical, indeed. Turning up the lights, positioned to spotlight her beauty, he selected some music. Mozart's *Masonic Funeral Music*, with its suitably dark, passionate, sobbing strings.

"With the door closed, the room is soundproofed," he said. "Feel free to make as much noise as you like. The music should work well as a backdrop."

Whipping the switch so it whistled above the swelling notes, he laid it across the round of her thigh. Harder, with more of a sting. She cried out, startled, eyes glazing over and hips writhing to reach the phallus. Bound to the wall loosely enough to move that much, she didn't have enough play for that, no matter how she tried. The blood roared in his ears along with Mozart's torment and his surging need.

Settling into his rhythm, he began switching her in earnest.

CHAPTER TWENTY-ONE

S HE'D THOUGHT THE little switch didn't hurt all that much. So slight in appearance. Nothing like the strap he'd used on her the night before. But, like the little den, what seemed innocuous held a deeper wealth of diabolical torment.

And Alec...he'd gone into some state she almost didn't recognize. Face contorted, eyes catching the warm lights with what her scattered thoughts and raging emotions insisted on seeing as demonic. That ravenous gaze devoured her slightest twitch, flaring in pleasure when she lost all control and fought to reach that damnable phallus he'd placed just out of reach. Deep red and covered with gnarled bumps like a polished walking stick, it tantalized her, brushing her swollen labia as she reflexively cringed away from the switch, every once in a long while catching her clit.

She discovered she wept, mainly because the tears clogged her throat, making her wordless pleas even more broken and watery. If asked—if she or her tormentor even retained the ability for human speech—she couldn't have said if she wept from the sting of the switch or from despair that climax, relief from the arousal that threatened to tear her limb from limb if not released, would remain equally as out of reach.

Worst, or most erotically excruciating of all, the entire

scene reflected back to her from the immense mirror. Alec in his shirt and pants—more casual than his suits, but still with knife-sharp creases, moving between her and her reflection, her body stark against the dark red wall, almost unrecognizable to herself.

He caught her attention, moving in, sliding the switch under her breast as he'd done before. She figured that out, that he liked to trick her into thinking he'd strike her there, or between her legs as he'd teased before. Again, a supreme mind-fuck because, even though she knew and trusted he wouldn't truly hurt her, an unreasoning emotional part of her didn't understand that and kicked into a maelstrom of reaction. Fear, arousal, orgasm, pain.

Staring into her eyes, he looked half-wild. Breathing as heavily as she, sweat beading his forehead, he ran his free hand down the underside of her arm, fingers gliding on her slicked skin, tracing the line of her muscle and the hollow of her armpit. As best she could, she leaned into the caress, absurd as it might be to seek comfort from him. He nodded, as if she'd confirmed something, and cast the switch aside.

Kneeling, running his hands down her straining legs as he did, he repositioned her ankles, reattaching them to the wall so the phallus pressed tight between her closed thighs. He moved her wrists down a notch, his breath harsh in her ears, even over the moody requiem chorus, the scent of his sweat and desire heavy as cologne in the small space.

Then he paused for a long moment, hands holding her wrists against the wall, and turned, pressing a fervent kiss against her temple. She almost thought he'd say something, but he didn't. Instead, he walked away, stripping off his shirt to reveal his gorgeously lean torso, and dropped into a leather chair where he could watch her without obstructing the view of her bound and naked self.

"Lower yourself onto the phallus," he ordered. "Fuck it for me, but don't come."

Feeling stunned, even stricken—and wildly naughty—she bent her knees so she made contact with the ugly thing. Made of some hard plastic, the rounded knobs bumped against her, stimulating without satisfying. More than enough, though, to send her out of her mind. She groaned at the impossibility of holding back the orgasm that boiled through her body with an enormous static charge.

"Don't do it," he warned, voice icy. "And eyes open, either on me or the mirror. Move or I'll get out something that will really hurt."

Fixing her eyes on him, so devastating in his stern handsomeness, she fought to obey, pumping her hips and sliding slickly along the phallus, concentrating on holding the climax she longed for at bay.

Smiling in that thin-lipped cruel way of his, he drew down the zipper of his pants, releasing his cock and stroking it slowly as he watched her, both of them moving to the insistent drive of the dark music.

"So beautiful," he murmured, as if looking at a work of art. She trembled, grateful, starving, needing more. Then shuddered hard as the orgasm nearly broke through. "Don't stop moving. You know how much I'd enjoy an excuse to punish you further."

"Alec," she pleaded, voice faltering.

"Are you asking permission?" He cocked his head, assessing her. "You understand this is mine to give or deny?"

"Yes." She caught back a sob. "Yes, Sir!"

"You've been good." He rose, leaving the pants open, cock thrusting out, which made him that much more animalistic, and stopped just in front of her, bracing his hands on either side of her head, not touching her, holding her gaze. "All right then. Come now."

As if he'd in fact commanded her body, the orgasm crashed through her, shattering in its intensity. She would have screamed, but he had her mouth, drinking in the ferocity of her climax, ravaging her lips with his and holding her anchored to the world.

When he released her mouth, she sagged in the restraints, rocking with the aftershocks, unable to muster the energy to wonder what he planned next as he unscrewed the phallus and unhooked her ankle cuffs from the wall, slipping off her heels as he did. Lifting her knee, he pressed it high and back, securing it with a broad black band he extracted from a hidden slot. Then did the same with a tight strap around her waist and also under her arms.

Holding her chin, he made her look at him. "Are you in there?"

"Right here." She parted her lips, hoping for a kiss, but he stroked her throat, adding to the shudders racking her.

"Pay attention. How does that feel? Too much pressure on your wrists, anywhere?"

She felt as if nothing of her body existed except the parts

that throbbed for his touch. Probably not an answer that would satisfy him. "So far, so good."

"And this?" He raised her other knee slowly, her weight settling into the three straps holding her to the wall. It constricted her chest and increased the sensation of helplessness. He pressed the knee back, splaying her open, but watching her face. "Does this hurt?"

"I'm flexible," she panted out.

He smiled, a flash of feral enjoyment. "Oh, darling, I've noticed."

Once he had her fixed in place, he moved quickly, shedding the pants and putting on a condom. Bracing himself again, he poised the head of his cock at her defenseless entrance and stared her down, face rigid with barely controlled passion. Not icy now, but raging.

"Only when I say you can, yes?"

"Yes." She sighed out the agreement, willing to promise anything, then sucked the air back in when he thrust hard into her, slamming his hips against hers, penetrating impossibly deep. Though she'd just come, the near-brutal shock threw her close to climax, like a spark set to a rocket. She clenched her teeth against the keening sound coming deep out of her.

Alec pulled back, kissing her with all the gentleness lacking a moment ago, coaxing her through it. As she recovered, softly, sweetly he moved in and out of her channel, stroking in long glides, lulling her, so she rode up on steadily increasing levels of arousal. Each time he seemed to ease deeper into her and she had no ability to resist, only to yield more.

Without warning, he slammed hard into her again.

She screamed and she thought she heard him laugh, low and wicked.

Managing to struggle back the orgasm, she found his mouth near her ear, his head bent and breathing hoarse as his hips pinned her against the wall. Raising his gaze to hers, he gave her a taunting smile. "More?"

Could she stand more? "Yes, please?" she answered, before she knew she would.

Holding her eyes, he slid back, working his cock in that gentle rhythm again, seductive, almost hypnotic. After a few strokes, she stopped bracing for the assault—as if she could in her helplessly open state—her body sinking into the building tension, rising to and following his lead.

"'Deliver my soul from the sword,'" he almost chanted, eyes dark with passion, his face contorted by the effort, panting the words in time with his meticulously controlled thrusts and the thrumming music. "'My darling from the power of the dog.'"

The tension built to unbearable levels and she returned his kisses with a ferocity of her own, begging him without words for that deliverance.

"This time, together," he ground out, and she clenched her fingers into fists, preparing for the moment when he'd break her apart. He watched her carefully, never altering the rhythmic, slow thrusting.

She never saw it coming. He slammed into her, throwing his head back in a shout that the damned might utter, and she fell into the flames after him, her body immolated and emptied.

COMING BACK TO herself, she found he'd already unstrapped her legs from the wall, his sweat-slicked body holding her up as he reached to free her wrists. Overcome, she pressed a kiss to the hollow between his pecs and shoulder, holding her mouth against his skin.

"She lives," he said, but his voice was gravelly. He undid the last of the bands and supported her to the floor, then sprawled beside her, chest heaving. "Give me a moment and I'll get the cuffs off."

"No worries." Sliding up against him, she put her head on his shoulder as she'd fallen asleep the night before, loving that his arm automatically bent to pull her closer. Her body sang with an exquisite kind of exhaustion, as if she'd been somehow purged. "That was intense."

He only grunted, but his fingers stroked her waist, not to soothe, she thought, but to savor.

"Was that more Faust you were quoting?"

He rolled his head toward her. Frowned. "I don't recall. What did I say?"

"Something about the power of the dog."

"Psalms." He laughed, staring up at the ceiling again, without music or humor. "Damn me, what you pull out of my psyche." He didn't sound happy about it.

"Are you religious?"

"Not beyond your typical childhood indoctrination. Why?"

"You seem to have a thing about heaven and hell." Paradise and damnation.

"Perhaps you put the fear of God in me."

"Surely that's my line."

He looked at her with concern and turned enough on his side to brush her hair out of her face. "Did I hurt you? Too rough? Too much?"

A funny question, from the man who'd switched her into a frenzy and fucked her past sanity, but she understood what he meant. She laid a hand on his cheek, then ran her fingers through his close-cropped hair. "You were perfect."

"Surely that's my line," he echoed her and smiled, more his daylight self.

It made her laugh and she kissed him, sinking in as he responded, the meeting of mouths somehow impossibly dreamy and romantic. Especially in that room decorated like the inside of a womb, with Mozart's demons still hissing in the background, shadows of Alec's darker, gothic nature.

"So, I did the math," she said.

"Clearly I didn't keep you well enough occupied."

"It was easy math. If I'm only the second woman you've been with in New York and that affair was vanilla, then have you used all this stuff on anyone else?"

He considered her long enough that she thought he might not answer. "Maybe I used it without full-sex. I mentioned that possibility."

"Yes. But I don't think so. Am I wrong?"

"Why does it matter?"

"I'm not sure. I'm asking. You don't have to say."

"My heart wasn't in it," he replied, so softly she wouldn't have heard him had she not been inches away. Something about his tone, the pain in his eyes, broke her own heart a little. Feeling the need to comfort him, she kissed him, unsurprised when he gathered her close and wound his hands through her hair. Finally he broke the kiss, a glint of impatience in his eyes, the door to his soul firmly closed again. "I wish someone would shut off that bloody music."

SHE DIDN'T WALK into her own apartment until nearly nine o'clock. After another long bath, they'd ordered pizza and lolled on the terrace, keeping conversation to light, impersonal topics, almost by tacit agreement. Alec had been as carved out by their encounter as she, not arguing that much when she insisted she'd be fine if he sent her home in his car without accompanying her.

The ride had given her some time and space to assemble her thoughts, away from the charisma and sexual distraction of Alec's presence. They'd been together just over twenty-four hours and it had been more intense than relationships that lasted weeks. He probably understood more about her secret heart than any lover she'd had. And she—she'd seen into him, too.

Though she wasn't sure what to make of what she'd glimpsed.

Kiki set aside her tablet and gave her a long look when she walked in dressed in last night's cocktail dress. "I should say something about this spectacular spin you've put on the walk of shame, but you don't look the least shamed."

Amber flopped onto the couch. "He very nearly killed me, but I would have died happy."

Intrigued, Kiki wrapped her arms around her knees and paused whatever movie she'd had on in the background. "That good, huh. What you hoped for?"

"Better." Now that she was home, ramping down from the high that was Alec, she seemed to be melting into the couch. "Omigod so much better. Beyond the realm."

"Uh-oh."

"What?" She found she had the energy to sit up after all. "There is no uh-oh."

"If you say." Kiki picked up the tablet again.

"Tell me why you said it then."

"Is this only about sex, or are you falling for this guy? This much older guy who happens to be your boss, I might point out."

"I don't fall for every guy I have earth-shattering, multi-orgasmic sex with."

"Actually, I'd argue you've never really fallen for any guy, ever."

Harsh, but possibly true. "Counter-argument—any other sex was just never this good."

"Yeah, you keep telling yourself that."

"I will." She pushed up off the couch as it seemed to be threatening to suck her in again. "And on that note, I'm crashing."

"Wore you out, did he?"

"Oh honey—you have no idea."

"I would if you shared some details." Kiki patted the couch invitingly. "Tell Kiki a bedtime story." She narrowed her eyes when Amber hesitated. "See? Big warning flag. You want to hug the experience close and keep it secret. You're falling bad. You didn't save a little memento, did you? Tell me you didn't."

"Don't be silly." Gathering her dignity around her, she closed herself into her room. Opening her old ballerina jewelry box, she got out the rose she'd saved from the bouquet out of the stash in her bag. She centered it on top of the coaster from the bar where they'd talked. Nothing wrong with a couple of keepsakes.

Didn't necessarily mean anything.

CHAPTER TWENTY-TWO

ALEC GOT TO the office early. The flat had seemed too big without Amber's vivacious presence, a realization that irritated him. They'd both agreed she needed to go home. Hell, he'd made the rule himself. Many good reasons for her not to spend the night in his bed and then go home to dress for work so they then could begin the pretense they hadn't been tangled together in the most intimate ways possible.

The night apart should have given him some much-needed distance. Instead, he'd missed her immediately and even now struggled against the impulse to see if she'd come in yet, to stop by her cube and say good morning. Far too dangerous, as the sight of her would bring his simmering thoughts of her sizzling to the surface. The gulf of days until Friday felt immense and he struggled against the deep-seated dread that she'd have sated her curiosity and decide against continuing.

Which would likely be the best, all around. If and when she did, he would be gracious, wish her well and send her on her way.

No dwelling on what he'd do after that.

As soon as he thought Lily might be in, he headed to her department—making sure to take the long way around instead of the treacherous route that would lead him past Amber's cubby. Lily glanced up in surprise when he rapped on the doorframe, then smiled and waved him in.

"Alec. Just the man I wanted to see. Have a seat." She raised an eyebrow when he shut the door. "Trouble?"

"Nothing like that. How was your weekend?"

"Restful, for once. Lovely weather. Coffee? No—tea." She poured herself coffee and set the Mr. Tea going. Leaned on the sideboard. Outside her corner office windows, the city skyscrapers gleamed silver and glass as she looked him over. "You look better."

"Oh?"

"Yes. More relaxed. A relief."

"I didn't know you were concerned." Or that his tension had showed so clearly.

"I was." She handed him the tea and a saucer for the bag. "In fact, I'd hoped to corner you for one more drink and some pointed questions last Friday, but then you took off like a bat out of hell."

"Pointed questions about what?" An icy shiver of warning slid down his spine. Lily, of all the partners, was the most observant.

"Perhaps it's moot." She sat behind her desk and lifted one shoulder, then decided to forge ahead. "Are you happy here?"

Not what he'd expected. "Yes. Very much so."

"I've wondered. I'm sure it's difficult—new city, new clients, recovering from divorce is awful—but I've been worrying lately that you're...restless."

A brilliant euphemism, if there ever was one. Still not what she meant, he thought. "Restless?"

She scowled at him. "You and that poker face. Look. Bill, Hai and I greatly value what you've brought to us, to your department and the firm. If you're being courted by a competitor, I hope you'll tell us, give us the opportunity to sweeten the deal here. We'd go a long ways to keep you happy. Change up your staffing, projects, whatever."

Rather astounded, he stirred his tea. Then shook his head. "You've worried for nothing, though I confess I'm flattered. I have been out of sorts, but it's nothing do with work." *Not exactly.*

"Good." She blew out a relieved breath. "You know, Alec, I consider you a friend. If you need a shoulder..."

"Thank you. I appreciate that."

"All right then. I won't take that as a brush-off, since you do seem more relaxed today and I know you're a private man. Still—the offer stands. So, why did you come to see me? Please don't tell me you've found other account discrepancies."

"No. Not that. Though I did look them all over, just in case," he added, to needle her.

She held up her hands, palms out. "Thank you for not telling me you were. I wouldn't have slept a wink for fear you'd find something else."

"You run a clean department. Not your fault you missed what Curlew was up to."

"You and I both know that's not true." She tapped her glossy nails on the desk, clearly still annoyed with herself. "At least it's in the lawyers' hands now."

"However, along those lines, and with an eye to shaking up some staff, I've come to the conclusion that you should bring

Amber Dolors over to your team."

She sat back in her chair, considered. "Why?"

"You like her work. You said you decided to advance Chris to replace Curlew and would thus need someone junior to fill the hole. I think she'd flourish under your mentorship."

"What did she screw up?"

Bugger it. "Not a thing." He had to work to keep the anger out. Protective much? An excellent reason right there to get her out from under his supervision. "She does excellent work. I thought you wanted her on your team."

"I do. But you're competitive about keeping the good people. It's not like you to hand over someone out of the blue. If she's got issues, I want to know about it."

"She doesn't. I promise. I rather thought of it as a promotion for her, though any salary changes would, of course, be up to you."

Lily pursed her lips, sharp gaze digging into his brain. "Out with it. What's the problem?"

"No problem. You only just finished promising me whatever staffing changes I asked for."

"And now you're defensive. Don't give me the runaround. If this is because she's female, I swear to God, I'm going to—"

"It's not," he cut her off and she raised her brows in surprise at his sharp tone. "Bloody hell," he muttered and swallowed down the bitter tea. Steeped far too long. "Look. You offered to listen as a friend. I hope this will go no further."

"All right."

He scrubbed his hand over his scalp. A private man, she'd called him. Unbearable to say this. "I'm attracted."

Lily took a moment to process that, then nodded, not all that surprised after all. "She's a pretty young woman."

"Indeed. I find I can't trust my judgment around her."

"I see." She swiveled idly in her chair. "Are you planning to act on it?"

"That wouldn't be fair to her." Enough truth that he could say it with a stone-cold expression.

"No, it wouldn't," Lily replied in crisp tone, then pointed a glossy nail at him. "She's easily half your age."

"Believe me, I'm aware."

"This is the right thing to do then. I'll set it up. Not a promotion but a very tasty lateral for her. And you'll make noises that I stole her for my team."

"Milking the situation for a team victory? And you call me competitive." He rose, relieved to be done with it. "Very well then."

"Alec?" She stopped him before he opened the door. "Thank you for confiding in me. You're doing the right thing. The honorable thing."

The image of Amber bound to the red velvet wall, screaming as he pounded into her, flew through his brain.

I only wish.

THE WORKWEEK WAS agony. Though she understood, knew, that Alec maintained that cool distance as a direct result of the rules they'd agreed to, it still ate at her. They'd barely seen each other all week, much less spoken. Of course, her desk move to Lily's side made it that much less likely that she'd run into him by chance. And easier for him to avoid her, a treacherously insecure voice whispered. After all, he'd be far from the first guy to bail after the bang.

It would just be the first time she really cared.

By Thursday night, Kiki had enough of her, pointing out that she might as well be having an affair with a married man, sitting home, sulking and pining. "Are you totally sure he's not married?" she asked.

"You think he hid the wife in his closet?" Amber tried to make it a joke, but it came out in an irritated snap that had Kiki throwing a paperback across the room at her. "Ow!"

"Don't give me that. He could be one of those guys with a fuck pad designed to bag sweet young things like you while the wife and kiddies are off in a tidy suburban in New Jersey."

"I work with him, remember? He's divorced. Everybody knows it."

"Do they? Maybe he's still married and she's cooling her heels in London, awaitin' for hisself to com'ome."

"Was that supposed to be a Cockney accent? Because you sound like an idiot."

"And you're not thinking straight."

"Bite me."

"Isn't that Alec's job—or is that only whipping?" Kiki shrieked with laughter when Amber winged the book back at her, missing entirely. "So touchy."

"Just…don't give me shit about this, okay?"

"For how long?" Kiki held up a hand and gave her a serious look. "I mean it. I'll cut you the slack to work this out of your system, but it's my job as your friend to yank you back from the abyss."

That gave her an odd chill. "The abyss? Of what? A smidge dramatic there."

"You know what I mean. This is totally unlike you to be so gone over a guy. You're in deep, really fast."

"Funny. Here I thought I haven't even seen him all week."

"And yet you have your bag packed to spend the weekend with him."

Amber leveled a cold glare on her friend, to cover the flash of embarrassment. So she'd been picking out things to wear. Sue her. "Is spying on me part of your job, too?"

"Oh, you mean I shouldn't have noticed your overnight bag on the bed and sex outfits strewn around the room? My bad."

"What are you saying, Kiki?"

"Nothing. I've said it. Go work this out of your system. But…"

"Spit it out."

"Remember that's what this is. Sex. Something you wanted to explore and you know I support that. But this thing with your boss can't go anywhere. Sneaking around isn't a basis for a healthy relationship. The power imbalance alone is seriously problematic."

"It bothers you that he's older."

"A lot of things bother me. Think past the kink!" She snorted at herself. "I'm going to paste that to the fridge as a reminder. Good tagline."

"Stupid tagline. I don't even know what it's supposed to mean."

"It means that you should think about who you are together out of the bedroom. I'd say this even if you didn't have the master/slave thing going—"

"It's not like that," Amber interrupted.

"And," Kiki talked over her, "if you didn't have the age difference thing, plus the work thing, you, my friend, are obsessed with this guy. Tread carefully."

The accusation pissed her off, which meant she needed to think about it. "I don't think I'm obsessed."

"Obsessed people never do." Kiki nodded wisely.

"Is that even a thing? That's not true."

"Okay." Kiki snorted. Got up and hugged her. "It sounded good. I have to go in early tomorrow for a breakfast meet, so I won't see you. Promise you'll still check in?"

"Yes. Don't worry."

"Don't be stupid."

CHAPTER TWENTY-THREE

B Y FRIDAY NOON, she began to feel nervous about having
worn the outfit. The one he'd specified—the pencil skirt
suit and the pink ruffled blouse—for that night. But then, they
hadn't spoken all week. She'd barely glimpsed Alec in passing,
which had to be deliberate. Lily kept her busy with new
responsibilities and she liked the work. Still, she'd feel better if
Alec had given some indication of continued interest. That he
expected her to come over that evening. What if she showed up
at his door and he gave her that look of bland distaste he
assumed when someone screwed up a task?

The power imbalance alone is seriously problematic.

Whether Kiki had intended it or not with her little come-
to-Jesus lecture, she'd instilled some doubts, sapped Amber's
confidence. Alec had been pretty clear about keeping it all on
the QT until they figured out if they'd burn out fast or not.
What if he'd decided they already had—would he tell her? Or
was the total lack of communication him telling her?

And since when did she let herself angst over a guy this
way?

Oh yeah, since Alexander Knight gave her that look.

You, my friend, are obsessed with this guy. Tread carefully.

She felt pissed enough to storm into Alec's office and demand to know where she stood, if she also didn't feel perilously

close to weeping—something she had little success controlling, particularly if she had anger mixed in. She'd thought she'd been a mess last Friday afternoon. Over the course of an intensely sexual weekend and a workweek of uncertainty and insecurity, she'd transcended to an entire new level of fucked-up.

Just fabulous.

"You okay?" Lily stopped by her desk, tipping her glasses down her nose to frown at her. "I know it's against the rules to tell another woman she looks tired, but…"

Amber laughed. "Just a long week." She waved at the computer screen. "Steep learning curve."

"You're doing great. Why don't you go home early? You've earned a reprieve. I'll get someone else to do the notes for the partners' meeting."

"No, that's okay. I kind of like that job."

"Smart of you. I know some of the junior staff consider it drudge work and I'm aware they're happy enough to pawn it off on you."

"True. I get a lot of good insights into how you all see things. I learn a lot from just listening."

"That's why you're going places."

Okay, Amber told herself as she headed for the fishbowl a little before four. No big deal. You've worn this outfit any number of times. It means nothing. Get a grip.

She situated herself in her usual spot, busying herself with setting up the laptop. Hai Lin and Lily came in, deep in conversation, saying hello in an offhanded way. Bill greeted her more enthusiastically, asking how she liked her new responsibilities. Because she was answering him, Alec slipped in without having to acknowledge her presence, his gaze passing over her with cool disinterest. He chose a different chair than usual—one with his back to her, the lines of his shoulders relaxed under the crisp lines of his suit. She didn't realize she was scowling at him until she caught Lily watching her from across the big conference table with a concerned look.

She rubbed her temple, pretending to a headache, which seemed to satisfy her new boss.

So far, the getting-a-grip thing wasn't going all that well.

Fortunately the meeting got started and she focused on getting everything down. They had a number of new clients to discuss, a charity event the firm had been asked to sponsor, the vacancy on Alec's team to fill. Everyone seemed to be in the mode of finishing out the week and getting home, so discussions went fast and no one suggested cocktails after, to her immense relief.

Short-lived relief, as Alec left so fast she missed his departure while she was looking at the screen.

Back at her desk—at least she'd escaped a cube—she waffled. She no longer ordered his car, so she didn't know if he'd left completely or not. Go by his office? Go home?

"See you Monday, Amber," Lily called out, sunglasses on and bag slung over her shoulder as she locked up her office. "And please, go home already!"

She tried not to take that as an omen. Needing a better one, she carried her water bottle to the other side of the floor, filling at the dispenser there and using the excuse of proximity to walk past Alec's office for the first time all week. Closed up and dark. *Well shit.*

What she wanted most to do was call Kiki for advice. Except she knew exactly what Kiki would say—that she was being stupid and you don't show up on a guy's doorstep unless you know you're wanted. Particularly not with your overnight bag. She should go home. Go do happy hour with Kiki somewhere.

And the dreary prospect of those options decided her. There was only one thing she really wanted to do, bad idea or not.

Weird, though, to take the subway to his far-classier neighborhood and walk the few blocks to his building on the Upper East Side, carrying her laptop bag on one shoulder and her overnight on the other. The white-gloved doorman gave her an icy once-over, and it hit her that he wouldn't know her. A different one had been on duty the week before. When she'd been naked under Alec's coat—a memory that added heat to the flush of embarrassment of having to beg admittance.

"Can I help you, miss?" He asked, subtly positioning himself between her and the entrance.

"I, ah, am here to see Alexander Knight." *Please let him have called down that he expected me.*

"Is he expecting you, Miss…?"

No such luck. "Dolors. Amber Dolors."

A woman stepped out of a cab, elegant in designer silk and dripping with jewels. She cast a look at Amber that left her feeling absurdly scruffy, and swept past the doorman, who tipped his cap and bowed slightly at her passage.

He turned his attention back to Amber, friendly smile fading. "I'll call up to Mr. Knight's."

At least he let her step inside the lobby, but kept his eye on her as if she might try to sneak past him. This was a bad idea. One that grew worse by the moment as time slowed to an agonizing pace and Alec didn't answer. Not home. Or avoiding her.

"Sorry, Miss Dolors—it seems he's not in." The man gestured to the street, and took a step to usher her out again. Swept out like unwanted refuse.

She should have called first. Could have, with his number still in her phone, but she felt like she shouldn't. Drawing up her dignity, she thanked the man and walked ahead of him out the doors.

And nearly crashed into Alec coming in.

"Amber!" He rocked back on his heels, seeming surprised to see her. He wore the same suit he'd had on at the partners' meeting, as crisp as if he'd just put it on. A dark and brooding look in his eye.

"The young lady came to visit, Mr. Knight." The doorman made the obvious information sound like an offer to get rid of her.

"Of course, I should have thought to notify you that she might. Apologies, Sean." He gave her a funny half smile that faded as he took in her expression. "Care to come up then?"

It was on the tip of her tongue to say no. To storm out maybe. Or suddenly remember another appointment. Apparently that, too, showed on her face, because he stroked a hand down her arm and decided her by leading her to the elevators. Not quite a demanding grip, but close. "At least for a drink, since you're here."

Not exactly what she wanted to hear. They rode up in awkward silence, as two other people entered the elevator also. When the others exited, Alec impatiently pressed the doors closed, sliding her an apologetic look. "I didn't expect you so early."

"When exactly did you expect me?" It came out meaner than she'd intended, a product of too much bottled-up emotion. Pissed, embarrassed, stupidly hurt—a lethal combo for her. When the doors opened, she didn't move, staring fiercely at the panel of buttons, willing herself not to cry.

Alec put a hand on the doors to keep them from closing, assessing her. "Coming in?"

"I kind of think I should go." A tear spilled over and she dashed it away with the back of her hand, wishing he hadn't seen it. "It's been a long week."

He smiled, rueful, and held out a hand. "Come in for a glass of wine at least. I clearly made a muddle of things."

Okay, fine. She'd just look more stupid if she left. But she didn't take his hand, partly because she needed hers to get rid of any more escapee tears, and stalked past him after he unlocked his door, then paused, uncertain what to do with her things.

"What's this?" he asked, taking her overnight bag and weighing it with a quizzical lift of his brows. Trying to keep the tone light.

"In case I stayed overnight." She grabbed it back and dumped it on the floor, setting the laptop bag next to it, staged for the possibility of a quick exit, and made herself meet his gaze evenly. "Just a precaution. So you wouldn't have to buy me more expensive hairbrushes."

"I see. It's a lovely evening," he said after a pause, giving up the teasing tone. "Why don't you go sit on the terrace and I'll bring out some wine." *And collect yourself,* he didn't have to say out loud.

A welcome reprieve, probably for them both. She went without another word and let herself out. Too restless to sit, she shrugged out of her jacket, tossed it on the table and went to lean on the rail, studying the glitter of fading light on the buildings, the green shimmer of Central Park. Abandoned trying to think it all through and just zoned for a few minutes.

Alec joined her, tieless now but still wearing the deep gray vest over his white shirt, and handed her a very full glass of white wine.

"Cheers." He clinked his equally full one to hers and sipped, watching her over the rim with that same assessing expression. A shadow behind it. The silence stretched on. Probably her turn to say something. Preferably something calm and sane, but he beat her to it. "You asked when I expected you—honestly, I didn't know whether to expect you at all. I'd rather convinced myself you wouldn't show."

"Why?"

He shrugged one shoulder, gave her a self-deprecating smile. "I wouldn't have been surprised if you'd had done with me."

"I wore the outfit," she pointed out and he winced, his gaze dragging over the blouse with heat before he turned his attention to the view.

"I know. I saw. You look—" he searched for the word out

in the skyscrapers, "—lovely." The evening, her—his standard fallback description. And not what he'd been thinking before he changed it. Something hungrier, given his tone.

"Really? I don't see how as you didn't look at me during the partners' meeting. Not once."

"I can't," he snapped, eyes flashing to hers, staring her down, the haunted shadows in his gaze smoking into flame. "Sometimes I could swear I smell you and I get hard, start thinking about dragging you into the nearest closet. You think I don't see you? I make excuses to myself to pass by your desk—just close enough to catch a glimpse. When I saw you'd worn that blouse today, I nearly lost my mind. I actually began imagining excuses to ask you into my office and working the logistics of what I could do to you with no one seeing. In the partners' meeting, I'm thinking not about the numbers but pivoting my chair and telling you to strip, right there.

"It's either tell myself you're not in the bloody building or go insane trying to keep my fucking hands off you." He dropped his head and stared down at the long drop. "And now I've hurt you, which I didn't intend."

She sipped her wine, cold and delicately floral, probably outrageously expensive. Nothing compared to the mind-swirling desire his words evoked. He always looked so cool, she'd never guessed at his thoughts or that they continued to torment him so. "I'm the one who's sorry. I got all worked up, feeling insecure, and Kiki...whatever."

"What about Kiki?"

"I really don't want to get into that."

"Thinks I'm not good for you, does she?"

"She doesn't know you, does she?"

"An excellent point." He stared out at the city, thinking, the fire contained but burning. Brooding. Thunderclouds gathering. Dark Alec.

"So what now?" *Tell me to strip, Alec.*

He glanced at her. Away again. Face and voice in that carefully neutral mode. "What would you prefer to do? If you want to go, I understand. Maybe you should. That's part of why I stayed away this evening. Part of me hoped you'd find me gone and leave again."

"Why?" Her mouth had gone dry with dread. But he'd said he wanted her. In devastating, erotic detail.

His lips curved in that cruel ironic smile and he turned to face her, leaning an elbow on the rail. Not relaxed, though. Coiled. "Perhaps the monster always hopes, somewhere in its twisted heart, that its prey will escape."

"Do you want me to go?"

"No. But I think you should want to."

"Are you saying you don't want me anymore?"

"How can you ask that?" he demanded, sounding strained, the temper rising again. Dark Alec seething close to the skin.

"You run hot and cold on me, Alec! You say you can't look at me at the office, for wanting to touch me, that you think of ways to be with me, and here we're alone and you're still not looking at me or touching me and—"

She broke off when he took the wineglass from her and threw it against the wall, following it with his, so both shattered, along with her nerves. He turned on her with a hard, nearly angry look that made her step back. Eyes locked on hers, he took advantage of the momentum, pushing her back and crowding her into a shadowed corner under the overhang, behind a fake potted palm. When her back bumped against the wall, it startled her and she squeaked. It seemed to send him over the edge because he curled his fingers in the front of her silk blouse, set his jaw, and ripped it open, buttons flying. Her breasts, encased in the pink lace bra, were exposed to his ravenous gaze.

"I'm looking," he grated out. He seized her wrists and stretched them over her head, pinning them there with one hand and using the other to flick open the front clasp of the bra. Cupping her naked breast, he squeezed, tight, and she writhed under the grip. "I'm touching." He leaned in hard, his erection pressing against her belly, the brick wall grating against her back through the silk. "Now tell me to stop."

Instead she moved her hips against his, wild for more. "Don't you dare stop."

"You know the penalties for giving me orders." He pinched her nipple and she gasped but held his gaze, defiant.

"Do your worst."

The words seemed to shred what control he'd clung to. With a growl he began tugging up her skirt, working the tight sheath until it bunched around her waist. He cupped her bottom, vising on her, then pushed his hand inside her panties, delving into her cleft from behind, shoving her hips against him. She moaned, he sank his teeth into the side of her neck, grinding her pinned wrists against the brick.

All the anxiety, the hurt and anger, swirled together into a desperate passion. She thrashed against his grip, thrilled that he didn't let her go. Instead he impatiently yanked at her panties, grunting in satisfaction when the delicate lace snapped. They fell down her leg, a tumble of wet, shredded silk, to settle at her ankle. Something she barely noted before his fingers speared into her from the front, rough, working her with merciless ferocity. His mouth fastened on her throat, sucking on her skin with vicious tension, his teeth sinking in so she cried out.

He moved his mouth to hers—finally—but it was less a kiss than a silencing. She writhed, wanting him inside her, unable to move enough to even raise her thigh. He managed to push a finger into her channel, cupping her mound with his whole hand, driving her up relentlessly, giving her no option but to climax with dizzying speed and intensity.

With a curse that sounded almost foreign, his accent had gone so thick, he released her wrists, dug in his pocket and ripped open his pants, just enough to release his cock and get the condom on. "Put your leg around my waist," he ordered, pinning her wrists on either side of her head. "I can't be gentle."

"I don't want gentle." She barely finished the words before he'd pushed deep inside her. Fast, hard, nearly brutal. Clenching her teeth to keep from screaming as a new orgasm built on the last, she watched his face, the way his gaze stayed riveted on her as he fucked her with a wild intensity.

"I want you every second of every day." His thrusts punctuated his words, thick and guttural. "That's not the problem."

With a hoarse, bitten-back shout that contained a note of surprise, he convulsed, his body racked with the climax grinding against her. As if he'd set her off, she followed right after, burying her teeth in his shoulder through his pressed shirt, the scent of starch and aftershave filling her brain as surely as his cock stretched her and his body covered her.

Releasing all the tension, she gave up and drowned in him.

CHAPTER TWENTY-FOUR

HARD UPON THE heels of glorious, blessed release came chagrin, remorse and crashing guilt. His shoulder throbbed where Amber bit him and her breath came hard and uneven, with little hitches of emotion, her bare breasts crushed against his chest and her body trembling, even as he had her still impaled against the wall.

"Fuck me," he groaned, rational thought creeping in, tail between its legs, lagging far behind the more potent drives that had taken him over.

"I'm pretty sure that was me," Amber replied, voice strained. She had her head tipped back, gulping in air, staring blindly up at the twilight sky. Realizing he still had her in a death grip, he eased out of her, the relieved sigh she made grating on his conscience. Flushed, more than half-naked, she looked as if she'd been ravished by a maniac. A bite mark stood out on her pale, arched throat—only serving to make him feel that much worse. He tried to pull her blouse together, staying close enough to shield her from prying eyes. Nice time to think of that now. The flimsy thing had torn and only one button remained, dangling by a thread. So, he worked at tugging down the far-too-tight skirt, then spotted her ravaged knickers hanging off one slim ankle.

Stricken, he braced himself and searched her face, dreading how she might weep. She'd looked so lost, being kicked out of the lobby of his building, some of her spirit showing in the angry set of her jaw, but those big blue eyes that changed shades with her moods had been pale with hurt and humiliation. Then she'd started crying in the elevator, trying not to, but too up-front with her feelings to disguise it, and he'd been at a total loss.

Instead of more tears and recriminations though, she gave him a cat-in-cream smile, eyes deep as the twilight and full of amusement as she observed his efforts without helping. "Damn, Alec. You are hard on a girl's clothes." She tilted her head, studying him, and her expression changed. She laid her palms on his cheeks. "If you're thinking about apologizing for this, stop right there." She kissed him, sweet lips asking a question, parting to invite him in, to have more. He swayed into her, completely overcome.

"We should get inside," he managed, between returning her kisses. "Change clothes." He'd likely ruined his trousers. Fair enough.

"And hey—I have something to change into." She said it lightly, but raised her eyebrows. Testing his reaction.

"I'm glad you do. I'm sorry I'm such a bleeding idiot. Let's change and have another go at the conversation we need to have."

"I really want that wine now. Too bad it went the way of my panties." She gathered her blouse together and held it as she kicked the ruined knickers into the corner. Inside, she scooped up the duffel bag, incongruously decorated with a blue cartoon pony that seemed to have rainbows for its mane and tail, and headed for the guest bathroom. No wonder Sean had been dubious about her. She could have been a boarding school refugee. And he the sugar daddy bent on compromising her. He found the broom, sweeping up the glass he'd broken in whatever fit had taken him, throwing it and her ruined knickers in the dustbin. They would start this over again.

Not only had he more than half convinced himself she wouldn't show, that the once had been enough for her, he'd reconciled himself to that reality. Decision out of his hands and all for the best. But no.

"I scraped the hell out of my hands." She walked back into the room, holding them out for him to see. She'd changed into that white sundress she'd worn when they worked that Saturday together, and she'd brushed out her hair so it gleamed like honey. A portrait of innocent loveliness—with a bite on her slim throat, red marks from his bruising grip on her wrists and angry scratches up and down the backs of her hands and arms.

Unable to think of a proper apology for such a transgression, he said nothing as he turned on his heel and went for the first aid kit, pulling other useless things out of the medicine cabinet to find it before he tossed it on the master bath counter. Amber leaned in the open doorway, watching quietly. He'd scraped up her mouth, too, her lips puffy and cheek chafed from his beard scruff, and he recalled how he'd silenced her, drinking in her frantic cries.

"Are you all right?" she asked in a gentle voice, as if he were the one who needed soothing.

"I'm not, no. But you're the one who needs taking care of, not me. Since I am the one who scraped the hell out of your hands, among other things. Sit."

She'd regained her native insouciance, making a little O of her lips and mouthing a silent *oh-kay*. She hitched herself onto the dark marble counter, bare feet swinging, and gave over her hands with total trust, as if he'd never hurt her. Some of the scratches were deeper than others. One bleeding, but most already scabbing over, angry against her pale skin. It made him feel somewhat better, to disinfect them, to clean the grit, the grime out of them.

Or, at least it spared him thinking for a few more minutes about what he'd done.

"Owie!" She sucked in a breath when the peroxide sizzled in the deepest cut and he had to shake his head.

"You fuss at this but not when I'm brutalizing you?"

"That was sex. You understand that. Totally different. Although…" She ducked her head to catch his eye, hair sliding over her smooth shoulder. "It's sexy in a different way, having you doctor me. Tend to me."

"Amber darling…" He didn't know what to say.

"If you don't stop acting all guilty, I'll just get pissed again and we'll be back to where we started before the make-up sex."

An aghast laugh tore through him. "You call that make-up sex? That was hardly disciplined domination. Not at all what you asked for from me."

"Oh, stop that!" She did look angry now, righteously so. "I know what I want from you. I have safewords, don't I? That's why I have them. Did you hear me say either one?"

"No," he realized. So practiced at this—or he had been once—and he'd never thought of it. Of course, nothing that had gone before had ever been like this. "But that wasn't a scene. I was…" He didn't know what he'd been.

"You were as into it as I was." She turned her hands to lace her fingers with his. "I like that best, when you're so gone that you're no longer so…studied about it. It feels more real. Less like something you're indulging me in."

"You're impossible," he murmured, kissing the backs of her hands. They tasted of peroxide and cream, underlaid with her leafy scent. He moved to the bruises forming on her wrists. "I'm not meant to leave marks such as this through carelessness."

"Except then you kiss them better." Her voice had gone mellower, her body pliant and inviting. "Totally worth it."

"The least I can do for you. Tilt your head."

She complied and he moved her hair out of the way, dabbing the bite with disinfectant—bruising, but at least he hadn't broken the skin. He kissed the angry mark and she trembled, making that sexy croon of encouragement. Impossible not to touch her.

"Your breasts—are they bruised, scratched?"

"You'd better check," she purred and untied her halter, lowering it to reveal the pink-tipped globes. Reddened, yes, and showing signs of rough use, alas, but not so bad. Nevertheless, he kissed them thoroughly, covering every millimeter of skin, as she shifted and sighed, running her fingers through his hair.

"I was quite rough with you—everywhere."

"Oh yes. I might have terrible bruises down below, the way

you went at me."

"Let me see." He knelt down, pressing kisses to the tops of her feet, her pink-polished toes like candy, and skimmed the full skirts up her pretty thighs.

"Was that the fantasy?"

He glanced up at her, confused. "Fantasy?"

"The one you promised me, if I wore that outfit."

"No. Nothing so planned." He pushed her skirts up and she obligingly lifted her bum, settling it—also showing some scratches—naked on the counter. "No knickers this time?"

"It seemed smart to leave them off for the time being, knowing how you are."

"Probably wise." Spreading her thighs, he examined her. Red and swollen. Also slick and aroused. Irresistible.

"It was one of my fantasies," she whispered, then moaned when he licked her.

"Tell me about it."

"You know. The stranger in the dark alley. Oh, Alec." Her breath hitched as he sucked lightly on her clit, kissed her there.

"Keep going." He settled into a soothing rhythm, one meant to take her up slowly, an apology for the harshness of before. "What does he do to you?"

"Just like you did. He has to have me. Takes me by surprise and pushes me against the wall, tears my clothes away. He's rough, squeezing my breasts, telling me I have to take it. I don't want to like it but I do. He won't let me go, pins my wrists and rams into me, hard like you did. Over and over. He doesn't care about my pleasure, just takes. He's wild for me and I can't help myself and, oh God, Alec…"

She came apart, clutching at his head, thighs tightening and sea salt fluids filling his mouth. Letting her ride it out, come down easily, he gentled her through it. Then looked up to find a dreamy smile on her lips.

"It's not an easy fantasy to want," she said. "Not very feminist. But I got to have it anyway, with you. So, thank you."

"I didn't do it for that reason."

"Which makes it even better." She bent, breasts swaying heavily, hair falling around him, and kissed him, an angel giving a benediction, then deepened it, savoring. "I like tasting myself on your mouth."

"I like having you in my mouth."

She smiled, radiant. Her naturally happy self. "This is why we're a perfect couple."

He shook his head at her. "Let's try for that conversation again, shall we?"

"You haven't changed clothes yet."

"I will."

"Can I pick them out?"

"I beg your pardon?"

She gave him a cheeky grin, reminding him that she inexplicably enjoyed when he said that, and jumped down from the counter, smoothing her skirts, then tying up her halter. The realization that he could easily have her again, simply by spinning her around and bending her over the counter, that she would be naked and ready, had his already hard cock aching. She raised her eyebrows, reading him easily. "Or are we not done yet?"

"Talk first." He bore down on the determination, clinging

to that rational thought that had deserted him earlier.

"Okay. But I get to poke through your closet." She bounced out of the bathroom, leaving him to discard his clothes, clean up and give himself a stern talking to. When he walked out into the bedroom naked, she sat on the side of the bed, next to the clothes she'd laid out—a pair of worn jeans and a dark green T-shirt.

"This is your special selection for me?"

"Yes. I've never seen you in jeans. And the green will bring out the hazel of your eyes." She tracked him as he pulled a pair of clean boxers out of a drawer and worked them on over his raging hard-on. "Sure you don't want to do something about that?"

"I feel certain it will keep."

"You have a bite mark, too. I should tend it."

"Leave it—it's no more than I deserve, treating you as I did."

"Are you sure you're not Catholic? All of the guilt," she added when he cast her a questioning look.

"Positive. Although, as for that, the C of E does a fine job. That's not the problem." He put on the jeans and shirt, still bemused by her choice.

"That's what you said earlier. Right before you fucked my brains out. Are you going to tell me what the problem actually is?"

For all her sexual confidence, she had an uncertainty in her expression, something a bit waifish as she posed the question, sitting on the heavy bed equipped with rings meant to restrain her for any number of debaucheries. A girl with rainbowmaned ponies on her overnight bag and bruises he'd placed on her. He simultaneously wanted to rescue and ravish her.

He held out a hand and she slipped off the bed with a smile. Instead of taking his hand, she ran her hands up his chest, much shorter than he, with them both barefoot. "It's a great color on you. A good look. Not that you don't rock the suit porn, but it's nice to see you kick back a little, too."

That gave him pause. "Suit porn?"

"Oh yeah. All those very crisp, very formal, very masterful suits you wear?" She slid her hand down and cupped his still-hard cock through his jeans, giving him a smoldering look. "Suit porn. Ask any girl."

"I believe I need that wine." Removing her hand— masterful restraint right there—he tucked it in his and led her down the hallway. They settled on the terrace, evening growing deeper, and sipped fresh glasses of wine by candlelight. "All right," he said, taking the lead, "before we got sidetracked, you were telling me that Kiki feels I'm not good for you and you were unhappy with how I've treated you also."

"I'm fascinated that's what you took away from our earlier conversation." She narrowed her eyes. "*You* were going to explain what this problem is that you've referenced twice."

"You were upset when you arrived," he persisted. "Before, I suspect, the incident with the doorman. Worked up and feeling insecure, you said. Why?"

She took a deep breath, a long sip of wine, and set her glass down. "So. Okay. I know I agreed to the no-contact all week rule, and I get that it's part of the sex thing, the dominance and all of that. But I'd like to call Morpheus on that."

He had to keep himself from smiling, she charmed and fascinated him so much with the way she thought. "All right."

"The thing is, it wasn't sexy for me. It was just crazy-making, having no control of that aspect. Don't get me wrong—because I totally get off on you pulling power plays in other ways, which I'm sure you know full well, as good as you are at fucking with my mind that way—but that didn't work for me. I need more."

"Such as?"

"Don't ask me to tell you how I feel and then go imperious."

"Sorry." He raked a hand through his hair. "You're right, of course. This verges into what my problem is, as I rather thought it would. I set the rule of no contact during the workweek to protect you. No, don't tell me you don't need protecting. I am experiencing a distressing lack of control where you're concerned—which is entirely my problem—so I thought it might be easier to, over the course of the workweek, to create the illusion for myself that..."

She looked half-amused, half-irritated. "That I don't exist."

He sighed. "In a word, yes."

"Well, it worked, because that's how I felt and I didn't like it."

"I see that now. I can only ask for your forgiveness. If it's any comfort, I didn't like it either."

"And it didn't solve your problem. You said you still wanted me every second of every day."

"Trust *you* to remember that part."

"It was one of my favorite parts. And not only because you

said it while fucking me senseless."

"So you continue to mention."

"You seem like you need the positive reinforcement." She scooted closer and laid her hand palm up on the table so he'd hold it. Such slim and delicate fingers. "Alec—is there some other reason you don't want this? I mean, I know I'm younger than you are and I'm maybe not as sophisticated as other women you've dated. Is it that you're only sexually attracted to me and you don't want to know me other than that? Do I—" She hesitated. "Are you embarrassed by me?"

That dug into his heart. A muddle, indeed. "No, darling." He squeezed her hand. "If we were to go public, I'd no doubt be the envy of every man alive."

"Then let's go public."

"No." He tapped the back of her hand when she opened her mouth to protest. "Not yet. The stakes are too high and I am already struggling with the guilt of debauching you. I shall never get over ruining your career prospects on top of it."

"I'm the one who pushed for the debauching," she pointed out with a sly smile.

"As I clearly recall. However, you would enjoy a ruined career far less. Still. Let's come up with a workaround. What do you propose?"

"I want better communication."

"I can't talk to you at the office. Maybe at some point, but have mercy on me there."

"Okay. Can we text?"

"It seems a very bad idea to have incriminating texts between us. What if someone happened to read them?"

"We'll use an emoji system, like Kiki and I do." She hopped up. "Where's your phone?"

He told her, bemused by her rebounding energy. "I thought this code was to remain a secret," he couldn't help teasing as she returned with both phones.

She scooted her chair next to his and laid their phones on the table. "You shall be admitted to our society and taught the language of the gods. Woe unto ye who fails to treat it with honor. I need to add the emoji keyboard to your phone. Here." She showed him her screen, which appeared to be an exchange of various smiley faces, a pair of girls kicking out their legs, a flamenco dancer and…

"Is that a jester?"

She laughed. "Exactly. That's kind of an inside joke."

She looked so gorgeous by candlelight. He tucked a lock of her hair behind her ear, limiting himself to that chaste contact for the moment. "Do I get to know?"

"Well, Kiki and her family belong to this church. Kind of a Universalist thing—I don't really know—but they're very much into embracing people of all kinds and bents. This one older gentleman in the church, who's in his nineties, and so very well-meaning, was talking to Kiki about making sure that people know they'd be welcome. He told her that they accepted everyone—gays, lesbians, cross-dressers, trans-jestered…" She trailed off with a sparkle in her eye, waiting for him to get it.

"Oh dear."

"Yeah. I mean, he's a wonderful man. Only he didn't quite get it. So it's funny. We send it to each other, for a laugh."

"You sent that to her just a bit ago."

She nodded. "When I was changing clothes. To let her know I was happy and wanted her to have a fun evening."

He trailed a finger down her cheek, golden pale in the soft light, realizing she meant it. That she wasn't jollying him along by saying she hadn't minded what had happened. But it concerned him that she didn't take it seriously enough. That she was too naïve to know better. "It worries me that I seem to have no control lately. That's my problem, my personal hell. I'm afraid of hurting you and that the only solution is to stay away."

CHAPTER TWENTY-FIVE

HIS CONFESSION TOOK her by surprise, particularly paired with the haunted look in his eyes. He'd seemed more relaxed, amused by the emojis and her stories, better after he'd tended to her and satisfied himself she was fine. But he kept circling back to the same thing. Part of his obsessive nature, most likely. The negative aspect.

"Okay, I have three things to say to you and I want you to listen to me," she said. He got that look—there, that was more him, offended at being given orders—and she returned it with interest. "We're still under Morpheus so don't try that. We're negotiating, which means I get to take a strong stand, right?"

Despite the flicker of irritation, he gave her an amused nod and a wave to continue.

"First of all, I'm not made of glass. I'm flesh and blood and I heal just fine. Secondly, you've never been out of control. Not once. In fact, you pretty much ordered me to tell you to stop— are you saying you wouldn't have?"

He looked affronted. "Of course I would have."

"Exactly my point."

"But I hurt you."

"This might be a newsflash, which I can't imagine how it could be, but I like that. No—I love it. Most important, if you hurt me in a way I didn't love, I would say so. Give me some goddamn credit, okay? I might be young, but I'm not a complete idiot."

"You're not, no."

"That's right. Also, the whole point of me having safewords is that I should be able to tell you to stop and you'll know I don't mean it. It's not fair that you changed that rule. I want to be able to beg you to stop and know you won't. Isn't that part of you trusting me?"

He closed his eyes briefly. "Right you are."

"Thirdly—"

"Wasn't that three already?"

"Yes, but you distracted me and forced me to add an extra. Finally, while I very much respect you and trust that you know what you're doing in general, this staying-away-from-me solution of yours has not worked. Big fail there."

"I beg your—" He bit it off when she grinned at him, then threw up his hands. "Fine. Finish your point."

"I believe I will." He looked so adorable, so flustered in a way he rarely ever was, that she climbed onto his lap, straddling him and sliding her hands around the back of his neck. Though suspicion glanced over his face, he reflexively set his hands on her hips. She feathered kisses over his cheekbones, scraping her teeth lightly over his five o'clock shadow. "I think we need more time together, not less. I want weeknights, too. At least a few."

"No. That's nonnego—ow!"

She licked the ear she'd nipped to stop him. "Morpheus. Negotiating, remember? How can that work if you pull the nonnegotiable card?"

"That's not exactly how I'd intended you to use that safe-word," he muttered, sounding grumpy, but his hands slid over her bottom, stroking her skirt where her panty lines would be. He loved that she wasn't wearing any, that much was clear.

"That's how I interpret it." She scooted a little closer, so the thrust of his erection through his jeans pressed against her mound. He hissed out a little breath. "Bottling up isn't working. I think that's what's happening. You keep bottling up and repressing and then it..." she rocked her groin against him, "...explodes."

"Is that what you think then?"

"It is. I want you to tell me something."

"I appear to be at your mercy."

"A heady sensation. Where did you go tonight, after work?"

He frowned. "After work?"

"I went by your office and you were gone, but I got here before you did. Where did you go?"

"Why do you wonder?"

Aha. Evading. She'd known something lurked there. "I'm gathering clues about you. Discovering how your fascinating, twisty mind works." She leaned in so her stiff nipples brushed his chest. He didn't show that he noticed, except that his hands flexed on her hips. "Tell me where you went, what you did."

"I...walked home. Through the park. And stopped to watch the ducks at the pond off 59th."

"Just watched them?"

He shrugged, hands moving up to her bare back, stroking her skin, making her want to purr. "They won't let you feed them, you know. Reminds me of home, when I used to walk home along the Thames. Before that, growing up, I'd walk on the beach when I had something on my mind. Being near the water—it helps settle my thoughts."

"What had your mind roiled up?"

"You know the answer to that."

"Yes, but it makes me feel better to hear that you're as worked up about me as I am about you."

He trailed his fingers down the bumps of her spine. "I find I think of little else."

She kissed him, long and deep, the way he liked it.

"What's that for?"

"A reward." She smiled. "I like knowing that about you. I want to know something else."

He groaned but waited for it.

"What is it about me that gets to you?"

"Fishing for compliments, darling?"

She wriggled and he pinched her bottom lightly. "I love compliments, so feel free. But no—I'm working on a theory here. While it does wonderful things for my ego to imagine that I'm simply so beautiful you can't resist me, I don't think that's it."

"No?" He lifted her hair to pull it over one shoulder, stroked her cheek on the other side, over her shoulder and down her bare arm, then cupped her breast through the light cotton. "But you are very beautiful."

"Thank you. What else?"

"Sensual. Lovely. Intelligent. Full of vitality. How many need I list?"

"It's a good list. I think there's something else you haven't said."

He tensed. Still caressing her breast, but wary. "Do you plan to enlighten me?"

"All of this, what we do, the fantasies, dancing the lines of what's right and wrong—it's about the taboos, isn't it?"

His thumb passed over her nipple, hand tightening on her, though he didn't reply. She was getting to him.

"I think it's feeling like you shouldn't do to me what you want to do that's driving you crazy. You see me as innocent somehow."

"You are an innocent."

"Not hardly. Certainly not as much as I was a week ago."

He winced at that, so she took advantage of his distraction to unfasten his jeans and release his cock. He clamped hands on her wrists. "Amber," he warned. "No using the Morpheus umbrella to break the rules."

She licked her lips, deliberately, loving that he couldn't help looking. "I know what happens when I break the rules. I'm telling you I want that. Make me less innocent. Cross my lines." She squeezed and he huffed out a laugh, then forced her hands away and pinned them behind her back. Arching into it, she ground against him. She'd never stopped being wet for him, but moisture surged, hot, needy. He nipped her nipple through the dress. "Oh God, yes, Alec."

"You're incorrigible."

"Is that another word for naughty? Are you saying I'm a bad girl?"

He hissed through his teeth, losing that reserve by the moment. "You're baiting me."

"We're not at work. I'm wearing white, but I'm not a virgin. Except in one way." She wiggled in his grasp and made a helpless sound. "Please be gentle with me."

His face had settled into those rigid lines. "Are we done negotiating then?"

"Yes, Sir. I'm totally at your mercy."

"Is that so?" He pulled on her wrists, making her arch further, his accent creamy. "Then I have a taboo or two to break."

He lifted her off his lap, telling her to keep her hands clasped behind her back, then fastened his jeans, daring her to object. She wouldn't though. He'd slid into his masterful mode, beyond the doubts that plagued him, and she flung herself after, her body a morass of need at the prospect of what he'd do to her.

Setting a firm grip on her wrists, he marched her to the bathroom—the bathing chamber—and made her stand in front of one of the chrome-framed mirrors. Untying her halter, he slowly lowered it, revealing her breasts, then unzipped the back of her dress and lifted it over her head.

"Don't move," he whispered in her ear and took the dress away.

She had no choice but to stare at her naked reflection—and all the iterations of her body from various angles, caught in the various mirrors.

And anticipate.

He finally came back in, carrying her hairbrush and a few other things, sexual tension riding the lines of his body. He'd changed into one of his black suits, wearing it with a black shirt and tie. It made her smile, knowing he'd listened to what she'd said and did it for her. His gaze flashed to hers. "Eyes forward, darling." He showed her a crimson velvet jewelry box. "I bought something for you."

"You did think about me."

His gaze swept over her, making her shiver. "Every second of every day." He opened the box and took out a set of cuffs, pale gold this time, and fastened them on her wrists and ankles. They were lined with a thicker, softer felt than the others and fit her snugly. Perfectly, even. "These suit your coloring better." Linking the cuffs together behind her back, he studied her in the mirror. "Graceful. Made specifically for you." He ran his hands over her breasts and down to her crotch, fingers dipping into her lightly, so she leaned back against him and moaned. "Mine," he murmured, and kissed the bruise he'd left on her neck.

"Yes."

"And now I'll have more of you."

"What are you going to do to me?"

He smacked her bottom with the back of the hairbrush and she gasped. "Speak when spoken to." Reversing the brush, he ran it through her hair, expertly pulling it into a ponytail that he then braided tightly, weaving a gold chain through it. He draped it over her shoulder to dangle on her breast, letting her see the gold hook at the end. "I do enjoy long hair. Soon you'll know why."

The uncertainty began to get to her, the mind-fuck well and truly sinking in. He teased her nipple with the hook, smiling when she whimpered, then brought it behind her back, pushed her bound wrists up, and attached the hook to them. It made her arch her back and stretch her throat, her breasts thrusting vulnerably forward. He took something else out of the box, matching gold, dangling and catching the light in her peripheral vision.

Coming around in front of her, he teased her nipples into harder points. As if they could be. She tried to breathe into it, guessing what was coming, but the bite of the clamp took her by surprise. Sharp pain. Along with the swift, aching need that followed.

"Does that hurt?"

"Yes, Sir," she gritted out, going with the truth. Hoping he wouldn't freak.

"Good." He slapped the clamped breast lightly and she sobbed a little. Both with the weakening sensation of erotic pain and the relief that he'd gotten his head on straight again. "Not so bossy now, are you?"

"No, Sir." She bit her lip when he fastened on the other clamp and she gave in to the need to struggle against it, feeling on the edge of frenzy, her bound hands tugging sharply on the braid. "Please, Sir—I'll be good!"

"Yes, you will. Because you'll have no other choice." He slapped the breast he'd just clamped, not hard, but in a way that made her nipples throb. "And you may as well resign yourself, as I'm far from done with you."

With a hand on her wrists he guided her to one of the complex metal apparatuses, moving her slowly, but whatever dangled from the nipple clamps bobbed as she walked, sending shooting sparks that went straight to her rioting pussy.

"Don't you dare come," he warned, sounding cold and cruel. "No orgasm for you, not for a long time yet."

He released her wrists, from each other and the braid, and stretched her over the bars that faced yet another mirror. Fastening the cuffs so her arms spread forward and out, he bent her over another bar, adjusting the height so it fit under her hips and raised them high. When he spread her legs, fastening her ankles wide apart, she was forced onto tiptoe, most of her weight on her hips and wrists, the rest of her dangling helplessly. Picking up the braid, he hooked it onto a bar behind her head, forcing her to arch her neck again, meet her reflection. A chain of golden balls dangled from the clamps on her nipples, swinging with her distressed breathing.

Checking her position, he ran his hands over every inch of her, casually teasing her, adjusting the apparatus so she could barely move. Looking satisfied, he gave her bottom an affectionate smack, then took some lube from a shelf. Holding it so she could watch, he squirted some onto his fingers, gave her a significant smile, then applied it to her vulnerable anus.

She couldn't help flinching at the unaccustomed sensation, reflexively trying to evade his probing fingers, which felt so strange going up inside her virgin passage.

"Alec," she whimpered.

He met her gaze in the mirror, adding another finger and pushing it in, widening her. "You asked for this," he replied in a severe tone. "You can beg and plead all you like, but I'll have this from you." He worked his fingers in and out of her. "I'm taking it and you can't do a thing about it."

Serious mind-fuck. The double message came through loud

and clear, that he acknowledged her complaint and wouldn't stop unless she safeworded. It gave her a glorious sense of freedom to let it all work on her. The pain in her nipples, the helpless immobility, the way he had her so wantonly displayed as he invaded her intimately, looking so severe and remote in his suit.

"Please stop," she whimpered.

"But I've just started. It will get worse."

"I'll do anything."

"Oh yes. Yes, you will." He removed his fingers and wiped them. Then picked up a hose looped on the wall, coated the nozzle with lube and pushed it into her. "Dirty girl," he whispered.

The metal was cold. The water that jetted into her warm. The reflection of her face had gone pale in the mirror, her eyes enormous. She moaned and bit her lip, feeling more exposed, more out of control than ever in her life. And more aroused.

It filled her, adding pressure. How far would he take it? Maybe too humiliating.

"Morpheus, Sir?" she whispered.

He paused. Turned off the stream of water and caressed her hip. "Too much?"

"Just, can I do the rest in private—pick it up from there?"

"Of course." He took something else from the shelf and lubed it up, watching her closely. The jet of water stopped and he slipped the nozzle out of her, then deftly replaced it with the other device, one that stretched her wide before it popped in, sealing the fluids, the pressure, inside her.

"Game on?" he asked and she nodded. Alec braced himself

on an upright and leaned over her, dark and deadly, reaching under her to tug on the nipple clamps. She shuddered, fighting the bonds.

"Please don't do this," she begged him, meeting his gaze.

"I hear the words." He slid his hand down her taut belly, cupped her mound and caressed her, fingers bracketing her clit so he made her crazy but not enough to make her come, ramping the intensity back up again. "But you're so very wet. You crave this. Admit it."

"No." The vicious tension rode through her at his light touch, all of the scenario sending her reeling. "Let me go, please!"

"You're mine to do with as I wish. My helpless captive."

He worked the butt plug with the other hand, pumping it slightly, so the pressure built impossibly higher, watching her struggle not to come. "This is what you'll do for me and then we'll revisit. I'm going to release you and you'll take yourself into the water closet and empty yourself for me. Nice and clean." He released her bonds as he spoke. Then handed her the tube of lube. "You'll need this. Use plenty—you'll be grateful you did. Put the plug back in and meet me in the bedroom. Don't try to escape or things will go much worse for you."

Shaking enough she could hardly walk, she obeyed. Unable to form coherent thoughts, in some kind of out-of-body delirium, she relied on following instructions, emptying herself in private and then reinserting the plug. The big bath was off the hallway that led to the master bedroom and he'd darkened all the lights, leaving only a soft glow from the master to guide her. Anticipation and trepidation both wound through her gut, the ache in her nipples from the swaying weights sinking down to seep out between her legs, slicking her thighs. Absurdly nervous to enter the room, she hesitated in the doorway, feeling much like she'd been summoned to the principal's office.

With all the dark fantasies that entailed.

"Hands and knees," Alec's voice snapped out and she obeyed reflexively, dropping to the plush carpet with a surge of longing. "Come here."

She crawled across the floor to where he sat in an armchair, shrouded in shadows. He'd lit candles, but only a few. Not enough to dispel the sense of intimate mystery, of vague threat, and that only the two of them existed in the world. The curtains stood open to the city, the towers of lights glittering. She halted at his feet, the black leather of his shoes a soft gleam in the dimness.

"Show your obedience," he whispered. She bent and kissed the shoe, soft and cool under her lips, while the rest of her melted in the lava of need. He brushed a hand over her head, running the braid through his fingers, then wrapping it around his fist. Lifting her to her feet, he directed her to the window, arranging her so she faced out, her palms flat against plate glass, the nipple clamps clinking musically, the dizzying drop of the city spread all around. "Can they see you, do you think?" he asked in her ear, stroking his hands down her flanks. "Are they watching, knowing what you're letting me do to you? What you can't stop from happening?"

"I don't know." But she could imagine it and it worked her as much as his casually possessive hands.

He leaned into her, crushing her against the glass, mouth feeding on her neck and hands clamping her front and back, making her squirm. Then he took her wrists and slid her hands down the glass, walking her hips toward him until she was bent in half. He tugged on her braid, the hook clinking against something else metallic and then tightened, pulling on the butt plug that already stretched her. She whimpered, unable to stop from resisting, which only pulled on both.

"Stay still."

He wandered away, silent on the thick carpeting. She tried to stay still, but the position made that impossible. Her curved back ached to straighten, her scalp protested, but when she tried to relieve them, the plug in her ass dug in deeper, echoed by the throbbing in her nipples. Complete mind and body fuck.

The frantic mewling sounds must be coming from her, because he murmured something soothing, running a hand over her hip and down her thigh. Attaching something to her ankle cuff, he spread her legs wide apart, and attached the other. Something rigid that didn't allow her to close her straining thighs.

"So lovely." He palmed her bottom, sliding a finger into her empty channel and stroking. "So totally helpless. My little virgin."

With her head craned back, she could see his dim reflection in the glass as he stood behind her, watch him slide his cock into her slick passage. The dual penetration seemed like it would split her apart, so intense. She moaned and tried to pull away, but he sharply smacked her ass and pushed in deeper.

"You wanted this." His voice had frayed, gone dark and ragged. "By God you'll take it."

He thrust in and out of her and she lost herself to all but that, clinging to the edge of control. Just when she thought she'd go insane from it, the braid released and he cupped her mound, working the plug free.

Then slid into her there.

He was larger than the plug had been. And longer. Filling her more deeply. So darkly intimate. His clever fingers worked her clit, sending her into an ascending frenzy of need.

"Please," she gasped, unable to frame more than that. "Please."

"When I say." He thrust in and out, the sensation so intense, shattering. Unreal.

With his other hand, he gathered her breasts together, squeezing them, and she cried at it, a long stream of pleas. The forestalled orgasm seemed as agonizing as any of it. He accelerated his pace, smacking into her hips so hard she had to brace against the glass.

"Now!" He shouted, simultaneously dragging off the clamps and pinching her clit, ramming to the hilt inside her.

She screamed. Flung far from the earth, fired into orbit by the incredible release. Rocket fuel. Nuclear fission.

She blasted into tiny fragments of who she'd been.

CHAPTER TWENTY-SIX

H IS KNEES THREATENED to buckle and he barely managed to stay upright through possibly the most intense orgasm of his life.

What is it about me that gets to you? Amber had asked, half-curious ingénue, half-sensual woman teasingly perched on his lap. She never let up, forgiving him everything, excusing him nothing. Pushing him to do his worst.

Daring him.

And now he'd buried himself in her deliciously tight ass. A bit more innocence stripped away. Devouring her the way he'd wanted from the first moment he laid eyes on her.

What is it about me that gets to you?

He had no idea. He only knew she did.

She might be helpless under him, shackled, speared, tormented and subdued, but she'd taken him prisoner. Worse, behind those searching blue eyes and determined questions, her canny brain knew it and exploited him ruthlessly. She shuddered under him, drooping, her hands sliding against the glass. Did she know the external window treatment kept anyone from seeing in—or did she trust him that much?

Likely the latter. She trusted him beyond reason. A thought that terrified him.

Easing out of her and stripping off the condom, he

wrapped her around the waist and helped her to the chair, then divested her of the spreader bar and cuffs. She lolled bonelessly, a pale slim figure against the dark leather, eyes nearly closed, completely exhausted.

"Come to bed, darling." He brushed her cheek and she smiled without opening her eyes.

"Gonna stay right here," she murmured. "Can't move."

"All right then." He managed to scoop her up, a surge of deep affection filling him at the way she curled into him, soft, curvy, impossibly sensual, winding her graceful arms around his neck and kissing his cheek.

"Thank you," she whispered. "I'm so glad it was you. You're perfect."

He laid her on the sheets, the same pale champagne color as the cuffs he'd had rush designed and then had resolved never to use. The colors suited her—he'd had that right, if nothing else. He unbraided her hair and spread it out across the pillow. Her breathing had already softened into deep sleep and he shucked off the suit, too wrung dry to do more than drop it on the floor. Suit porn. She never ceased to surprise and delight him.

He managed enough energy to snuff the candles, then slid into bed with her, wrapping himself around her, breathing in her scent and loving how she snuggled into him.

Perfect.

HE WOKE BEFORE she did this time. She looked more like an angel than ever, face soft, peaceful in sleep, one slim hand curled under her cheek, hair kinked from the tight braid in a glittering cascade, shades darker than the sheets. The mark on her neck stood out livid against her creamy skin—stirring both regret and desire.

His typical mix with her, it seemed. And yet, even with that, he itched to roll her under him, to watch her innocent eyes darken with her wickeder nature, for her body to go pliant under his, offering him everything in her artless, trusting way.

As if she sensed his sharpening thoughts, she opened her eyes. A drowsy blink followed by a radiant smile. "Hi."

He couldn't help smiling back, the taint of regret sliding away. "Hi."

She scooted closer, pressing her warm naked breasts against him and sliding a long thigh between his, rocking her hip against his erection. "Look who's up."

So beautiful, with that mischief sparkling in her eyes. She parted her lips as he leaned in for the kiss, welcoming him into her mouth with a soft *mmm*. Indulging himself, he traced the curving landscape from her shoulder to her waist, the rounded hip, the slim thigh, so delicately soft on the inner curve, her cleft wet and hot. She gasped, that enticingly sweet sound as he pushed a finger inside her welcoming heat, spreading her thighs and pulling her onto her back.

With a sly glance, she reached for the bedside stand, freed the condom from its foil and sheathed him with it. Then guided him into her, expression going sublime as he went deep. She pushed the sheet down his thighs, using her feet to kick it off of him. "I want to watch this," she purred into his ear.

For himself, he watched her face as he set a lazy tempo, the pleasure clouding the blue. She enfolded him, fingers dancing over his back, savoring him as he loved to do with her. Digging into the muscles of his shoulders, the backs of his thighs, scraping over his ass. Her deep moans increased from warm whispers to erotic openmouthed cries. He increased the speed, raising her knee to penetrate deeper, rewarded by the way her eyes rolled back in her head.

The climax shouldered into him, demanding release, and he held out, waiting for her. She focused on his face, dragging her nails down his chest and lifting her hips to meet his thrusts.

"Kiss me, Alec," she commanded, glowing with the power she wielded.

Helpless to resist her, he bent to obey, the orgasm tearing loose as their lips touched. She cried out her pleasure into his mouth, body flexing in waves that buoyed his. She clung to him, clamping onto him with arms, legs and her rippling wet heat, offering a sensual comfort that flooded him with a release far more than sexual.

"I'M STARVING." SHE walked naked into the bedroom, hair wrapped in a towel and skin flushed from her shower.

"No surprise as we never ate dinner."

She tipped her head, thinking. "You're right. See what a cheap date I am? Tons of kinky sex and all for a glass of wine. I'm not counting the one you broke—that's on you."

"Perfectly reasonable. I clearly owe you. What would you like—shall we order up?"

"No. I want diner breakfast. Something very greasy and American." She rummaged in her bag, yanking out a pair of shorts and a T-shirt, then tossed them on the bed and gave him a look. "In public."

"Amber…"

She wiggled into a pair of scandalously sexy red lace knickers and slipped on a matching bra, casually plumping her breasts as she adjusted the fit. "I'm serious about this, Alec. I want to be able to go out and have breakfast with you on a gorgeous Saturday morning. There's, what, over eight million people in the city and something like one point five in Manhattan alone. What are the odds we'll run into someone we know?"

"Am I allowed to factor in Murphy's Law?"

"No." She pulled the shorts over her long legs, whipped the towel off her wet hair and yanked the shirt over her head. It was hot pink, had a woman's face on it and said WE ARE THE MEDIA. She looked him over. Cocked her head. "I love that you wear a button-down shirt even on a weekend morning."

"And what's the one you have on?"

She glanced down, pulled it out from her body to look. "That's Amanda Fucking Palmer. Indie rock star. She's married to Neil Gaiman, a name you should recognize by now. We can discuss over breakfast. Out."

"You're terribly pushy for a supposedly submissive girl."

"You know the saying—submissive whore in the bedroom, pushy broad in the drawing room."

"I'm pretty sure that's not how it goes." But she amused him, making him smile with her irrepressible spirit. "Besides, we're still in the bedroom."

She put her arms around his waist and rubbed against him like a cat, a teasing smile curving her fresh lipstick. "Unless you're planning to make use of it, I want you to feed me."

"I see. Still a reasonably cheap date." He squeezed her pert bottom and she winced. "Sore?"

"A bit. What I get for having your enormous cock rammed up my virgin ass." She gave him a sunny smile.

"Such a pretty mouth. Such a filthy one."

"You like it. You can't resist me."

"True. Very well then, as I'm clearly doomed, let's go and have breakfast."

"Yay! Let me just comb out my hair."

"I need a shave."

"No, don't." She scraped her nails along his stubble. "I like the shadow. Very sexy."

"You think everything is sexy."

"You were the one who said the everyday can be sexually fraught. I happen to agree."

They walked out through the lobby, the day bright and busy indeed. Amber threaded her arm through his when Sean opened the glass doors for them.

"Good morning, Sean! Thank you," she sang out. Completely incorrigible.

"Is there anyone you don't enjoy teasing?"

"Hush. I'm having a *Pretty Woman* moment here."

"You don't know who Sinead O'Connor is, but you've seen that movie?"

"Every girl has seen that movie. Classic Cinderella and don't bug me about the details." She slid him a speculative look. "You know, you could pull off that Richard Gere look, if you went silver—with your pretty brown eyes."

"I'm not that old." *Yet.*

True to her word, she picked an old-fashioned-style diner and insisted on sitting at the counter. Making happy sounds as she drank her mocha with whipped cream on top, spinning on the stool, long legs bare and ending in sparkly sandals, she looked both gorgeous and terribly young. The ponytail she'd pulled her hair into, not wanting to take the time to dry it, didn't help. She perused the laminated menu—then ordered an absurdly large breakfast—and badgered him to do the same.

He enjoyed himself, he discovered. Letting her draw him into telling stories of London and his family. After they ate, they walked along the wrought iron fence that bordered Central Park, Amber insisting that they'd be swallowed up among the thousands of people thronging the place on a sunny weekend.

"Carriage ride for you and your daughter, sir?" One of the men with the horse-drawn carriages called out.

Bloody hell. And there Amber went, with that delighted mischief on her face. With her arm already looped through his, she squeezed against him and gave him a huge smile. "Oh, Daddy! Can we? Please please please?"

He glared at her, but she only pressed her breast against his arm, enjoying his discomfort.

"Fine then." He helped her into the carriage. "But I'm going to paddle your bottom for that," he hissed into her ear as he settled beside her.

"Promises, promises." She looped a slim thigh over his lap and snuggled against his chest. "You're the best Daddy ever."

"Stop that. You'll scandalize that poor bloke."

"It's his own damn fault for making assumptions. Besides—" she slipped a hand between them to brush his hardening cock, "—it turns you on."

"You turn me on," he corrected, but relented and took the kiss she offered, sliding a hand along her silky thigh, letting her stroke his erection behind the visual barrier of her leg. Completely irresistible. "And I know you enjoy yanking my chain."

"Yes. Yes, I do. Because, if I yank hard enough, dark Alec comes out to play."

Bemused, he tugged her ponytail. "Dark Alec?"

"You know. Right now you're sunny Alec. Happy. Laughing. Relaxed. And then you get that edge, like when the cabbie called me your daughter. Then you go all intense and demanding. Kind of angry, kind of severe with it. Like you get in scenes. Dark Alec." She nuzzled his neck, bit lightly. "Mmm."

"You make me sound to be Jekyll and Hyde."

"Very British," she agreed. "Let's make the cabbie drop us at the pond, so we can watch the ducks."

"What are you up to?"

"I told you. Gathering clues."

The park teemed with people, children carrying balloons, musicians playing, couples lying in the grass, heads pillowed on each other as they read, cops riding by on glossy horses. All of it a circuslike atmosphere that infected him with a foreign sense of giddiness. As they returned to the lower end, near the duck pond, he asked the cabbie to stop and tipped him, though the man gave him a black look.

"You should be ashamed of yourself," the cabbie muttered.

"Why's that?" Amber nipped up, inserting herself under

Alec's arm.

"You should be more careful, sweetheart. How old are you, anyway?"

"Are you planning to card me?" She'd gone from gamine to ice queen in a flash, staring the man down. "Oh, wait—I know! Instead of that, you can just mind your own fucking business. And watch that assumption thing. You know what it does." She slapped her hip. "Except I think you're the only ass here."

"That was hardly necessary," Alec said as they walked down the grassy bank.

She took his hand and picked a bench overlooking the lake. "You're the polite one in this relationship."

"And you my defender?"

"I don't like anyone trying to make you feel bad about us." She cast him a long look. "You do enough of that on your own."

"He was jealous, darling."

She brightened. "You think so?"

It made him laugh, surprising, since the incident did rankle. "Undoubtedly. As I predicted, I am the envy of every man we encounter."

"Good. I want you to be proud to be seen with me." She turned to him and searched his face. "You're not going broody on me, are you?"

"Is that dark Alec?"

"Connected, but not the same, I think. However, I'm willing to offer up my tender flesh for you to take out your frustrations upon."

"Noble of you."

"I'm selfless like that."

"I think we'll give your tender—and already abused—flesh a bit of time to recover."

"So much for that promised spanking."

"Hush."

"No one can overhear. Besides, I have another plan."

"Color me terrified."

"For later. For now we're digesting that amazing breakfast. And you're telling me why you got divorced."

The shock curdled the amazing breakfast in his gut. "I'll do no such thing."

"I'll withhold sex." She tried to give him a serious look, but couldn't maintain. "Okay, I need a better threat." She turned on the bench and draped her legs over his lap. "It's the elephant in the room that distracts me. I just want to understand more about you."

"You seem to have me pretty well nailed."

"I thought that was me." She smiled impishly, reminding him of how she'd said the same thing the night before. "Look, I'd tell you about mine, but there's nothing interesting to tell."

"No? Why no long-term relationships then?" It surprised him that he asked, unaware that it resided still, in the back of his mind. Judging by the look on her face, he'd surprised her, too.

"That's bothering you?" She toyed with his shirt collar, thoughtful. "I don't think there's any one reason. The sex was part of it. I didn't like it when the guys acted as if what I wanted was messed up. One guy called me a nympho, which pissed me off."

Hurt her feelings, too. That showed clearly in her eyes. Enough so that he lifted her chin and kissed her softly. "There's nothing wrong with the way you enjoy sex. You intimidated him."

"Maybe," she breathed. "I don't intimidate you."

More than she knew, but not in the way she meant. "No. You delight me."

"Another told me our problem was that I had a hair-trigger orgasm. That was a weird fight."

"And a sign he had no idea how to handle a woman with your passionate sexuality."

"See?" She wiggled closer. "You get me. I'm not sure anyone else ever has. I'd say that's really why no long-term. I think that maybe…" She hesitated.

"What?"

"I think I was waiting for you. You might be it for me, Alec." She shrugged off the import of her declaration. "Which is why I don't plan to let you brush me off. Why I want to understand where you're coming from."

Staggered, he stared at the water, the same blue as her eyes. Tried to assemble a response to that.

"I mean that in a non-stalkery way," she added. "I also know I just broke about seventeen different relationship rules by moving too fast, making you feel crowded. That's probably another reason I haven't really cemented with another guy— I'm not good at playing games. I'm pretty honest about how I feel."

He caressed the rounded muscle of her calf, skin so smooth

in the sunlight. "I had noticed that about you."

"Well. I don't want to screw this up for the wrong reasons, at least." She tried to sound brisk, but a thread of that insecurity he'd glimpsed ran beneath. "However this works out in the end, at least you know you don't have to worry about me losing interest and gallivanting off…like your ex-wife did?"

The laugh escaped him and she smiled at having gotten that response. "Do you have a reason to guess that or are you throwing darts blind?"

"Educated guess. It's pretty clear that she ditched you and since no sane woman would, she did it for a stupid reason. And I think it blindsided you, left you wounded because you never really processed the why of it, so you've kind of been quietly hiding from the world."

"Ah. So you think to trap me in a public setting and force me to bare my soul."

"You said looking at the water clears your mind, makes you happy. I was mainly thinking of that. You know, you've never said her name out loud to me. That might be a place to start."

"Tessa. Her name was—is—Tessa."

Amber leaned her elbow on the back of the bench and propped her head on her hand. "Did you do the dom/sub thing with her?"

Utterly relentless, with true concern in her eyes. He stroked the velvety skin of her calves, her lovely, delicate ankles. "We did, yes. It's not much of a story. At first, we only dabbled, but over time, she became…consumed by certain aspects of it. She quit her job in order to be my slave. Wanted to be kept chained all the time. Gagged and subservient. Every man's dream.

Hardly something for me to cite as the beginning of the end."

"Was that what you wanted?"

He flicked a glance at her face. She watched him, intent, compassionate. "The money wasn't a problem by then—I was making plenty for us both."

"But?"

"Well, it doesn't make for interesting dinner conversation, does it?" He laughed at himself and focused on her toes. The second much longer that the first, an asymmetry he found vastly appealing. "It's difficult to explain. But I didn't want it, no. I wasn't happy."

"Because the sex, the kink, was more important to her than you were."

He hadn't thought of it that way. "Perhaps so. The other piece was..."

She stroked the back of his neck. "What?"

Did she have any clue still of the devil that crawled through him, voracious and violently consuming? "She had no boundaries left. She'd crossed the border into self-destruction and I became afraid that I would hurt her and she wouldn't stop me. I couldn't trust her not to stop me."

"Oh, Alec. You go dark, yes. But never once have I been afraid with you."

She didn't know. He cleared his throat. "At any rate, I couldn't give her what she wanted. She felt I was being obstinate—that I could but wouldn't. That I refused out of selfishness. Some of the types of imprisonment she craved...they were unsafe. I couldn't justify them to myself, even if I, personally, had been into those scenarios. I failed her in that."

"They must have been extreme, if you felt that way." She raised her eyebrows back at him. "What? We might not have been lovers that long, but I know that you're a generous one. I know we have the dynamic set up that you pretend to take from me what you want, but I'm well aware how much attention you pay to pleasing me. Like I told you about the suit porn and you put on the suit for me. Even when you're rough you make sure I'm into it. I suspect you'd go to lengths to fulfill every dirty fantasy I dared to tell you about. It's also already really clear to me that you'd refuse to do anything that would endanger me. I think it would take something extreme for you to not want to go along with it, for you not to find it hot yourself."

Such an old brain in her young head. Had he fully realized that about her? "You're correct—I went along with some, but after a time it felt as if I had become an abstract to her. That I was merely the device for her own head trip. She ceased to be my companion, then stopped being my lover in any interactive sense. She craved the role, not me." The blue of the lake burned his eyes.

"I'm sorry, Alec." Amber ran her hand over his hair and brushed the back of his neck. "I can't imagine how terribly lonely that would have felt."

CHAPTER TWENTY-SEVEN

L ONELY.

As usual, she'd seen right through him. He'd thought of himself as lonely since moving to New York, but it had started long before that, hadn't it? Odd to have that perspective, telling Amber this story he hadn't fully shared with anyone, not sure why he had. Except that it felt right. Amber's caressing touch on his neck soothed, her bottom snugged against his leg, skin under his hands. So very present in her physical affection. Funny to think about Tessa and those last years, the remoteness in her face, disconnected even during intense scenes. Perhaps more so at those times.

"So, you told her you wanted out?" Amber prompted softly, making him realize he'd fallen silent in his thoughts.

"No." It had never occurred to him, in any material way, that their marriage would end. "I proposed a compromise."

"For her to go elsewhere?"

She nodded when he glanced at her. "It's very you—and logical. Keep the marriage intact by having her seek the severe kink somewhere else. You implied as much, by saying you'd become the role to her, not her partner or lover. I'm thinking she took the out and kept going?"

"Ah, now there you would be wrong." Some boaters paddled by, happy, shouting in German at one another. "I hurt her deeply by proposing it."

"Wow. Really?"

"Yes. I should have known better. In retrospect, I understand. She felt I'd betrayed her and failed her as a husband and dom. Which I had." *You're only playacting. If you were really my dom, you'd want to keep me to yourself, under lock and key.*

"Oh, horseshit."

"I beg your pardon?"

Amber took a fistful of his shirt and tugged him in for a long, hot kiss that made his head swim even more than retracing the boggy emotional territory had. "God, I love it when you say that. And I cry bullshit on Tessa and her lame excuse."

"Do explain."

"Look." Amber sat up straight, crossing her legs tailor style. "You say you tried to make this work for years, right? How long did she do the slave thing?"

"Just over three years."

"And what did she do for you during that time?"

"Do? She did everything—the housework, meals, any task I set for her. That was part of it. She wanted tasks and restrictions. I sometimes had to invent things, to keep her busy."

Amber heard him out, then shook her head. "That's not what I mean. That was all part of her shtick. All satisfying her fantasy, what she wanted. What about what you wanted—what did she do to give you that?"

He didn't know how to answer that and Amber raised her brows, nodding. "Exactly. See, she made it seem like she was being your slave, doing all that shit for you, but it was all to indulge herself—and keep you roped into perpetuating her fantasy. When you offered her the out, you blew her hold on you. She thought she had you in the thumbscrews, but you changed the rules and slipped out. I'll bet she was severely pissed."

"You could say that."

"You know what else?"

"Dare I ask?"

"Ha. I think that you subconsciously knew that, too. You hate being pushed around, that's core dark Alec. You're also a thoughtful man with a tremendously loving nature, much as you cover that over. You wanted her happy. You needed out of that cycle. So you found a way for her to pull the escape clause, have it be her idea—and freed yourself from that particular hell."

The way she saw it followed the general lines of what had happened, but put a different color on it all. "I'll have to think about that. Though it surprises me that you use that metaphor."

"Hell? Just getting into your métier." She casually draped her legs over his lap again. "I like having you touch me. I went and read up on Faust last week."

"Did you now?"

"Yes. Since I couldn't talk to you, I thought I could at least learn something more about you that way. Interesting choice—the bored and dissatisfied philosopher who surrenders moral integrity for worldly pleasure."

With her satin skin under his hands and that erotic charge she seemed to stir in him on a constant basis, it seemed particularly apt. "Isn't that what I've done?"

"Depends on the spin. I'm no Gretchen, an innocent whose life will be destroyed."

"Which remains to be seen…"

"Besides, if anything, I seduced you."

"Which is not how the world would see it."

"Yes, well, the world is full of sexism, particularly toward young women. That's beside the point, however."

"I wondered if you had one."

"Don't be snarky." She lightly punched his shoulder. "What's important is which ending you choose."

"The story ends where he's condemned to hell for eternity, incidentally discovering it's been one of his own making."

"Or—" she gave him a fierce stare, "—he's saved, both by his own work and through Gretchen's intervention. There's lots of ways for this to turn out."

"Ah."

"Exactly. Perhaps you need a new metaphor. I have an idea." She paused, thoughtful.

"Never say you're not giving voice to what's on your mind."

She wrinkled her nose at him. "You would think me amazingly discreet and reserved if you knew all the things I think and don't say."

"Terrifying to contemplate."

"If I ask you a question, will you give me an honest answer?"

He met her earnest gaze. The beautiful and unspoiled Gretchen, willingly consumed by lust. "I have always been honest with you."

"I know—but you might be tempted to cushion my feelings here, knowing you."

That sparked his curiosity. He cupped her cheek and rubbed a thumb over her lower lip. "Ask."

"Do you mind—now that you've told me this story, of how it went down with Tessa—does it bother you, what I want from you? The dom/sub kink?"

"Isn't that why we're together?"

She frowned, a line between her fine eyebrows. "I wondered if you thought that."

"It's true."

"If anything, it's what brought us together, but that's not all of it. Not anymore."

"Regardless, my honest answer is an emphatic no. Not only do I not mind, you've brought the joy of it all back to me. It is part of who I am and I missed it. Bottled it up, as you wisely pointed out." He took her wrist, wrapped his fingers around it, delighted to feel her quick tremble at the gesture. "I'll have more, as long as you'll have me."

"Okay—here's my rule then." She raised her brows, no longer frowning. "Don't make me pull out my negotiating safeword. I'm leaving that side of things up to you. You set the pace, do what you want to. I'd hate myself if I thought I'd trapped you into some scene you weren't into."

"You shouldn't concern yourself with—"

"With you and your happiness? Too late. Besides, I like it better that way." She wiggled her bum against his thigh. "Having everything be your idea."

"All right then."

"However—don't sigh like that—I want to do something for you. I need to shop for some supplies. Can I meet you back at your place in a couple of hours?"

"What are you up to?"

"Special surprise. Taboos to tweak. You to do."

She had that mischievous look, the one that would make him fear indeed for his immortal soul, if he believed in it. No, his damnation was a different sort altogether. *If I yank hard enough, dark Alec comes out to play.*

"Can I stop you?"

"You may borrow my safewords," she offered with a benevolent wave of her hand. Then she swung her legs off his lap and stood. "I'm off to shop."

"Let me give you some money." He reached for his money clip.

"Eyew. Creepy sugar-daddy vibe with that."

"Not at all. I've ruined several bits of your clothing and promised to make good on them. You must allow me or I shall feel guilty about doing so."

"You and your guilt. Fine then. If only to ensure you'll feel free to rip them off in the future."

"Very practical."

"That's me." She bent down and kissed him. "See you soon."

He watched her go, her brisk walk down the path jaunty, ponytail bouncing. Then he stayed where he was, looked at the water, and thought about endings.

AT LEAST SHE hadn't told him she was falling in love. Of course, she'd implied as much, hinted at the danger and all but declared her intentions. Alec, in his inimitable fashion, had heard only what he wanted to. Or, at least, only directly acknowledged that much. It wasn't always easy to tell if she'd gotten through to him, he covered his thoughts so well behind that cool reserve.

If only she could have been a fly on the wall when he offered Tessa an open marriage.

She knew something of how that dynamic worked from watching the long, slow demise of her parents' marriage. People were funny that way, determined to use the emotional hooks they'd sunk deep to keep the other captive, hating the other person but unwilling to set them free. Her parents had played it out in a nonsexual way—so far as she knew—but Alec's story had fit that same pattern. It wasn't fair to hate Tessa for it, this woman she'd never met. Screw fair, though. She hated Tessa on principle, for putting that misery on Alec's face.

Thinking of him, she pulled out her phone and sent him the jester face, just to see what he'd do. She also sent Kiki a row of dancing girls. Enough said. Kiki sent back a sleeping face, so she left her alone. Alec hadn't replied, so she tucked the phone away.

She'd made it six blocks from the park before her phone whistled. He'd sent a heart with a bow around it. How could she not fall for this guy? He'd probably spent all that time searching through the umpteen emojis, picking the right one. Her phone whistled again and she puzzled over the image of the shirt and tie he'd sent until, laughing, she realized it was suit porn.

A man passing her on the sidewalk gave her a flirtatious smile, which she returned. Yes, she was happy. Her body ached in places, in salacious ways, and she savored the delicious secret of the extraordinary sex she'd had, that only she and Alec knew about. Now it would be her turn to blow Alec's mind, and she knew exactly how to do it. Giving him a taste of things to come—besides him—she sent him a lollipop emoji. Let him wonder about that one.

Yeah, guy on the street—eat your heart out.

She ended up spending more than she'd imagined, between Dylan's Candy Bar and the sex and costume shops—along with the impulsive stop at the bookstore. But then, Alec had handed her a substantial amount of cash. Without blinking, which meant he didn't see it as all that much. She wouldn't worry about it then. If he didn't give it much thought, she wouldn't either. She'd catch up to him eventually, as she had no intention of ever being someone's penniless slave.

Serious heebie-jeebies there. Interesting, too, that she and he seemed to be of the same mind on that. On many things, actually. Circle back around to the perilously sweet, falling sensation. She'd never been in love, but the certainty filled her. The way she quickened at his least glance, the brush of his hand. Erotic compatibility, yes, but far more. She liked teasing him over breakfast and walking in the park.

It had hit her hard, during his story, when she knew she had to ask if he wanted an out on the kink. She would have agreed in an instant, to be with him. Blew Kiki's whole theory that she'd crushed hard on the dom vibe. That might have been the doorway, but he was the home inside it. She'd stepped over the threshold and found herself wrapped in his heart. The mirror of how it had gone with Tessa. Alec had started as the role, the abstract for her.

Now he was everything. Her first love.

She'd bide her time until she'd wooed him into feeling something of the same. In the meantime, she'd use his lust for her without mercy.

If he wants out, though, I'll let him go.

She sailed up to the doors, carrying her many bags, and gave Sean a sunny smile. He did not like her—or was, more likely, offended by her—so she asked him how his Saturday was going, just to torture him into having to talk to her. She had to knock on Alec's door. Dammit, hopefully he'd come back home. If he hadn't, she'd camp out on his doorstep rather than have the stinking doorman think she'd been kicked out.

Alec opened the door with a smile and a suspicious eye for her packages. "I suppose I should give you a set of keys."

"Really?" A huge concession for him, that maybe they weren't only having a brief fling. Practically a declaration of affection, from him.

"It only makes sense. And I've offered you keys to my flat, not to the city. It's not that exciting."

She set the bags down, went up on tiptoe and hugged him, gratified when he kissed her in his long, slow lazy way, sending her always-simmering desire for him into slow boil.

"It *is* that exciting," she murmured against his mouth. "It means a great deal to me." She stopped herself from saying anything more. "Now let me go. I have to get ready. You can wait for me in the living room."

He studied her face. Glanced at the bags again. "Should I be afraid?"

"If I'm on target, you'll love this. If not, we'll stop. Those are the rules, right?"

"She says, as if she's ever used her safewords in a sexual scenario."

"I did, too."

"To save your pride, not for any other concern."

"But I would," she insisted.

"I shall believe it when I hear it," he responded drily.

"Well, then, this will be a good opportunity for you to demonstrate."

"Possibly." But he sounded unconvinced. Dark Alec, seething just beneath the surface, not liking the loss of control. Good.

She had the perfect lure for him.

CHAPTER TWENTY-EIGHT

H E WAITED FOR her, wondering what the hell she had planned. Something diabolical, with her sharp, creative and perverse brain. He'd given thought to it, her question of what Tessa had done for him, to please him. And had slowly realized their relationship had never been about that, not in essence. Even with Tessa being determinedly submissive sexually, everything had been about keeping her happy.

Not easy to do. He'd discovered over time that she hadn't been a happy person in many ways. And, in the way of some fundamentally unhappy people, she'd looked for external solutions. At first it had been about money and the things. Fancier homes and more expensive clothes. Gifts from him had assumed enormous significance—and never quite lived up to expectations, making her birthday and holidays something he'd begun to quietly dread.

She'd given up job after job, searching for the perfect one, then only quitting entirely would satisfy her. With all of the attendant expectations of what sexual slavery would give her. How a good dom would know how to take away her worries and concerns, so she'd be free to be happy.

But, seeing it all through Amber's clear-eyed gaze, it seemed so obvious. He thought he'd failed Tessa as a dominant—but he hadn't been what she wanted on any level. Funny that it made him feel better to know that. As if it let him set down some load he'd been carrying.

Being with Amber…it took him back to how it had been with Sasha, the playful fun. The games without the baggage.

All the better to fret over what Amber had in mind. A whisper of her movement alerted him, so he stopped pacing and made himself sit. Then regretted the choice as the sight of her nearly sent his blood pressure through his head.

Sweet bleeding Jesus.

She slinked around the corner and posed—no other word for it—leaning against the doorframe and licking a colorful lolly. Yanking his chain and yanking it hard, indeed.

She wore her hair in twin pigtails, high on either side of her head, curled into ringlets and with ribbons added. Her outfit was pure schoolgirl, from the white blouse knotted kerchief-style at her waist to the pleated skirt, over-the-knee black stockings and—fuck him sideways—patent leather shoes.

Face clean of makeup except for glittery pink lip gloss, she'd managed to look younger than usual. The picture of innocence, but for the sultry challenge in her eyes. He didn't know whether to be fully ashamed at her insight into him, truly angry that she tried to play him this way—or terrified that she'd send him into an oblivion he couldn't return from. Regardless, he did not intend to give her chain of any length to yank on this scenario.

"Morpheus," he said. "Absolutely not."

She dropped the lolly to her side and stood straight, if anything, exasperated. "Shouldn't you have said *Lolita* then?"

He nearly snapped at that, digging his fingers into the arms of the chair to anchor himself. But she had him there. He couldn't insist on a veto without voicing the very word that emblemized everything he felt most guilty about.

"Fine. But we're not doing this. Not going there."

"Alec." She sighed with impatience. "You were the one who told me that no fantasy is too dark, no taboo that can't be broken—between consenting adults. I'm not a minor. I'm not some innocent schoolgirl, but I know I represent that to you in certain ways. You wouldn't be this affected if it didn't have a big charge for you. I'm very happy to work that charge out. More than that, I'm dying to. It rocks my world, too."

Bloody hell.

"No one here but you and me. No one to know but us." She swayed closer, cocking her head and licking the lolly again. "You want this. Don't try to deny it. Say I can go ahead."

His temples throbbed in time with the painful echo in his rock-hard cock. She had him there, wrapped around her delicate pinky. As she moved forward, the short skirt showed slices of bare thigh above the stockings. His brain melted, filled with a high whine, and he lost his tenuous grasp on right and wrong.

"Show me your knickers then." His demand came out hoarse.

She suppressed her delighted smile and managed to look shocked. "Mr. Knight! I don't think I should do that. I'm a good girl."

"Are you now?" He patted his knee, luring her in to be seduced and devoured. "Don't good girls do what they're told?"

Acting hesitant, dragging her feet, she sidled closer. Fidgeted with the hem of her skirt. Gave the lolly a long, slow, completely salacious stroke of her tongue. His vision went black at the edges.

"My daddy said I should be careful of strange men."

If he ever recovered from this—what had she called it? The "mind-fuck"—he'd pay her back in spades. A glint of that, probably dark Alec, must have shown through because Amber paled a little. It made him crave her that much more.

"If you sit on my lap," he coaxed her, "then we can get to know each other and I won't be a stranger. Come here this instant or I'll do more than look at your knickers."

She visibly trembled. Hesitated. Then gingerly perched on the very end of his knee. She smelled of the thick candy sweetness of the lolly and strawberry lip gloss, watching him with wide eyes only partly assumed for the role. Setting a hand on her stocking-clad thigh, he nudged her closer, then slid his fingers up under the flippy skirt. She put a hand on the hem, holding it down, keeping him from raising it.

"I don't know, Mr. Knight," she whispered. "I feel funny. What happens if I let you see my panties?"

He kept his hand under her skirt, stroking her soft skin, finding the edge of her knickers over her hip. Cotton. And was that a bit of lace? Knowing her, she'd picked out something such as rosebuds or unicorns. He burned with the need to see them. To rip them off.

"Why don't you give me a little kiss?" He pushed on her back, tilting her into him, using the hand on her hip to slide her even closer. "Just on the cheek. So we can be friends."

"I guess that's okay." She brushed her lips, sticky sweet, against his cheek. He put his hand on her neck and held her there, turning his head and taking her mouth. She squeaked, struggled a little and then gave in with a moan, opening her mouth to his tongue, all hot woman there. Sex and candy.

He used her distraction to get his hand between her thighs, though she held them tight together. Totally soaked. If he'd had any doubt what the scenario did for her, he had none now. He turned his hand, wedging her thighs apart, and she squealed, still holding the hem down and squirming on his thigh. "Oh, Mr. Knight," she gasped. "I really don't think you should—"

"You're not being a good girl at all." He stroked her through the sodden knickers, working the cotton up into her folds. "I think you need a spanking."

"No, please." She looked genuinely stricken. "I can't let you do that."

"Yes, you can." He took the lolly from her and set in on the end table. "Look what you've been doing with a strange man. Kissing him. Letting him touch your knickers. You should be spanked for being bad, yes?"

"Yes," she breathed, completely overwrought, hips moving in unconscious pleading.

"Over my knee."

She resisted a little, whimpering, but let him arrange her over his lap, her bum high over his right knee, breasts pressed against his calf where she dangled to the floor. Gorgeous, with her skirt riding high above the tops of her stockings. Rapt, he lifted the skirt slowly, pulling it up to her waist. White cotton knickers with little pink hearts, trimmed in pink lace.

Not innocent Gretchen, though, but his Mephistopheles. Tormenting him with tricks at every turn.

She'd gone still, breathing hard, cunt hot against his leg even through his trousers. He fondled her bottom through the fabric and she moved under his hand, moaning a little, breath hitching with little hiccups.

"Very pretty knickers. You see? You could have shown me when I asked and saved yourself a spanking. But now I have to take them down to do it properly."

She made a sobbing sound. "Please don't, Mr. Knight. I'll be naked."

"Yes, you will. Naked and helpless."

He held her still with a hand in the small of her back, letting her kick and squirm as he worked the knickers down her stockinged legs, leaving them to dangle around her ankles. She went limp when he slid his fingers into her slick heat, then lifted her hips beseechingly when he pushed a thumb just inside the tight clamp of her vulva, stroking her clit.

"So naughty," he murmured, and she made a sound of helpless longing. One that increased in volume and desperation when he took his hand away. The perfect white skin of her bottom showed a few scratches still, from the brick wall the night before, and the sight inflamed something in him. Giving in to the tide of it, he smacked her bum, the erotic sting burning through his hand and lasering into his completely fucked brain.

THE FIRST SMACK startled her. The pain settling in after the shock blasted through her. His hand came down again. The sensation of flesh on flesh was somehow more intimate, more emotional and mind-blowing than anything else he'd used on her. She tried to duck the blows that came down hard, fast and relentless, but he held her tightly in place.

This on top of the scene, the game-playing that worked so deeply into him and swept her up in it, made her unravel in some profound way. She kicked and wept, begging him to stop. Though he paused now and then, to rub her heated flesh and taunt her for her tears, to delve into her swollen pussy to tease her, calling her naughty in that cool British tone, he'd go back to spanking her.

The orgasm took her by surprise. Especially as she came while he was spanking her, not with his clever fingers inside her. It took her hard, clean, and made her cry out. He stopped, rubbing her bottom and making a tsking sound.

"Oh, my dear Miss Dolors. Do you know what kind of girl comes during a spanking?"

She couldn't answer, gulping through tears, thoughts shattered.

"Answer me." His tone was curt.

"A...a naughty one?"

"Yes." He helped her to sit up, bare bottom on the scratchy material of his pants, his hand going up her skirt again, long fingers gliding into her. "A very naughty, very sexy young woman. Open your blouse and show me your titties, love."

Blinking through tears, rocking herself on his relentlessly teasing hand, she obeyed, hands shaking as she untied the blouse and showed him she wore nothing beneath.

"So lovely," he breathed, then cupped her wet cheek and kissed her. "You're going to show me how sorry you are, aren't you?"

"Yes, Mr. Knight." Something in his expression made her quake inside.

He handed her the lollipop. "Show me how you lick it."

She did, aware of how she'd teased him with the image before, touching her tongue tentatively to it, aware for the first time of the consequences of baiting him too far.

"Do it right," he growled. "Like you do to a man's cock. I know you know how."

Feeling a new desperation to please him, she did, dragging her tongue along the colorful candy, he watching her like the rapacious monster he claimed to be.

"On your knees." He pushed her down between his spread thighs, not giving her the opportunity to obey, and opened his pants. His beautiful cock thrust free and she bent over without being told, licking the crown the way she'd tongued the lollipop, holding his gaze. He'd gone rigid, apparently mesmerized, so she sank down, relaxing her throat and taking him all the way in.

In the next moment he had her on the floor, hands rough on her, shoving up her skirt, lifting her hips as he pumped his fingers into her. He watched her, curling his fingers up inside her, thumb pressing her clit, other hand holding her ankle, holding her open as the next climax hit, wrenching in its intensity. "Again," he demanded.

As if helpless to disobey, her body followed suit, climbing higher and breaking on yet another peak. He pushed her knees wide apart, and stood over her, staring fixedly at her nakedness, one stocking fallen below her knee, her skirt tangled around her waist. He shucked off his pants and, whipping on the condom he got out of his pocket, knelt between her splayed thighs, brushing the skin with an expression of reverence.

Then met her eyes, his dark chocolate in the extremity of his desire, and slid into her. He'd forgotten about his shirt, so she fisted her hands in it and tore it open, enjoying the turnabout and the way his face clenched. Especially when she dragged her nails down his chest.

With rigid control that belied the wildness in his face, he stroked in and out of her, keeping it slow until she caught up. Which happened faster than she'd have thought, after those bone-breaking orgasms.

Of it all, though, she loved this best. The feel of him inside her, his skin against hers, the sinuous slide of his body and the intent way he watched her face, measuring, anticipating. They'd transitioned from the game now, back to being just them, twined with each other, saturated in the delight of how they fit. Like minds coming together in a profound meeting and understanding.

He quickened, tightened, gasped. "Oh, love…"

"I'm with you." She wrapped her arms around him and let herself fall.

CHAPTER TWENTY-NINE

NEITHER OF THEM said anything for some time. He felt curiously incapable of thought. Emptied out. Purged on some level, aware mainly of her immediate presence, limbs tangled with his, her breath slowing, heart thudding in the same rhythm as his, her slim, supple body under him. Vaguely he contemplated moving. Knew he should.

Instead he buried his face in the scented crook of her shoulder, breathing her in and filling those spaces she'd opened up.

He'd seen this, in others. The emergence from that zone. But he'd never quite experienced it himself. Had never sought or expected it. Hadn't known he needed it.

Somehow Amber had.

And he wasn't at all sure how to process that.

"I can hear you thinking," she said in a dry tone, but she also stroked his hair with gentle affection. "Amazing, since that was off the charts."

"Indeed." Though she'd made no complaint of being crushed, he rolled off of her and focused on the ceiling. She sat up, thoroughly bedraggled, one pigtail drooping, the ribbons dangling over a naked breast that showed through her open blouse. "Do me a favor and take your hair down, would you?"

She smiled, entirely pleased woman, but did as he asked. "Such a simple thing, to yank your chain so very hard."

He closed his eyes, which didn't help, since the images had apparently been burned onto his retinas. "I'm rather bruised and bloodied from said yanking, so I'll thank you to leave off for a bit."

"I can do that." A whisper of movement as she leaned over him, her silky hair spilling over his chest, her lips brushing his. "I'll go change clothes and then how about I scrounge something to cook for supper?"

He cracked an eye open, relieved to see her without the erotic symbolism that had so completely gutted him. She looked ravished still, but less as innocence defiled. "You want to cook?"

"Did you think I don't know how? I'm actually a decent cook, particularly if I feel like I have the time." Amber smoothed her fingers over his cheekbones, his brow, and he let his eyes close, absorbing the sensation of being cared for. Wondering that it felt so foreign, yet welcome. Water on parched soil. She kissed him again, lightly, as soothing as her touch. "Why don't you have a shower or a bath, then join me in the kitchen, keep me company?"

She was being gentle with him. Taking care of him and giving him room to recover from the mind-fuck she had to know she'd delivered so exquisitely. Something else he didn't know how to process. He waited until he heard her messing around in the kitchen, then took her suggestion and went for a shower, blistering hot, to bring him back to himself.

He felt exhausted, beyond the physical challenges of satisfying his insatiable young mistress. She'd pried him open, getting him to talk about Tessa, then widened the wound, a scalpel to his heart with a stroke as clean as ripping apart his shirt, leaving him no ability to hold back. No reserve, as she so frequently accused him of having.

She'd put on the shorts and T-shirt again, singing as she chopped vegetables. Some song he didn't recognize. Possibly by the rock star she wore. Something about getting a tattoo that said she's living in the moment, which seemed an ironic juxtaposition. She turned and smiled, registering that he'd put on the old jeans and green shirt she'd picked out. After all, he'd not had them on for long.

"Stir fry okay? I've got rice steaming, but I don't know how to make curry. I'll have to learn, so I can attempt to counterfeit London curry for you. It's started to rain, so at least we have that much ambience."

He lifted her chin, bemused and dazzled by her. "You remembered that?"

"Of course. I told you. I'm making a very serious study of you, collecting my clues." She set down her knife and caressed his cheek. "You shaved."

"Yes. I'd gone past scruffy. Sorry."

"I like you both ways." She raised on her toes and pressed her soft lips to his cheek, slowly inhaling. "You smell of almonds and wood."

"My shaving soap."

"Mmm. Yes. Delicious. I opened some wine."

And had poured herself a glass, too. He sat at the breakfast bar and poured a glass for himself, watching her so at home in his black-and-chrome kitchen. A place he'd rarely spent any time. Her presence made the place cozier, reminding him of times spent chatting with his mother and sisters as they prepared holiday meals, though their kitchens were nothing so sleek. For once, the stab of nostalgia, of homesickness, felt less a pain than a pleasure.

"I was thinking tomorrow we should drive out to the beach," she interrupted his thoughts by saying.

"The beach?"

"New York is an island." She flashed him a cheeky grin. "It doesn't take that long to get to a nice one I know of. We could go early, have lunch and walk on the sand a bit."

"And if it's raining?"

"Even better—not so many people."

"All right then." He stopped himself from saying *whatever you want.* Even though he knew in his heart that it was true. He hadn't been able to deny her from the beginning.

"Good. I think it will be good for you, help with the home-sickness, to see the ocean again."

And that was why.

"YOU *CAN* DRIVE!" Amber exclaimed, running her hands over the smooth leather of the passenger seat.

"I never said I couldn't." He gave her a sideways glance of amused irritation as he backed the car smoothly out of the reserved space in the parking garage. He'd been thoughtful, a bit withdrawn, since the mind-blowing scene that had rocked them both the previous afternoon. Not in broody-Alec way, though. He'd been more relaxed than she'd known him to be and casually affectionate with it. They'd eaten, watched part of a movie, then thrown in the towel and gone to bed.

He'd made love to her in a completely vanilla, extraordinarily ardent way that had her wondering what was going on in his head. And left her hesitant to ask.

"You won't drive on the wrong side of the road, will you?" she teased, just to see how he'd respond.

"I shall endeavor to keep my wits about me." He patted the hand she'd set on his thigh, enjoying the feel of his muscle flexing through his pants. "Which means this stays here. No distractions."

"If we'd had the car service take us, we could have distracted each other."

"I enjoy driving, recreationally. I see more this way. Appropriate, as you have me sightseeing."

"I love that you drive a Jag, too."

"How's that?"

"Because of course."

He laughed and she settled in, happy to have shaken some of his pensiveness. Having gone to sleep early, they'd awakened early also. The city traffic—between Sunday morning quiet and the continuing rain—remained light for the drive out to the beach. Alec stayed quiet, too, absorbed in his thoughts, but it was a pleasant silence between them.

It let her replay her favorite parts of yesterday and last night. He'd called her "love" twice during the kink scene, but she'd put it down to the role-playing, especially as he hadn't said it again, and she really doubted he'd meant anything beyond the pet name. Or one of the Britishisms that came out when he was over the edge. He'd never said the word before that she could recall and she thought she'd remember because of the exotic way he pronounced it—with a breath at the end. More like "luff."

She really wanted to hear it again, but she could be patient. Early days yet.

The steady rain had the beach deserted, and Alec gave her a questioning look as they pulled into the parking lot. "Not ideal weather for a walk."

"What—because it never rains in England?"

He laughed and tugged her over for a kiss. "You have a point there."

The chill breeze off the water made her glad she'd thrown some jeans into her overnight bag, and Alec had loaned her one of his sweaters—no, a "jumper," which cracked her up—and it felt like the perfect thing to be wearing. Warm, enveloping and smelling of him. He smiled as they walked hand in hand, the wind ruffling his hair. It had been the right thing to bring him here. They went a ways and then, as the rain picked up, turned back.

"Does Brighton look like this?"

"We're some distance from Brighton and that's more built-up. Piers and Regency buildings and lots of tourists. The beach by our house is much this way—dunes and shore grasses. The town is quite rural, much less so than this region. Country."

"And you're the only one of your sibs who left?"

"Yes. The only one not content to live off the family money." He ran his thumb over the back of her hand. "I was too ambitious for it."

"Did they understand?"

"Yes and no. They thought I'd gone quite off my head going to the States. My mother, in particular, has been nagging me to come home for a visit. Mostly so she can see for herself that I'm all right."

"So will you?"

He glanced at her, something opaque in his expression. "I've been thinking of it, yes. Perhaps later in the summer, around my birthday, would please them. Would you like to see England?"

"I would love that." She nearly said it his way. *Luff.* Pure, sheer happiness simmered in her that he'd suggested it. He'd stopped talking about them in the short term. Months away. Meeting his family.

"There's a restaurant back by where we parked." He nodded toward it, perched on an overlook, with sea-sprayed windows overlooking the surf. "Shall we eat, warm up and dry off?"

"Definitely." She raked her damp, snarled hair off her forehead. "Though I probably look like a sea hag."

He stopped and pretended to scrutinize her. Then cupped her face in his chilled hands. "You look indescribably lovely, as always." He kissed her lightly, which quickly turned hotter and deeper, making her forget the rain.

Luff.

The restaurant was as deserted as the beach, so they snagged a table at the windows. Alec insisted on beer with fish and chips, if she wanted to replicate the British beach experience. He pronounced the facsimile close enough and teased her into trying vinegar on her French fries. Ducking out to use the ladies', she sent Kiki a quick series of heart emojis. They'd talk later.

Neither she nor Alec spoke of the fact that they'd be at work again the next day. They'd figure it out. Get through it. Once he was satisfied they were more than a fling, they could come out of the closet, as it were. Maybe meet with the partners and figure out a way to let everyone know.

"Amber?"

She whirled around at the familiar voice. "Daddy!" Surprised, delighted, she jumped up to hug him. "What are you doing here?"

"I could ask you the same. I came out to look over some real estate in the area."

"Always working, even on the weekend. Don't give yourself a heart attack."

"You sound like your mother. And your stepmother." His questioning gaze went over her shoulder to Alec, who'd politely stood.

"Dad, this is Alec Knight." *Eesh. How to introduce him?* "We work together."

"Looks like that's not all you're doing together. John Dolors. Amber's father."

"Good to meet you." Alec shook her father's hand, all business genial, but that cool reserve had slammed into place. "Would you like to join us? We've nearly finished, but we could ask the server to bring up another chair."

"No, no. I already ate at the bar. Brit, are you?"

"Indeed."

"Yes, well." He put an arm around Amber. "Our little girl is very precious to us."

"Daddy." She kissed his cheek. "Don't embarrass me."

"Just letting him know you have family who looks after you. Though I wonder if your mother knows about this."

Now he was annoying her. "Seeing as how I'm an adult and not required to report on my activities, I'd guess not."

"I see. Why don't you walk me out to my car? Knight." He nodded and steered her out. Behind his back she caught Alec's eye and mouthed *sorry*. He simply sat and signaled the waitress for the check.

"So what's this about?" Her father started in, as soon as they were out of earshot. "And don't tell me you just work together. It's more than that—it's written all over both of you."

She managed to tamp down the gleeful surge of pleasure at that. Fairly easy to do, since her dad was getting under her skin and Alec had looked coolly pissed. "What it is is none of your business. That whole grown-adult thing, remember?"

"Nonsense. You will always be my business. Always be my little girl. I don't care how old you are."

"Fine. Yes, I'm seeing Alec romantically. It's only been a couple of weeks so I'm not ready to bring him over for family dinner and interrogation, okay?"

"Isn't he a little old for you?"

"I don't think so."

"Honey—think about it. When you're a middle-aged woman, he'll be an old man."

"You mean, when I'm his age, he'll be *your* age?"

That annoyed him. "Don't get smart with me."

"I was born smart and you encouraged me to act smart. Give me a little credit, Dad."

"What about babies, a family—will he give you that?"

She laughed, because the absurdity took her breath away. "We're dating, not picking out wedding china."

"You act like that's not important, but you don't want to wake up someday and discover you've wasted your youth on a man who can't or won't give you what you want."

"And you just assume I want marriage and babies."

"Don't think you won't."

"I do think that. I'm pretty clear on what I want, and babies are not on my radar."

"You're too young to know what you want."

"Oh, is there some magic age for that? I'm old enough to choose a career but not anything else?"

"You're full of ambition now, but that could change in an instant." He snapped his fingers. "You have to think about these things."

"Why?"

Her dad glowered. "Amber—"

"I'm serious. I've been seeing him for two freaking weeks—not even that, really. What the hell is wrong with living in the moment? I refuse to evaluate every potential relationship on whether he'll be suitable to replicate the life you and mom had. This is *my* life and maybe I want to do it differently!"

He went from angry to defeated, as fast as his finger snap. "Did we set such a terrible example? I know things were bad for a while, but..."

"No, Daddy. No." She hugged him again and he patted her

shoulder. "Just…give me some room, okay? Let me find out for myself what I want."

He set her back on her feet, pointing his chin at Alec who'd followed them out and was waiting for her by the wooden steps that led up to the restaurant. "And you think it's him?"

"I think—" She'd been about to say *I think he could be.* But she realized that would be prevaricating. "Yes. I'm pretty sure he is. I've found a great guy. I want to enjoy that."

"Humph. Well. Bring him over for dinner sometime then." He cracked a smile and waved at Alec. "So we can interrogate him properly."

CHAPTER THIRTY

"WHAT ARE THE odds, huh?" she said, walking up to Alec.

He didn't smile, however. Icy reserve deployed like a force field. "It depends—why did you pick that particular beach?"

Oops. "It's a favorite," she admitted. "But I didn't expect to see my dad there."

"Didn't you?"

"I wouldn't set you up that way. Why would I?"

"I can't imagine." He looked out at the ocean. Shook his head. "I think it's time to return home."

"Okay." She got into the car, trying not to give in to feeling rattled. The almost-fight with her dad, the very awkward introduction and now Alec. Clearly Not Happy. "I *am* sorry about that. You know fathers—overprotective."

"As he should be. I'd no doubt feel the same in his shoes."

She studied his profile. "Except you know there's no reason for him to be concerned. That I don't need protection from you."

"Don't you?" He flicked a glance at her. "One wonders what he thought of the mark on your neck."

"I made sure my hair covered it. And I used some foundation, too."

"Ah, so comforting. Wouldn't want your father to see what sort you'd hooked up with."

"I didn't say that. And that's not fair."

"No? You were happy enough to get him away from me."

"Because I thought you were uncomfortable."

"I was." He bit off the words. "Bloody *uncomfortable*."

"I already apologized. It's not like I set this up on purpose. In fact, I'm not sure why you're so pissed off."

He seethed, visibly growing angrier by the moment. That sense of being off balance dropped into stomach-clenching dread. "Alec—talk to me."

For a few minutes, she thought he wouldn't. Finally, he spoke. "You're obviously very attached to him."

Not what she'd expected. "Yes? I love him. He's my dad. Why are we fighting about this?"

"We're not fighting." But he had that set to his jaw and kept his eyes steady on the road, though the traffic hardly required that level of attention. "It gives me food for thought."

"What thoughts?"

"Your attachment to your father and your attraction to me. The games you enjoy playing. Your *daddy*."

She felt like she'd been sucker-punched. Once, in college, a drunken girl had swung her beer mug in a wild dance and clocked Amber on the head. Giving her the spins. Sickness foamed in her gut, a rancid combination of outrage, hurt and—worst of all—shame.

"It's not like that."

"No? What's it like then?"

"I don't have a sex thing for my father. I have a sex thing

for you."

"You can understand why I'm confused."

"No, I can't, actually."

"Because you haven't given it proper thought."

"You were the one," she said softly, so she wouldn't yell, "who said that all fantasies are okay. That what we did together wasn't shameful or wrong because we both enjoyed it and hurt no one."

He didn't reply. Just that muscle at the corner of his jaw, twitching.

"Have you changed your mind about that?"

"I don't know. I think it's not the same thing." He had a rigid set to his face. "It's a hard thing to look at a man, one you'd consider an equal under other circumstances, and have him wonder what you've been doing to his young daughter. Knowing at the same time that it's far worse than he imagines."

She took a deep breath. "I'm getting tired of this."

"Are you?" He sounded terribly cool. "Inevitable, I suppose."

"Stop that! That's not what I mean. I'm tired of you casting me in the role of despoiled innocence. I get that you're obsessed with Faust and his damnation, but isn't that a little overly dramatic?"

"Obsessed, am I?"

"Yes. Don't get me wrong, the myriad and delightful ways that obsessiveness manifests totally rock my world, but it's past time for you to get over yourself and accept that I'm a full participant in what we do together. I *want* what you do to me."

"You're too young to know what you want."

That washed in like an icy wave. "Funny—my dad just said those exact words to me."

"Perhaps you should examine the truth inherent in them then."

"Perhaps *you* should wake the fuck up and figure out that you are not my dad!" By the end, she'd shouted it, curling her fingers into her palms so the nails cut in.

She'd startled him with her anger, judging by the flash of white as he glanced at her and away, adjusted his hands on the leather-bound steering wheel.

"I apologize," he said stiffly, clearly not meaning it. "I regret to have failed you in this, also."

"Oh, knock off the crap! You haven't failed me in anything. I don't know if you could fail if you tried. But we are not acting out some Faustian cycle of damnation and innocence. Maybe it's time for a new metaphor. One that takes into account who I am as a person, rather than as a symbol."

"You're the one who keeps inserting that into our conversations."

"Because, so far, it's our common reference. Until we build more."

"That's it then, isn't it? We don't share references in common—different generations, cultures. Nothing beyond a certain sexual compatibility."

"You make it sound so distasteful." And it hurt her heart.

He raised an eyebrow at her. "Do I? I don't mean to. I'm recognizing the bare facts. It's the mat—"

"Don't you dare say that's the mature thing to do."

"Fine. I won't say it then."

They rode in silence for a while. He behind his wall of stone and she wondering how the hell to salvage this. If she could or should. Had she been wrong, all along? Did he only want her for what she represented—a nubile piece of ass, the forbidden fruit.

"You know, I never once felt any shame over what we did until this. I hate it that you do."

"Amber..."

"Let me ask you this. Why do we at least have the Faust metaphor as a common reference?"

He frowned slightly. More that she'd broken the silence he'd taken refuge in more than anything, she thought. "It's a classic."

"No, because I read up on it, so I could understand you. Did you study mine?"

"*Lolita*? You know I don't—"

"Not that," she cut him off. "You know—or you should—that I only picked that to poke at you. Maybe I shouldn't have because you completely missed the point."

"And what point is that?" he asked in a tone of infinite, and patronizing, patience.

"Morpheus. Gaiman says the story begins when the King of Dreams must decide whether to change or die."

"Ah, yes, the comic book."

"Fuck you and your condescension, Alec."

Stopped at a light, he gave her a longer sidelong look. Maybe paying more attention to her than his own angst for the first time since he started the fight. "You're upset."

"Thank you, Captain Obvious."

"All right then. I understand. This isn't working out—which I anticipated."

"You didn't anticipate this—you made it happen. You did everything you could to sabotage this from the beginning. I was falling in love with you and you only looked for an exit. Because you were afraid."

He didn't reply, staring hard at the cars ahead.

"Nothing at all to say to that?"

"I don't know what to say."

"You could tell me I'm wrong. That you've been falling for me, too. That you understand that's what about me that gets to you. That you know this has never been only about sex or about the taboos. For either of us."

He didn't reply. Only that moody flex of his jaw.

"I'm saying that this is a really excellent opportunity for you to tell me you care about me. That you see a future for us. I really need to hear that right now."

"I can't tell you that."

He might as well have driven a knife through her heart. She couldn't stand to be trapped in the car with him for another moment.

"Congratulations, then. You finally succeeded in running me off. I'll make my way home from here."

"Amber!" He reached for her as she opened the car door, but she'd surprised him and got out in time, the rain hitting her with a cold blast of reality. For once her timing was perfect—the light turned green and horns blared, forcing Alec to go through the intersection. She didn't think he'd follow, but to be sure, she went the other direction on the one-way, walking in the rain until she got chilled, then ducking into the subway and riding the train to her stop.

When she walked into their apartment, Kiki, ensconced on the couch, didn't look up from the manuscript she was reading, making a note in the margin. "Is the sex weekend over already? I didn't expect you home after all those hearts. So—are you in love?"

"I was stupid." Amber stood there, stricken. "We broke up, I think."

Kiki pretended to glance at the watch she wasn't wearing. "Right on schedule for you, huh?"

When Amber didn't answer, Kiki finally looked at her, and her expression crumpled in sympathy. "Oh, honey…"

And Amber burst into tears.

SHE'D LEFT HER things behind, including that ridiculous bag. Alec went about the place, picking up a discarded hair tie here, her earrings there, digging out the glittery sandals she'd worn to breakfast from under the coffee table. She'd left her cosmetics scattered on the bathroom counter, her shampoo in the shower, a pile of discarded clothes on the floor. A considerable diaspora of belongings, given her short occupation.

Seeing what she'd brought and hadn't got out stabbed at him. A red cocktail dress, in case they went out for dinner, he supposed, a lacy nightgown, a bikini, a pair of running shoes. All of it emblematic of her enthusiastic optimism, her faith in him. Prepared for anything, not having any idea what they might end up doing.

Hell, she'd been prepared for him to turn her away at his

door. As he'd eventually done—it had only taken a couple of days. Record time to break her heart.

Congratulations, then. You finally succeeded in running me off.

He packed it all carefully into her bag, as if by handling her things meticulously he could somehow make up for his clumsy behavior in the car. The way the words she'd needed to hear had stuck in his throat, trapped behind his anger and uncertainty. He'd have his driver deliver it all, so she'd have it for the morning, tie things up between them that way. She'd stormed out wearing his jumper, but he could let her keep it. Or burn it, judging by that last, viciously betrayed and devastated look she'd thrown at him.

Better for her to be angry. She was young and resilient. She might be upset now, but she'd get over him. Find someone more appropriate. Someone who wouldn't hurt her as he had.

He couldn't stew about it. He'd warned her from the beginning that he wouldn't be good for her and he'd proved it.

You made it happen. You did everything you could to sabotage this from the beginning.

Shaking off the accusation, the gut-scraping regret that he'd proven himself to be as unworthy of her as he'd ever predicted, he turned to repacking her shopping bags. He caught her scent as he folded the schoolgirl outfit, making him falter. She'd a few things in there she'd bought but hadn't used yet. Two sets of lingerie, in pink and black. No new pink blouse—he'd have to stop in the morning and buy one, make up for what he'd shredded and had no way of mending. Find a way to get it to her as a sort of farewell gift. Perhaps he'd find one of her bloody emojis to explain.

Oh yes, encapsulate the entirety of his regret in one cartoon image.

In the bottom of the bag was a slim, vivid book, the receipt tucked in the flyleaf.

A cover worthy of a Faustian tale, a bloodied hand in repose, virulent orange behind, bore the title *Preludes and Nocturnes*. Reflexively, he turned it over to read the back...*the home of Morpheus, the King of Dreams*. Ah. She'd bought it for him, he suspected. Planning to share it at some point.

Not realizing how quickly their implosion would arrive.

He should send it back with her other things. Pretend he hadn't seen it. Hadn't rifled through the rest of what she'd brought, mooning over her loss as the tomblike stillness of the flat settled around him.

Taking the book back to the living room, he poured a stiff whiskey, and sat down to read.

IN THE MORNING, he arrived at work as wearied as when dreams of craving Amber had disturbed his sleep. This time her cursed story had done it. *The King of Dreams must decide whether to change or die.* The metaphor didn't escape him—no doubt as she'd intended—Morpheus outliving his captors and his prison, waiting for it to crumble into nothing before he walked free.

He wanted to talk to her about it. Wanted to talk with her, full stop.

But it was over, as it should be, and he'd leave it there.

Joe gave him a funny look, possibly because he was later than usual, but only said good morning as he passed, Jean not at her desk, oddly enough. Alec booted up his computer, bringing up his task list to focus on the day ahead. His first conference call had been canceled and a new meeting scheduled starting in ten minutes. A prickle of foreboding crept up his spine—followed by Lily rapping on his doorframe. Her folded arms and the look on her face sealed the clang of doom rattling his brain.

"We need you in the goldfish bowl, Alec," she informed him. "Emergency meeting."

"All right then."

If she expected him to ask what this was about, he wouldn't. After all, he knew. Had known all along he'd face this moment, and the best he could do would be to meet it head-on and accept full responsibility for his actions.

Heaven has no rage like love to hatred turned/Nor hell a fury like a woman scorned.

There—he'd found a new metaphor at last. Perhaps Amber would approve.

Before he even entered the executive conference room, he could see Amber, pale and brittle, sitting at the table with the other partners and Tim from Human Resources. Amber had her hair up in that coil she probably thought made her look more sophisticated, but had the effect of showing off the fine bones of her face, making her eyes that much larger by comparison. She looked tired, waifish, and he thought she'd been weeping. She caught his eye, but he couldn't read the message. Oddly, he most wanted to sit next to her. Take her hand or pull her against his side. Comfort her as she eviscerated him in her just revenge.

He'd focused on her to such an extent that he failed to immediately register that his admin Jean also sat at the table, thin-lipped and a glitter of rage in her eye.

Lily closed the door, sealing in their conversation, though everyone passing by glanced at the unusual meeting with avid curiosity. Within an hour, everyone would know what he'd done, a public shaming he deserved.

"Alec," Bill began, then sighed. "I'm frankly at a loss at how to proceed here."

Tim cut in. "Bill—we have procedures and they're clear-cut. We should follow them. Alec. A complaint has been lodged against you that you've sexually harassed one of your direct reports and may have exerted undue influence on a junior colleague. Possibly causing that colleague to be advanced without merit and causing her professional reputation damage."

Which is it, he wanted to ask, *did I advance her without merit or cause her damage?* All a Christ-bleeding mess. He wanted to throttle somebody, though he had only himself to blame. Oddly, Amber caught his eye again and he nearly heard her think it. *Dark Alec.* "I see."

"Is it true?" Bill asked. "Are you having or have you had an affair with Amber here?"

He met Amber's gaze across the table. She'd lost no time filing the complaint with HR, not that he could blame her. Still. "I—"

"It's nobody's business," Amber cut him off. "I refuse to have this very intrusive inquisition into my personal life."

She glared at him, at his shocked silence.

"Amber," Tim said in a soothing tone. "You're not in trouble. We simply need to get to the bottom of this. If nothing has occurred, then we'll put this behind us. But Mr. Knight needs to respond to the allegation."

Everyone but Amber turned to him expectantly. Especially Jean, who wore an unpleasant smile. *Jig's up. Time to face the fires of hell.*

"Yes. I engaged in a sexual relationship with Ms. Dolors. I take full responsibility. The fault is entirely mine."

Bill and Hai Lin looked flabbergasted. Lily slammed her hands on the table. "How the *fuck* could you? We discussed this and you swore to do the right thing."

Tim turned to her. "You were aware of the relationship?"

"Alec came to me and said he was *attracted.*" She spit out the word. "He asked me to take Amber as my direct report to remove himself from temptation. Were you fucking her already then?"

"Yes."

"Goddammit, Alec—"

"Excuse me!" Amber stood up and raised her voice to cut Lily off, speaking directly to her. "With all due respect, Lily. I appreciate you as my boss and as my mentor. But don't talk about me like I'm some brainless idiot. Alec was not engaged in a sexual relationship with me, he never sexually harassed me. We engaged in a relationship together. It was consensual. As soon as we decided on our mutual attraction and acted on it, Alec took the appropriate steps to remove me from his supervision. There are no company rules against interoffice dating. I want to be on record stating that I have no complaint against Alec." She said the last to Tim and sat again. Picked up her bottle of water and drank, her hand shaking, not meeting his eye now. Instead she stared fixedly at her finger chipping at the water bottle design, holding her eyes open wide the way she did when she was trying not to cry.

"Why did you file a complaint, then?" He couldn't help asking her. Figuring he deserved to hear the answer.

"I didn't, thank you," she snapped, flicking a glance at Jean.

"I saw you," Jean said. "In Central Park on Saturday. We took the kids into the city for some sightseeing and I saw you go by in the horse-drawn carriage. He was all over her," she added in a tone of disgust. "And suddenly everything that's been going on here made a *lot* more sense."

"Such as?" Alec asked, aware of the ice in his own tone. Tim flinched a little and opened his mouth to intervene, but Jean beat him to it.

"We've all seen it, you giving her special favors. The McCloskey account. Suddenly she's privy to the partners' meetings."

A headache throbbed in his temple. Lily, who'd been tapping her red nails on the glossy table, clearly fuming, paused and transferred an incredulous look at Jean. "What? You've done everything you can the past year to get out of taking notes at the Friday afternoon meeting."

"It's still access to privileged information. And what about the McCloskey account?"

Tim looked between him and Lily. "Alec?"

He spoke to Lily. "You suggested I give Amber more responsibility. I did."

Lily groaned and rubbed her forehead. "Oh God. What a fucking mess. Yes," she told Tim. "I did. I was concerned that Alec was holding her back because of lack of faith in her gender. I didn't know then that…whatever. I still don't understand how you could do this, Alec. To us, to the firm, to Amber. Couldn't you keep it in your pants for God's sake?"

"Now, Lily." Tim frowned. "Let's steer this back to a civil discussion. If indeed Amber has no complaint, she has the right of it that their relationship is not in violation of company policy. If we can address Jean's concerns, then set some ground rules everyone can agree to, then they can continue to—"

"There's nothing to continue or discuss," Amber broke in, standing again and picking up her water bottle. Her gaze flicked up to meet his. Heartbroken. "I quit."

"No, you won't," he and Lily said in the same breath.

"Excuse me, the both of you," Amber replied in a tone that sounded more quietly enraged than respectful, "I did just quit, so you can't tell me what I will or won't do. I'll clear off my desk." Her glare passed over him, deep blue and glittering. She raised her chin and walked out.

He blew out a long breath and stood also, keeping an eye on Amber as she stalked, stiff-legged, down the hall to her desk. "I apologize to you all for this. If everyone agrees, I'd like to take this plan of action. Amber and I need to have a conversation. Then she and I will discuss with Tim and we'll bring a proposed resolution to the partners. At that time, we'll take Jean's complaint into account and settle that to everyone's satisfaction. If necessary, I'll resign from the firm."

"I think Alec's suggestion is a good one," Tim held up his hands like a referee. "I propose you clear your schedule for the day. Take some personal time and decide how you and Amber *both* would like to proceed. We'll meet in my office tomorrow morning, then take it to the partners. Please convey to Amber—though I'll contact her also—that I'm available to talk to her privately. Or would you like me to mediate your conversation with her?"

"That won't be necessary yet, though I'll tell her you offered."

"As will I," Lily inserted, in a warning tone. "If I get a whiff you've tried to intimidate her, Alec..."

He managed to suppress the laugh. Nothing and no one intimidated Amber. How long would it take her to clear her desk? He wanted to catch her before she left the building.

"I'll echo that warning." Tim leveled a stern look on him. "Jean, feel free to see me to discuss your thoughts further, but for now I'm asking you and everyone to keep this away from the water cooler gossip, okay? Let's demonstrate a bit of discretion and sensitivity here."

"We don't want to lose you, Alec," Bill said, holding up a hand to forestall whatever Lily had been about to say. "Either of you. But get this handled. If she comes back with a lawsuit..."

"Oh Christ." Lily put her head in her hands. "That's all we need."

"If it comes to that, I'll shoulder the financial hit. Whatever it takes," he told them. Hai Lin shrugged, as if it were all immaterial to her, and Bill nodded. "Lily?"

She tipped her glasses down her nose. "I'd want to know how this happened. I would never have expected this of you, Alec, of all people. Why did you do it?"

The bald question sank through his gut. *Why this is hell...* No. Not that. Not anymore.

"All I can offer is that I had to. I had to change or die."

CHAPTER THIRTY-ONE

H E CAUGHT HER just as she finished piling her few belongings into a box she'd obviously snagged from the copy room, everyone around her surreptitiously watching, without staring. The gossip would start up as soon as she left.

She flashed him a hard look as he walked up. "Come to see that I'm escorted from the building?"

"No. I'm taking a personal day—as are you—and we're going to talk."

"I'm not—"

He stopped her with his own hard look, raising his brows to indicate the many avid eavesdroppers. "Leave those things. Let's go walk in the park."

She huffed out an exasperated breath, but did as he said. Either out of reflex or simple expedience. They walked together out of the building, the marble-and-glass lobby nearly empty with all the morning commuters at their desks now. The click of Amber's heels echoed in the quiet, going faster than she usually did and Alec had the absurd—probably inadvisable— urge to take her arm to keep her from running off.

"I feel like I'm being sent home from school," she commented.

He laughed, surprising himself that he could. "It is rather

like that. Were you ever?"

"Once." She shook her head. "For a stupid girl thing. My best friend wrote something mean in my yearbook, so I wrote a similarly mean reply in hers. Only she took hers to the school counselor and I ended up looking like the bad guy. I cried." She gave him a look, defying him to comment. "My Achilles' heel. I cry when I'm mad, when I'm hurt, when I'm embarrassed or ashamed. I hate it. I nearly started bawling in that fucking meeting."

"But you held it together." He held the door for her and they walked out into the brilliant morning sunshine.

"Barely."

"Understandable, as the entire scenario was decidedly unpleasant."

She whirled on him. Stopped to face him on the sidewalk. "Don't you dare whip out the Brit equivalent of 'I told you so.' What do you want to hear—that you called it? That you were right all along, that you and I bumping nasties would lead directly to this? Fine. You were right. I was stupid. Happy?"

"Not even close to it."

"Well, welcome to the club." She sighed, rubbed her temple. "Look—you don't need to worry. I don't plan to complain to Tim. I'll sign whatever to guarantee I won't bring a lawsuit. Just let me complete the process of removing my unwelcome, perverted presence from your life."

"I'm sorry. For what I said. For how I've behaved. All of it."

She set her jaw and opened her eyes wide, staring at the stone wall.

"I think *you* were right," he said, quietly and steadily. "It played that way because I ensured it would."

She raised her brows, sarcastic. "You made sure Jean would see us in the park? You sly dog."

"Not that. Come. Let's talk this out." He touched her arm now, not her skin but the black sleeve of her suit jacket.

"The duck pond?"

"Where do you go, to clear your mind? It's occurred to me that I've been selfish—in that and other ways—always in my territory, as it were."

"I liked your places. I was happy to share that with you." Her tone made it clear that was no longer true.

"Is it all past tense then?"

She searched his face, uncertain, unhappy. "Why are you doing this, Alec? The guilt you're so good at wallowing in? We had this conversation yesterday. I bared my heart to you, told you I was falling in love with you—for the first time in my whole freaking life, I might add—and you very coolly said that you couldn't say the same. I wanted to believe it was more than what it was, that I meant more to you than some passing fancy."

"Amber—"

"No, I get it. So, I'm coping. I bawled on my girlfriend's shoulder, drank entirely too much wine and made myself sick on ice cream. I may have slept in your sweater, but I'll have it dry cleaned and sent to you. I can't say you didn't break my heart, but you were very clear from the beginning. All of that was on me. I accept it. I appreciate you being all gallant in that meeting, but we both know none of this would have happened if I hadn't pushed you into it. The wages of my sin, right? I get what I get. I might be hungover as hell, but I have my big girl panties on and I'm dealing. Please don't make it more difficult." She screwed up her face and heaved an exasperated sigh, then brushed away the tears that had started to fall. "Dammit."

"I suppose we'll have this conversation on the street corner then." He set his briefcase on a sloping stone window ledge, the person at the desk inside looking startled. Ignoring him, Alec opened it and took out the book. "I found this as I was packing up your things to send to you."

"Thanks for that. It was good to have my makeup this morning." She eyed the book. "You might as well keep it. I was going to give it to you. Or return it—I think I used your money to buy it anyway."

"I already read it. And ordered the others. I wanted to talk to you about it."

"Decent dinner conversation, at least?" She made it sound scornful, but he had her curiosity now.

"At the very least."

She transferred her gaze away, frowning as she caught sight of the person inside the window watching them. "Let's go to the park already." She pulled out her sunglasses, surreptitiously wiped her cheeks and started walking.

HE CAUGHT UP to her easily, carrying *Sandman* in one hand, briefcase in the other, looking ridiculously gorgeous in his three-piece suit and understated tie. So unfair when she looked dragged in from the gutter it felt like she'd slept in. Even though he'd been pretty much ambushed by that personnel meeting—God knows she'd been—he'd recovered with his typical aplomb.

She'd nearly hurled her water bottle at him for it.

Until he started defending her. Taking the noble stand, of course. Watching her with that compassionate gaze that felt like a caress. Only he could cut out her heart as concisely as he had and then have her wanting to hand it to him again. Only he could make her feel simultaneously cherished and meaningless.

He didn't say anything as they walked the blocks to Central Park. Giving her space to settle, most likely, as he did. Following along as if they were taking a stroll. Then giving her an interested look when she stopped and sat on a bench across from the carousel.

"It's a childish choice probably." She knew she sounded defensive. "But it makes me happy." Not many people rode it yet, just past ten on a Monday morning, but the lilting music played and the colorful horses pranced up and down, people smiling and laughing.

"You like ponies," he commented, sitting beside her. "The blue unicorns on your bag."

She made an indignant sound. "Rainbow Dash is a Pegasus, thank you. I'd think a classicist like you would know that."

"I didn't recall Pegasus having rainbows for a mane and tail." He sounded wry. Teasing her. It hurt her heart.

"She represents loyalty. Never mind—it's a dumb thing, too, I know."

"There's nothing stupid about loyalty." Alec set the book

aside and took her hand in both of his. "You showed nothing but to me and I came up empty."

"I gave it 'proper thought,' you know. The daddy sex thing. I think that was unfair. I never looked for a daddy. I fell for you, not some idea of who you'd be. That's your baggage, not mine."

"It is. I'm sorry for it."

The tears wanted to well up yet again and she stared hard at the carousel horses. "I hate that you're ashamed of me. What you said to me."

To his credit, he didn't deny it, but stroked her hand, tracing the lines of her fingers. "I hate it, too. I'm not proud of how I behaved. You said, in the car, that I was afraid. I don't think that's true. Or not entirely true."

She shrugged a little. "It really doesn't matter."

"It does." He raised her hand and kissed it. "You said that the King of Dreams's story began when he realized he had to change or die. But that's not what the stories are about, are they?"

"You really did read it?"

"It took some time to become accustomed to the flow of the graphics, reading down and sideways and diagonally. Rather like settling into the rhythm of Shakespeare, though—it creates its own lyricism. An almost poetic impact."

"Only you would say something like that."

"He quotes Marlowe's *Faustus,* near the end of this volume."

"I know. I thought it was interesting, how we intersected on that." That they'd traveled similar paths, if on parallel planes of their generations. Something he hadn't seemed to recognize.

"'It is a comfort in wretchedness to have companions in woe,'" he quoted.

"In other words, misery loves company. Is that what we're doing here—prolonging the misery?"

"I found the story horrifying—especially towards the end, with Morpheus having lost his power and the world in chaos. Nightmares come to life. Not light reading."

"It is horror," she pointed out.

"I think I know why you wanted me to read it."

Did she know? "Why?"

"You see me as him, the King of Dreams, as he is at the end. With everything he sought, but he's empty, without purpose. Feeding pigeons in the park."

"Well, if you can't feed ducks, at least you can feed pigeons." She tried to make it a joke, but she was searching her mind for the why of it. "I don't think that's true. I suggested *Morpheus* as a safeword long before I knew..."

"How empty I was?"

"You're not empty. Though you may bear a superficial resemblance to Dream, especially when you're broody." She couldn't help looking at him, meeting his somber gaze. "You're using my metaphor."

"Creakily perhaps. It occurred to me, sometime between last night and this morning, that I can see how I've been like your Morpheus, sitting patiently in my prison, waiting for the memories to die and the walls to crumble away. While the world passes by."

"You've hardly been entombed."

"It's felt something like that. My flat, without you in it, feels that way. I was so wrapped up in feeling out of control with you, resisting the temptation you represented to me, that I couldn't see past it to what was important—treating you as the gift you are. The young woman who appears at the end. You look nothing like her, his sister Death, and yet…" He paused thoughtfully.

"And yet?"

He stroked her hand and smiled ruefully. "She sets him free, doesn't she? Kicks at him and gets him to see what matters. I see it now in a way I didn't before—that the promise of paradise is worth anything."

The flare of hope rubbed like salt in her wounded heart. "Alec, I can't…"

He nodded, thoughtfully, sorrowfully. "I can understand that. I certainly don't deserve another chance with you. But I need you to know that I never, not for one instant, was ashamed of you. If anything, I was ashamed of myself."

"You have nothing to be ashamed of."

"I know that. Sort of." He smiled ruefully and trailed a finger down her cheek. "Except that I was so wrapped up in worrying about how badly I wanted you, fighting to under-stand why I couldn't seem to resist you, that I failed to recognize the obvious truth."

"What's that?" The hope began to feel better, rising up with the gleaming carousel horses.

"You know. You knew that day in my office, or the day you asked me why you get to me as you do. You called me obsessive, but I'm not. Not normally."

"You do have some OCD issues," she said, mostly to needle him. Because she needed him to smile, so she wouldn't start crying again.

He didn't smile though. Just gazed soberly at her, groping for the words. "I should have known what drove me so hard, why I never had a chance to resist you. With anyone else, I could have. But there was never a chance of not taking the opportunity to touch you, when you offered it." He ran his fingers over the line of her jaw, brushing down her throat, face intent as if he somehow tasted her through the tender touch that made her shiver to her bones. "You are what I need. What I can't make on my own. You're not innocence, but light.

"I don't know when or how it happened—" he stroked her collarbone, watching the movement, then met her eyes, "—but you must know that I love—I love you. Every second of every day."

Luff.

"Why tell me now—why didn't you just say so yesterday?"

"I couldn't see it then. Only when—insanely enough—Lily asked me why I couldn't keep it in my pants. I could have. But you already had my heart, so there was no point but to let the rest of me follow."

The hope bubbled over, becoming a laugh. "That has to be the most unromantic thing ever."

"I know. I know, love." He leaned his forehead against hers, closing his eyes. "You have no reason to give it another go, but I'm asking anyway. I know I'm moody. I'll try to change."

The carousel whirled, horses prancing up and down. "There's another song I like," she told him, feeling her way through, sorting all the ups and downs. "About a merry-go-round as a metaphor for life. How some things have to go up for others to come down. And one part says how the moon can't glow if the sky isn't dark enough."

He looked bemused. "What does that mean?"

"If I'm your light, maybe you're my dark. I've never minded it. You know that. You're the one who worried about it."

"True."

"I never asked you to change. I asked you to tell me that I'm more than the cliché. That I mean more to you than the taboo. More than arm candy."

"Darling—"

"No, you've told me enough for today. Or the hour, at least." She laughed at herself and kissed him. "But I might need to know it a lot. Remember that I'm learning how to do the long-term thing."

"Understood."

"One more thing—I want you to have dinner with my parents. They don't like to be in the same room, so that means two dinners."

He sighed. "A mighty penance, indeed. Perhaps I shall force my family upon you, as well."

A thrill of gladness came with that, along with a shiver of trepidation. "Will they disapprove of me—my age and so forth?"

"I won't care if they do."

"Ho-kay." She pondered. This was what she'd asked for. A

chance for them, to live in the moment and see how things went. "I'm ready. Sign me up."

Alec lifted her hand and kissed it, his breath brushing over her skin as he recognized the words she'd used at the beginning. But she understood much more of what she really wanted now, didn't she? Not reckless or stupid. Bold and brave.

"We'll take it as slow as you like. However you want to handle the office stuff, we'll sort it out. You can set the rules."

He meant it, too, and her heart overflowed. "I like it when you set the rules. As long as we can negotiate, of course."

His lips curved and his hands tightened on hers. "Naturally. There will be meetings. Tim offered to mediate for you with me."

"*That* would be an interesting conversation."

"Wicked woman. Of course you would think that."

"But you don't mind, because you're not ashamed of me, right?"

"No." He said it firmly, then feathered his fingers over her cheek. "I am the envy of every man alive. I don't want you to quit your job over this. Not for me. For you."

"I might—if I find a better one. After all, I need to catch up with you, so I can keep you in the manner to which you've become accustomed." She wiggled closer, angled in to brush his lips with a kiss. "We don't have to know everything this minute. Let's see how things go. Right now we have an unexpected day off and I believe you owe me serious make-up sex. Yet again."

"Alas for me. What have you in mind?"

"The other way around. You owe me that fantasy still." She

felt herself thawing, warming to the answering gleam in his eye. "And I'm wearing this suit. Perhaps you owe me a performance evaluation, Mr. Knight?"

"I bought you another pink blouse."

"Did you buy three?"

"I will." He slid a hand behind her neck and held her close, for a long kiss that heated rapidly. "Indeed, Ms. Dolors. I have a number of things to bring to your attention."

Look for these other books in the Falling Under series by
Jeffe Kennedy
Going Under and *Under Contract*

TITLES BY JEFFE KENNEDY

FANTASY ROMANCES

BONDS OF MAGIC
Dark Wizard
Bright Familiar
Grey Magic
Familiar Winter Magic
(Also Available in Fire of the Frost)

RENEGADES OF MAGIC
Shadow Wizard
Rogue Familiar

HEIRS OF MAGIC
The Long Night of the Crystalline Moon
(also available in *Under a Winter Sky*)
The Golden Gryphon and the Bear Prince
The Sorceress Queen and the Pirate Rogue
The Dragon's Daughter and the Winter Mage
The Storm Princess and the Raven King
The Long Night of the Radiant Star

THE FORGOTTEN EMPIRES
The Orchid Throne
The Fiery Crown
The Promised Queen

A COVENANT OF THORNS

Rogue's Pawn

Rogue's Possession

Rogue's Paradise

CONTEMPORARY ROMANCES

Shooting Star

MISSED CONNECTIONS

Last Dance

With a Prince

Since Last Christmas

CONTEMPORARY EROTIC ROMANCES

Exact Warm Unholy

The Devil's Doorbell

FACETS OF PASSION

Sapphire

Platinum

Ruby

Five Golden Rings

FALLING UNDER

Going Under

Under His Touch

Under Contract

EROTIC PARANORMAL

MASTER OF THE OPERA E-SERIAL
Master of the Opera, Act 1: Passionate Overture
Master of the Opera, Act 2: Ghost Aria
Master of the Opera, Act 3: Phantom Serenade
Master of the Opera, Act 4: Dark Interlude
Master of the Opera, Act 5: A Haunting Duet
Master of the Opera, Act 6: Crescendo
Master of the Opera

BLOOD CURRENCY
Blood Currency

BDSM FAIRYTALE ROMANCE
Petals and Thorns

Thank you for reading!

ABOUT JEFFE KENNEDY

Jeffe Kennedy is a multi-award-winning and best-selling author of epic fantasy romance. She is the current president of the Science Fiction and Fantasy Writers Association (SFWA) and is a member of Romance Writers of America (RWA), and Novelists, Inc. (NINC). She is best known for her RITA® Award-winning novel, *The Pages of the Mind*, the recent trilogy, *The Forgotten Empires*, and the wildly popular, *Dark Wizard*. Jeffe lives in Santa Fe, New Mexico.

Jeffe can be found online at her website: JeffeKennedy.com, on her podcast First Cup of Coffee, every Sunday at the popular SFF Seven blog, on Facebook, on Goodreads, on BookBub, and pretty much constantly on Twitter @jeffekennedy. She is represented by Sarah Younger of Nancy Yost Literary Agency.

jeffekennedy.com
facebook.com/Author.Jeffe.Kennedy
twitter.com/jeffekennedy
goodreads.com/author/show/1014374.Jeffe_Kennedy
bookbub.com/profile/jeffe-kennedy

Sign up for her newsletter here.
jeffekennedy.com/sign-up-for-my-newsletter